The Big Woods
1853–1873

The Big Woods 1853–1873

BOOK ONE

Al Lamanda

THORNDIKE PRESS
A part of Gale, a Cengage Company

The Big Woods #1.
Thorndike Press, a part of Gale, a Cengage Company.

Thorndike Press® Large Print Softcover Western.
The text of this Large Print edition is unabridged.
Set in 16 pt. Plantin.

LIBRARY OF CONGRESS CIP DATA ON FILE.
CATALOGUING IN PUBLICATION FOR THIS BOOK
IS AVAILABLE FROM THE LIBRARY OF CONGRESS.

ISBN-13: 979-8-88579-891-4 (softcover alk. paper)

Published in 2024 by arrangement with Alfred John Lamanda.

The Big Woods 1853–1873

Chapter One: 1853

Emmet Boyd held the reins on the team of mules while his brother Ellis guided them through the field. It was spring in the year 1853 and if the crop of wheat was to be a good one, the plowing and planting had to be done now before the heavy rains came and washed everything away.

In a separate field, their father, John guided another team of mules through dirt and rocks where he would plant potatoes and corn. Back at the cabin, their mother, Sarah, planted vegetables in her garden so there would be plenty to harvest all summer into fall.

Emmet was eleven-years-old and a stout lad, with sandy hair, blue eyes and broad shoulders for a boy his age. Working with his pa since he was eight, his hands were well-developed and calloused.

Ellis, eleven months younger that Emmet, was smaller, with the darker hair and eyes of his father.

Ellis stopped the team at the end of the row.

"What did you stop for?" Emmet said.

"Pa said to quit at the end of this row and go home to feed the hogs and chickens," Ellis said.

"Okay, I'll lead the team back, you go on ahead," Emmet said.

Ellis ran through the field about a thousand yards to the cabin, where ma was tending to her garden.

"Where's your brother?" Sarah said.

"He'll be along with the team," Ellis said. "I want to get a head start feeding the hogs."

"You mind yourself," Sarah said. "Those hogs are dangerous animals."

"I know, Ma," Ellis said. "You tell me every day."

In the field where John was plowing, he watched Emmet walk the team of mules home. He loved both of his sons equally and he would never choose between them, but Emmet was the more disciplined of the two.

If he told Emmet to work a field from sunup to sundown that was exactly what he would do. Ellis, on the other hand might take a few hours off to go fishing. Both were good boys. A man couldn't ask for finer sons.

There were two hours of daylight. John continued plowing for the next hour.

Emmet reached the barn and brought the mules in for the night. He gave them grain as he brushed them, then left them with hay and filled their water bucket.

Emmet met Ellis at the chicken coop where he was feeding the chickens. "Where's Ma?" Emmet said.

"She's inside fixing supper," Ellis said.

"We better wash up and help set the table," Emmet said. "You know how upset Ma gets if we come to the table dirty."

"Yeah," Ellis said.

They went to the pump outside the house They took turns working the pump, sticking their heads under the water and washing their hands with the bar of soap that was always beside the pump.

Sarah always set out clean towels on the clothes line for the boys and John. They grabbed towels, dried off and replaced the towels on the line.

"Let's go help Ma," Emmet said.

"What about the milking cow?" Ellis said.

"I'll do that, you go help Ma," Emmet said.

Emmet went to the barn to milk the cow,

Ellis to the house to help Ma.

Three years ago, when John built the cabin, he had the foresight to construct a separate room for the cooking stove so the house stayed cool in the summer months.

Ellis opened the closet where the dishes were kept and set the table. Four dishes, four glasses, silverware, serving platter, carving knife, salt and pepper and linen napkins.

By the time the table was set, Emmet returned with a gallon bucket of fresh milk. He carried it to the 'cooking room' as he called it and opened the lid on the five-gallon milk jug.

"Careful what you spill," Sarah said as she removed a golden brown chicken from the oven and set it on the wood table used for cooling.

John returned the mules to the barn, fed, watered and brushed them, then went to the pump to wash up for dinner.

The food was on the table when John entered the cabin. Chicken, potatoes and carrots, fresh apple pie and whipped cream made from the cream skimmed off the top of the milk container. Besides whipped cream, Sarah churned butter several times a week.

Before John carved the chicken, the family bowed their heads and John led them in prayer.

Then John carved the chicken and the family sat down to eat.

"Tomorrow is Saturday, boys," John said. "We work a half day because we need to go to town for supplies."

"All of us?" Emmet said.

"You can stay behind and do chores if you like," John said.

"Aw, Pa," Emmet said.

"Don't tease the boy, John," Sarah said. "When we return from town, you boys need a bath. We can't have you looking like orphans when we go to church on Sunday."

"We know, Ma," Emmet said.

"I might work a bit on the new room tomorrow," John said.

"No hurry," Sarah said.

John Boyd was a man who seemed to feel the need to work every waking moment. If he wasn't plowing, he was building something or repairing something, just always doing something. Even on Sunday, after services, he was always restless at the idea of doing nothing.

While Sarah and the boys prepared a picnic lunch, he would sneak off to the barn to mess with the harness for the mules or sharpen the plow blades and axes.

He was, in general, a restless man, never satisfied. He also hated crowds. Originally from the Ohio River Valley, where he met and married Sara, twelve years ago, he insisted the family move to a less crowded place when too many settlers moved in to suit him.

He heard of the Big Woods of Wisconsin, an open and unsettled place, inhabited by German and Scandinavian settlers. He and Sarah came from Scandinavian stock and three years earlier, they packed up and traveled a thousand miles in a covered wagon to find a new home.

They left in late winter and arrived in mid-summer and staked a claim to a piece of land that would become home.

They lived in the covered wagon while John cleared the land and began constructing a cabin. The work was hard, especially when winter came and snow halted construction. They had one thousand dollars when they left Ohio and spent much of it during the winter on food. Come spring, John continued building the cabin. By summer it was complete and he started on a barn, corral, henhouse and had yet to stop building something.

At thirty-five-years of age, John was in his prime and the need to do and build was his number one focus.

The new room John mentioned was a third bedroom, so the boys could have a room of their own. Sarah considered it a waste of time and wood, but John instated they would be men soon and men needed a space to call their own.

After dinner, after dessert of apple pie, Sarah and the boys cleared the table and washed the dirty crockery in the cooking room at the indoor pump and sink.

Then came one hour of schooling. Sarah insisted on one hour of school work every night before bed every night except Sunday. Emmet was an excellent student, Ellis not so much as he was a daydreamer. He was as smart as Emmet, but his mind tended to wander.

Tonight they studied math and history.

While they did that, John went to the barn to tinker.

By nine o'clock, the family was in bed.

Emmet was always the first out of bed. His eyes opened the moment the sun rose and he tossed on his shoes and went to gather the eggs in the henhouse for breakfast.

By the time Emmet returned with the eggs, Sarah had coffee going and bacon fry-ing in a pan. "Got the eggs, Ma," Emmet said.

"Go get you brother out of bed and wash up for breakfast," Sarah said.

"Where's Pa?" Emmet said.

"Tinkering," Sarah said. "Fill the milk pitcher."

One of the things John insisted upon was an indoor icebox. He purchased it from a catalogue and placed it in the cooking room in the corner. The bottom of the box held a large amount of ice that, as it melted would drip through a hole into a pan that needed to be emptied every morning. The interior of the box was cold enough to keep meats, bacon and milk ice cold.

The ice came from nearby ponds that would freeze over in the winter. John and the boys would carve out large blocks of ice, wrap them in burlap and transport them home in the wagon. They would stack them in the root cellar where they would stay frozen all summer. John would cut out a block as needed.

Breakfast was scrambled eggs, bacon, fried potatoes and bread toasted on the stove.

"You boys help your ma clean up while I hitch the team. And wash your face and put on a clean shirt," John said. "I want you presentable in town."

The ride to town took about an hour. The town, really wasn't one. There was a large general store, a blacksmith shop, a butcher shop, a small church and nothing else.

As John parked the wagon beside a dozen others, he said, "Must be fifty people here."

"John, there's room for everybody," Sarah said.

"I know, I know," John said. "You boys head on in with your ma, I need to see the blacksmith for a moment."

John removed a spare hoeing blade from the back of the wagon and carried it to blacksmith shop. The blacksmith, a powerful man named Stein had the proper equipment to sharpen the blade.

In the general store, Sarah greeted other wives from surrounding farms before shopping. She only got to town twice a month and it was the only way to catch up on what was happening in the world.

"Boys, have a look around," Sarah said when she started her shopping.

Emmet and Ellis went to the section of the store devoted to candy and toys. While they looked at the toys and the candy that was never allowed because ma swore it rotted their teeth, a girl of about ten was looking at dolls.

Her name was Beth Olson and she was a

Swedish girl new to the Big Woods, arriving a year ago with her family. She was an only child and doted on for it.

Beth looked at Emmet. "Your name is Emmet," she said.

Emmet, surprised, looked at her. "How do you know my name?" he said.

"I asked my ma," Beth said. "She knows your ma."

"What for?" Emmet said.

"I saw you last month with your folks in the store," Beth said.

"I didn't see you," Emmet said.

"I hid," Beth said. "I was shy."

"Hid from me?" Emmet said. "Why?"

"I'm eleven like you and I have my reasons," Beth said.

"Why did you hide?" Emmet said.

"When we grow up, I'm going to marry you Emmet Boyd," Beth said and hurried away, leaving Emmet confused and stunned.

Ellis, who was looking at some toys, said, "What did she want?"

"I don't know, she's just some dopey girl," Emmet said.

"Girls aren't good for much," Ellis said.

"Yeah, let's go find ma," Emmet said.

On the way home, wagon full of sugar, flour, salt, coffee and material for making clothes, John said, "We got time to get some plowing in before dark."

"John, the boys are tired," Sarah said.

"We sure are," Ellis said.

"No we ain't, Ma," Emmet said.

"What did I tell you about using the word ain't?" Sarah said.

"Sorry, Ma," Emmet said.

"I'll tell you what," John said. "You boys give me a solid two hours work and I'll give you the surprise I picked up for each of you at the general store."

"A surprise?" Ellis said.

"And you can have it right after you take your bath," Sarah said.

"Aw, Ma," Ellis said.

Emmet controlled the team while Ellis held the reins. They plowed six sections before they heard the bell ringing, ma telling them to stop work.

They brought the team in slowly, knowing what was at the other end of that bell.

Before entering the barn where two bath tubs filled with hot water awaited, Sarah trimmed Emmet and Ellis's hair with a scissors and brush.

"Alright, off with you two and don't come in the house until every inch of you is clean," Sarah said.

"What about Pa?" Ellis said.

"Never mind about pa," Sarah said.

Resigned to their fate, Emmet and Ellis entered the barn with clean clothes under their arms, stripped and got into the tubs. They scrubbed and washed their newly cut hair and got out when the water turned cold.

They dressed and went to the house where the aroma of fresh baked bread filled the house.

"Wipe your feet," Sarah said from the cooking room.

They wiped their feet and then went to the cabinet to set the table for dinner.

"Did you empty the tubs?" Sarah said as she went to the table.

"Yes, Ma," Emmet said.

"I got water boiling for your pa," Sarah said. "Think you can carry buckets to the barn without burning yourselves?"

"Sure, Ma," Emmet said.

It took six tripe to the barn to fill the tub with hot water for pa's bath and when they were done, pa was home.

"I believe I'll have a shave before my bath," John said. "But first, you boys come with me to the porch."

Emmet and Ellis followed John to the porch. "Now boys, my pa gave me my first ever jackknife when I was ten-years-old,"

John said. "It was his way of telling me I was on the road to manhood. With that thought in mind, I have a new jackknife for each of you. Mind you now, a jackknife is not a toy and must be treated with respect. If you can do that, it will serve you well."

John gave a small wood box to Emmet and Ellis.

"Thank you, Pa," Emmet said.

"Yes, Pa, thank you," Ellis said.

"I best take my bath before your ma skins me alive," John said.

Emmet and Ellis sat in chairs on the porch and opened the boxes and removed the three-blade, black jackknives.

"We're men now, Ellis," Emmet said.

"Yeah," Ellis said.

Fifty people attended service on Sunday morning. Sarah could see how uncomfortable John was with so many in the small building.

The reverend was also the owner of the general store, Mr. Nelsen, another Swede. His wife always made the coffee and doughnuts that would follow the service.

Emmet paid attention to Mr. Nelsen's message, but Ellis kept feeling his jackknife in his right front packet.

Beth sat with her parents in the same pew

as Emmet and she kept glancing at him. Once or twice, Emmet caught her eyes and she smiled and he quickly looked away.

After the service, everybody filed out and went to the two tables for doughnuts and coffee. The children had milk.

John went to talk to the blacksmith to see about his blade. Sarah helped Mrs. Nelsen serve coffee and doughnuts.

Emmet and Ellis grabbed a donut and a glass of milk and sat on the church steps. The doughnuts were still warm and flavored with cinnamon. Emmet bit off a piece of doughnut and washed it down with a sip of milk. Ellis broke off a piece of his doughnut and dunked it in his milk and popped it into his mouth.

"I'm gonna get another doughnut," Ellis said and went to the serving table.

"Don't let Ma hear you say gonna," Emmet said.

"You're doing it wrong," Beth said as she walked to the church steps.

"Doing what wrong?" Emmet said.

"Eating your doughnut," Beth said.

"How can you eat a doughnut wrong?" Emmet said.

"You're supposed to dunk it in the milk," Beth said.

"Says who?"

"Says everybody you stupid boy."

"The other day you said you wanted to marry me."

"I still do, but you're still a stupid boy," Beth said and walked away.

Ellis returned with another doughnut. "What did she want?"

"She doesn't like the way I eat doughnuts."

"What?"

"Never mind. Let's go behind the church and play with our jackknives," Emmet said.

"Yeah."

Chapter Two: 1855

"I tell you I don't like it," John said. "I don't like it one damn bit."

"Don't swear, John," Sarah said. "And so what if the town is bigger. We need a proper school and now we'll have one."

"Five years ago there wasn't ten people within thirty miles and look at it now," John said. "Must be a hundred people in these woods now and more coming every month."

"John, we have roots here now," Sarah said. "Solid roots and we're getting too old to start over every time the whim hits you."

"Who said anything about . . . I just don't like being crowded is all," John said.

"Can't we just enjoy the celebration without talk of crowds?" Sarah said.

John sighed. "Where are the boys?"

The celebration was the 4th of July, celebrating the birth of the nation. The town, still unnamed, now had a doctor that made house calls and a one room schoolhouse and there was talk of building a lumber mill, something that would save men a lot of backbreaking work.

Newspapers from Milwaukee, the largest city in Wisconsin were brought in by horse and made available to anyone who wanted a copy. John grabbed a copy and folded it away in his back pocket to read later.

"The boys are in the general store buying a treat for the fireworks," Sarah said.

"Sugar no doubt," John said.

"Their teeth are fine, John. Come on, let's get a good place to watch the fireworks," Sarah said.

Emmet and Ellis came out of the general store with twenty-five cents worth of hard candy in a paper bag.

At thirteen, Emmet was nearly as tall as his father and Ellis, at twelve, was nearly as tall as his brother. They walked to the church to stand on the top steps for a better view of the fireworks.

"Here comes your sweetheart," Ellis said.

"Shut up," Emmet said.

At thirteen, Beth was taking the shape of a woman. She came to the steps and stood next to Emmet. "Aren't you going to share?" she said to Emmet.

Emmet held out the paper bag and Beth took a hard candy. "Thank you," she said.

"It's getting dark, I'm going up to the bell," Ellis said.

"Ellis, you can't . . ." Emmet said as Ellis dashed into the church.

"Let him go," Beth said.

The sky was getting darker, the show would begin soon. "He shouldn't be in there," Emmet said.

"Go ahead and leave me then," Beth said.

"No, I'll stay with you," Emmet said.

"Good, or I wouldn't talk to you anymore," Beth said.

"Yes you would."

"I would but I'd be mad at you."

A red flare shot up into the sky, telling everyone the show would start in five minutes.

Beth moved a bit closer to Emmet as they waited for the fireworks to begin. Then, as the first rocked flew into the air and burst into a shower of red and gold colors, Beth reached out and took Emmet's right hand.

"What are you doing?" Emmet said.

"Holding your hand," Beth said.

"Why?"

"That's what married people do," Beth said.

"We're not married," Emmet said.

"Not yet," Beth said. "Watch the fireworks."

For the next fifteen minutes, the sky was ablaze with colors and patterns. Not until the last rocket exploded and faded from the sky, did Beth release Emmet's hand.

"My ma and pa will be looking for me," Beth said. Then she turned and kissed Emmet on the cheek and ran off.

Emmet didn't know what to think about that as he watched her run into the crowd. Ellis returned from the bell tower.

"Where's Beth?" Ellis said.

"She went to find her folks," Emmet said. "Ellis, promise me you won't tell anybody. She kissed me on the cheek."

"Why? What for?"

"I don't know."

Ellis shook his head. "Let's go find ma and pa," he said.

John sat in a chair on the porch with a cup of coffee and the newspaper. He turned the flame on the wall-mounted lantern to high so he could read.

The news of the day wasn't good.

Buchanan was running against John Fremont of the Whig Party. Buchanan, A Democrat promised he would keep the Union together no matter what. The slave states of the south were worried slavery would be abolished and that would cripple their economy.

John knew some black farmers back home in the Ohio Valley. They were decent, hard-working, Christian people and he never gave a thought to their skin color. To enslave an entire race because of their skin color wasn't just morally wrong, but against all of God's teachings.

Some southern states were talking about breaking away from the Union. There was even talk of war between the North and the South.

War would change the country. Not just the North and South, but the states and territories west like Ohio, Illinois and even Wisconsin.

"John, what are you doing?" Sarah said when she came out to the porch.

"Reading the newspaper."

"You know how that always gives you heartburn," Sarah said. "Come have some milk and go to bed."

The September harvest was the best year of the five years since John owned the farm. They had enough wheat, corn, carrots and potatoes to last the winter and the rest went to market. The way it worked was that on a certain day, freight wagons would arrive from Pepin, along with market buyers.

Last fall, John earned three-hundred-dollars selling to the market buyers. He expected to make more this year.

John, Emmet and Ellis toiled for days to get three wagons loaded to capacity for the big day in late September. John and Ellis drove one wagon, Sarah and Emmet the other. When one wagon was empty, John and Ellis rode home to switch the team to the third wagon.

After hours of inspection, bargaining and weighing, John drove home with three hundred and forty dollars in his pocket.

That night, after Emmet and Ellis went to bed, John and Sarah sat at the kitchen table to do their finances. They had a savings of two hundred and forty dollars. With the three forty they just earned they had five hundred and eighty dollars saved.

After paying the tax on the land of one hundred dollars, they had enough savings to see them through a bad year if one came.

"The talk is they need an extra hand at the mill after the harvest until spring. Mr. Jurgensen asked me if I could run the mill over the winter," John said. "I could run the boys to school and bring them home at night."

"How much?" Sarah said.

"Thirty a month," John said.

"Not for that, you won't," Sarah said. "You tell that cheapskate fifty a month or he can get someone else."

"Jurgensen won't got fifty," John said.

"I know, but he'll talk you down to forty," Sarah said.

"I'll ride over and tell him in the morning," John said.

John met with Jurgensen and over coffee they settled on forty dollars a month as a salary to run the mill. Jurgensen knew that John knew carpentry and worked hard at whatever he did. They settled the negotiation with a handshake.

As John and Jurgensen walked out of the mill, the bell at the church rang. It wasn't a call to service but a distress call.

John and Jurgensen ran to the church. Inside were Mr. Nelsen, the preacher, his wife, Stein the blacksmith and Mr. Noem, the owner of the general store.

"What's happened here?" Jurgensen said.

"Look," Nelsen said.

In a rear pew, a black man of about thirty years of age, was asleep or unconscious. He clothing was tattered and dirty. His shoes had holes in them.

"Is he dead?" John said.

"No, just passed out," Nelsen said.

"I think this man is an escaped slave," John said. "Look at his wrists and ankles. He's been in shackles."

"John's right, he's an escaped slave," Nelsen said.

"Get him some water," John said.

John shook the man. "Mister, wake up," he said.

The man opened his eyes, looked at John and jumped up in fear.

"Easy, mister," John said. "No one here is going to hurt you."

"Where . . . where am I?" the man said.

"Wisconsin," Nelsen said.

"I need to get to Canada," the man said.

"Mister, in the shape you're in, you're not going anywhere," John said.

The man tried to stand and nearly fell over.

"When did you last eat?" John said.

"I can't remember," the man said.

"I'll get him some food," Noem said and left the church.

"Just relax," John said. "We'll get you some food."

"I have to get to Canada," the man said. "No slaves in Canada."

"No slaves in Wisconsin, either," John said.

"Wisconsin, where is that?" the man said.

"North," John said.

Noem returned with a thick, roast beef sandwich and a pitcher of milk. As the man ate, John and the others went outside.

"Someone's bound to be looking for him," Stein said.

"Before we panic, we need to talk to the man and find out where he's from and how he got here," John said.

"John's right," Noem said.

"Okay, let's talk to the man," Nelsen said.

They reentered the church. The man had finished the sandwich and was drinking milk.

"What's your name, mister?" John said.

"I'm called George."

"And where are you from?" John said.

"Mississippi," George said.

"You're an escaped slave, aren't you?" John said.

George stared at John.

"It's okay," John said. "Nobody here believes in slavery. How did you escape?"

"I ran away with the help of what they call the Underground Railroad," George said. "I got separated when they come with the dogs. I got lost. I ran."

"How long have you been running?" John said.

"I don't know," George said. "Weeks."

"Jesus Christ," John said.

"They can't come here," Nelsen said.

"They can if they have a warrant signed by a judge," John said.

"But this is a free state," Nelsen said.

"That don't matter," Stein said. "If they have a warrant they can bring him back. I'm sure his punishment will be harsh."

"Nobody is to speak of this," John said. "George, I'll take you to Canada."

"I can't let you do that," George said. "All I need is some food and water and I'll be on my way."

"Do you even know where Canada is?" John said.

"North," George said.

"George, north of here is Lake Superior, ever hear of it?" John said.

"No sir," George said.

"I'll get my wagon," John said. "Reverend, bring George out the back door just in case someone sees him who doesn't agree with us."

Halfway home, John stopped the wagon and turned around. "George, come on up here with me," he said.

George climbed onto the seat next to John and they continued riding.

"George, what did you do back in Mississippi?" John said.

"On the plantation?"

"Yes."

"I was in charge of inspecting the tobacco plants in the field," George said. "Make sure the bugs don't get them before they ready to be picked and cured."

"Can you read and write?"

"Some," George said. "They taught me because I needed to work with numbers and such."

"What happened that you ran away?" John said.

"They whipped my wife," George said. "She worked in the kitchen. She had an accident and broke a bowl that belonged to the master's wife and she got whipped for it. Her cuts got infected and she died of the blood poisoning. That's when I ran away and found the Underground Railroad."

"I'm sorry about your wife," John said. "But we'll get you to Canada where they can't touch you."

"Why you helping me?" George said.

"Because you need help," John said. "That's reason enough."

Sarah, Emmet and Ellis were a bit shocked at the sight of a black man seated beside John when he arrived home.

"Sarah, Emmet, Ellis, this is George," John said. "We're going to help him get to Canada."

While Emmet and Ellis filled the bathtub in the barn with hot water, Sarah cut George's hair on the porch.

"Leave his beard but trim it," John said.

While George soaked in the tub, John brought him some clean clothes. "Mr. Noem, he owns the general store, he donated some clean clothes for you," John said. "And we have others for the trip."

"Mr. . . . I'm sorry, but I don't know you family name," George said.

"Boyd."

"Mr. Boyd, I don't wish to endanger your family," George said.

"You're not," John said. "Don't take too long, my wife doesn't like it when we're late to the dinner table."

Wearing clean clothes and shoes, George sat beside John at the dinner table and bowed his head when Sarah said grace.

"We saw black folks in Ohio," Emmet said. "They were farmers like us."

"They were free?" George said.

"What do you mean?" Emmet said.

"They haven't learned about slavery in school yet," Sarah said.

"What do you mean, Ma?" Ellis said.

As they ate dinner, Sarah explained about

slavery in the South.

"You mean somebody owns you?" Ellis said to George.

"I'm afraid so, son," George said.

"How can you own people?" Emmet said.

"Never mind about that now," John said. "We're going to help George get to Canada."

"How, Pa?" Emmet said.

"Well, son, you and I are going to take him in our wagon," John said.

"Can I go, Pa?" Ellis said.

"No, son, you have to stay and help your mother," John said.

"When?" Sarah said.

"Day after tomorrow," John said.

"We're leaving tomorrow," John said to Noem as the two men talked inside Noem's general store. "I need some extra powder, caps and ammunition for my plains rifle."

"You might need more than that, John," Noem said.

"What do you suggest?" John said.

Noem turned and opened the gun case where he removed an 1851 Navy Colt revolver. "Let's go out back and I'll show you how it works," he said.

"The extra plains rifle is in the closet," John

said. “Keep it loaded and keep it handy. Ellis, you mind your ma. You’re the man of the family until we get back.”

“How long do you figure, Pa?” Ellis said.

“A month,” John said. “George, let’s go if we’re going.”

Sarah and Ellis watched the wagon roll to the road where it kicked up dust. They watched until it was no longer visible.

John sat in the middle and worked the reins. George sat to his right, Emmet to his left.

“Mr. Boyd, I can never repay you for this,” George said.

“Sure you can,” John said. “When you get to Canada, if you see someone in need of help, help them.”

“That’s what it says in the good book,” Emmet said.

“I had a good book,” George said. “I lost it somewhere when I lost my satchel.”

“You can keep the one I have with me,” John said. “We have another at home.”

“I couldn’t,” George said.

“George, when you get into Canada, you have to start thinking about what you can do instead of what you can’t,” John said.

Emmet looked at George. “Pa says that a lot,” he said.

■ ■ ■ ■

"Where are we, Pa?" Emmet said as John studied his map in front of a campfire.

"Maybe fifty miles north of Saint Cloud," John said. "George, you'll be in Canada in ten days or so."

Stirring the fire, George said, "Sure is cold at night this far north."

"You never been this far north before," Emmet said.

"I never been out of Mississippi before," George said.

"Emmet, stir the cookpot," John said. "I'm hungry."

Emmet stirred the stew in the large pot. "It's ready, Pa."

"George, let's eat," John said.

The next day, they went hunting for fresh meat. John was an excellent shot with his Hawken .50 caliber, plains rifle. He shot four rabbits and then said, "We'll ride on for a bit."

A few miles north, John stopped the wagon and stood up. "Emmet, get down and find some throwing stones," he said.

Emmet jumped down and found a few stones.

"See that big clump of brush over to the

left?" John said.

"I see it, Pa," Emmet said.

"When I tell you to, throw the stones into the brush," John said.

John carefully loaded the Hawken rifle and looked at Emmet. "Now, son."

Emmet threw three stones into the large clump of brush and a dozen chickens flew out. John aimed at the plumpest chicken at shot it out of the air. "Go get it, Emmet," John said.

Emmet ran to the chicken and picked it up and brought it to the wagon.

"Now take off your hat and go into the brush and gather up the eggs," John said.

"The eggs?" Emmet said.

"Chickens are chickens no matter where you find them," John said.

Emmet went to the brush and crawled inside. Ten minutes later he returned with a hatful of eggs. "Look, Pa," he said.

"That's how my pa taught me," John said. "We got dinner for tonight and breakfast for the morning."

"This is a good spot to make camp," John said. "Creek for water, plenty of firewood and just about forty miles to the border."

"I'll get some wood, Pa," Emmet said.

"Let's cook those two rabbits we hunted

today," John said.

"I'll skin them," George said.

"I'll see to the mules," John said.

After a hearty meal of rabbit stew and crusty bread, John, Emmet and George went to sleep beside the campfire/

They slept soundly until a boot kicked John in the side, waking him with a start.

"Easy, mister, no sudden moves," a man holding a Sharps 1852, carbine riffle said.

Another man, carrying the same rifle stepped forward. "All we want is your nigger," he said.

George and Emmet sat up.

"Pa, what's happening?' Emmet said.

"Tell your boy to be quiet," the first man said.

"Emmet, stay still," John said.

The second man pointed his rifle at George. "You, nigger, get up," he said.

"What do you men want?" John said.

"Mister, we can shoot you and be in our rights for helping a nigger escape into Canada," the first man said.

"Minnesota is a free state," John said.

"And still has to follow the extradition laws," the second man said.

"Now mister, if your nigger ain't standing with his hands up by the time I count five, I'm gonna shoot your boy," the first man said and aimed his rifle at Emmet.

George stood and put his hands up.

"Get the chains," the first man said.

"He makes six when we get him back in the wagon," the second man said.

"Nigger, turn around," the second man said.

"I'd appreciate it if you didn't aim that rifle at my son," John said.

Grinning, the first man cocked his rifle. "If you don't shut up, your boy ain't gonna have much of a head left," he said.

Under his blanket, John removed the Navy Colt from his belt. He slowly cocked it and waited for the second man to grab George, then he flung the blanket away and shot the first man in the chest.

The second man turned to John and John shot him twice in the chest.

Emmet stared at John as John stood up with the Colt aimed at the first man.

"You kilt me," the first man said. "Over a nigger."

"No, because you threatened my son," John said.

"You kilt me," the first man said and closed his eyes.

"Son, make us a pot of coffee," John said. "George, there's a shovel in the wagon, we have to get these men in the ground."

After the two men were buried, John said, "We best find their wagon. It can't be far."

Before burying them, John went through their pockets and found a set of keys and two wallets and put them in the wagon.

"Let's go," John said.

"Where?" George said.

"Find their wagon," John said.

Less than three hundred yards away, they found a prisoner wagon with five black men imprisoned inside.

"Pa," Emmet said.

"I know, son," John said.

John removed the keys from the wagon and unlocked the cage. "You men can come out," John said.

The five men in the cage didn't move.

"He's a friend," George said. "You can come out."

"It's alright men, come out," John said. "We'll get you something to eat. George, see what supplies are in that wagon we can use."

As they ate breakfast, John said, "Can any of you men ride a horse?"

"We can ride," one of them said.

"Two to a horse, one of you rides with us and we'll make the border by nightfall," John said.

"Who are you, mister?" one of the men said.

"Name is John Boyd. This is my son Emmet and this is George," John said. "Now we got some miles to cover to get to Canada."

Around midnight, they reached the river that separated Canada from Minnesota.

"George, you shouldn't have much trouble crossing," John said. "Those two men had some money. Take the money and supplies and don't look back."

"Mister Boyd, I haven't the words," George said.

"Remember what I said, if you see someone needs help, extend a hand," John said. "That's all the payment needed."

John and Emmet stood on the bank of the river and watched George and the others wade in and cross over to Canada.

"Son, let's get some sleep," John said. "We go home tomorrow."

When John and Emmet arrived home, Sarah and Ellis ran to greet them. Sarah hugged John and cried and Ellis hugged John's leg and Emmet laughed and rolled his eyes.

That night, after supper, John and Sarah

sat in chairs on the porch and something happened that Emmet and Ellis didn't understand until many years later. They were washing the dirty crockery at the pump in the cooking room when they heard crying coming from the porch.

They listened for a moment, thinking it was Ma that was crying and then they were shocked when they realized it was Pa.

They went to the window in the living room. Pa was crying into Ma's chest and she held him close and patted his hair.

"You did what you had to do, John," Sarah said.

The next day, John went to town and met with Noem, Jurgensen, Stein and Nelsen in the church. John told them about the two men that he killed.

"I feel that it should be reported to the law," John said.

"John, it was self-defense," Noem said. "They threatened to shoot your boy."

"I didn't say otherwise," John said. "But I killed two men helping George escape to Canada and I feel it should be reported to the law."

"John, you've committed no crime in the eyes of God," Nelsen said. "But the eyes of the law might not take too kindly to helping a slave escape to Canada."

"He's right, John," Stein said. "Why make trouble for yourself?"

"Besides, it happened in free territory, not the South," Noem said. "They can't do anything to you anyway. Best just forget it."

"How can I forget I killed two men?" John said. "I'll send a letter to the U.S Marshal in Milwaukee," John said.

"It will take a month to get there," Noem said.

"I'm not going anywhere," John said.

November passed quickly. John, Emmet and Ellis worked to complete the extra bedroom and finished the day before Thanksgiving.

At Thanksgiving dinner, John said, "Emmet, as soon as we build you a dresser, we can move your bed into the new room."

"Maybe not, John," Sarah said.

"Why not, Ma?" Emmet said.

Sarah looked at John. "Because we may need that room for a new baby," she said.

"Now? After all these years?" John said.

"As they say, good things come to those who wait," Sarah said.

"A baby?" Emmet said.

"What kind of baby?" Ellis said.

"We'll just have to wait and see what the good Lord sends us," Sarah said.

"We'll have to take a trip to Pepin to see

the doctor," John said.

"Can we go, Pa?" Ellis said.

"We'll all go," John said.

Pepin was a settlement of about four hundred people. Originally a French trading post, it was now a stopover for farmers within a fifty mile radius before the goods and produce were shipped east to bigger towns and cities.

About one square mile, it was the largest town Emmet and Ellis had ever seen. Several buildings, including the church and town office were made of brick.

John parked the wagon at the doctor's office. "Boys, we may be a while," John said. "I'm giving you each a quarter to spend at the general store across the street there."

"Thanks, Pa," Emmet said.

As Emmet and Ellis crossed the street, Sarah said, "You know they're just going to buy sugar."

"I know," John said.

John and Sarah had to wait twenty minutes for Doctor William Adams. He was a small man in his forties, with greying hair and moustache.

Adams had a nurse and she stayed in the room while John stayed in the waiting room.

In the general store, Emmet and Ellis

looked at the candy in the long counter. "Ellis, I think we should use the money to buy Ma a present," Emmet said.

"What kind of present?"

"I don't know," Emmet said. "I brought my allowance money. I have an extra dollar. What did you bring?"

"Seventy-five cents."

"So together we have two dollars and fifty cents," Emmet said.

"But what do we get her?"

"Let's ask the lady at the counter," Emmet said.

In the doctor's office, after examining Sarah, he met with them in his office.

"Mrs. Boyd, you're as strong as an ox," Adams said. "This being your third delivery, I would expect it to be an easy one. I would like to see you several more times before the baby is due next July."

After leaving the doctor's office, John and Sarah were surprised to see Emmet and Ellis waiting in the wagon.

"We thought you two would be off somewhere stuffing yourself with candy," John said.

"We decided," Emmet said.

"Decided what, son?" John said.

"We'd rather get this for Ma," Emmet said.

"Ellis held out a small, giftwrapped box to Sarah.

"For me?" Sarah said.

'Open it, Ma," Emmet said.

Sarah removed the giftwrap and opened the box. It contained a one ounce bottle of lemon verbena perfume. "Boys, I love it but this cost more than fifty cents," she said.

"We spent our allowance money, Ma," Emmet said. "Don't be mad."

"How could I be mad at my two men?" Sarah said.

"Well, I was saving this as a surprise, so now is the time," John said.

"What surprise?" Sarah said.

"It's a long ride home on an empty stomach, so I thought we have lunch at the restaurant in town," John said.

"What's a restaurant?" Ellis said.

At the end of the block was a small restaurant with a dozen tables. It was the first time Emmet and Ellis had been in a restaurant and the first time for John and Sarah since before Ellis was born.

The luncheon special was beef stew with potatoes and carrots and crusty bread. Not that the stew was any better than the stew Sarah made at home, but the idea of someone bringing it to them was such a unique experience that Emmet and Ellis thought it the best meal they ever had.

The two-hour ride home seemed to pass in a blink as Sarah played a game with Emmet and Ellis of picking a name for the new baby.

November was mild, but December came in like a roaring lion. By the second week, three feet of snow covered the ground. John, Emmet and Ellis did all the shoveling to clear the barn and the chickens and hogs were relocated to a stall inside the barn.

There was a good woodstove in the barn and they kept a fire going to keep the animals warm, especially at night when the temperatures dropped to well-below freezing.

Ten days before Christmas, the weather broke and the temperatures hit the mid 40's during the day and much of the snow melted. On a bright morning, after breakfast, Emmet and Ellis widened the paths by shoveling the melting snow, while John worked in the barn.

As he shoveled the path in front of the house, Emmet noticed a rider approaching the house. He was a tall, straight man and he was riding a massive horse.

"Ellis, get Pa," Emmet said.

Ellis dropped his shovel and ran to the

barn. A moment later, John and Ellis walked to the house.

The rider arrived and he dismounted. He had a Colt revolver on his hip and a Sharps rifle on the saddle. "Mr. John Boyd?" he said.

"I'm John Boyd," John said.

"I'm Marshal Sam Titus from Milwaukee and I received your letter."

"Emmet, Ellis, take the marshal's horse to the barn to keep him warm," John said.

"Obliged," Titus said.

"Let's go in the house and have some coffee," John said.

Ten minutes later, Sarah served coffee to Titus and John at the table. Then she and Emmet and Ellis joined them.

Titus removed John's letter from a pocket and unfolded it. "I discussed this matter with Governor Bashford before riding here," he said.

"The Governor of Wisconsin?" Sarah said.

"He's my boss, ma'am," Titus said. "The names of the two men you sent are wanted outlaws, working as escaped slave hunters, the worst kind of scum. Excuse my language, Mrs. Boyd."

"One of them pointed his rifle at me and said he was going to shoot me," Emmet said. "That's when my Pa shot him and the other man."

"I know, son," Titus said. "I came here to tell your pa that no charges will be filed against him."

"Oh thank God," Sarah said.

"I helped George and five other escaped slaves get into Canada," John said.

"Who's George?" Titus said and winked at Sarah.

"Marshal Titus, will you stay for lunch?" Sarah said.

"I'd be pleased, ma'am,' Titus said.

Christmas Eve brought a large snowstorm that dumped two feet of new snow on the ground. While Sarah, Emmet and Ellis decorated the tree, John shoveled off the roof.

Christmas morning was a bright, sunny day, filled with excitement for Emmet and Ellis. After breakfast and before gifts were opened, chores needed to be done. Emmet and Ellis fed the mules, chickens and hogs and gathered up the eggs, while John shoveled snow.

Then gifts were exchanged. Sarah got a new sweater and boots, John a new hat and gloves, Emmet and Ellis got sweaters, hats and gloves.

Dinner on Christmas was always served at

three o'clock. John had hunted a large wild turkey and Sarah cooked it perfectly and the family enjoyed a feast.

A week later, they rang in the new year.

CHAPTER THREE: 1856

March saw the weather turn warmer and John, Sarah, Emmet and Ellis took another trip to Pepin to see Doctor Adams.

Sarah was showing now, being four plus months along.

The visit went well and Doctor Adams pronounced Sarah fit and healthy. Afterwards, they returned to the restaurant and enjoyed a lunch of ham steaks, with apple pie for dessert.

Before leaving Pepin, John purchased a newspaper.

That night, after supper, John sat in his chair by the fire and read the newspaper. The Presidential election was just six months away and things were heating up dramatically. Slavery was the main focus of the debates. Keep or abolish.

The argument to keep was based upon economics. Those in favor claimed the economy of the South would collapse if they had to pay wages to workers to do the work being done by slaves.

The argument to abolish was based upon the idea that no man had the right to own another man, that it was against the very notion of the freedom the country was founded on.

John had the feeling the entire election would go the way of those in favor of keeping slavery.

In April, John, Emmet and Ellis readied the fields for planting. The work, as usual, was hard, but Emmet, fourteen now was nearly as tall as John and Ellis, a year younger was nearly as tall as Emmet. The work seemed just a bit easier.

Sarah, five months pregnant now, had a glow about her that even the boys noticed.

Once the planting was done, John resumed his job at Jurgensen's lumber mill. School had reopened and he took Emmet and Ellis to town with him every morning so they could attend classes.

The one-room schoolhouse had desks for twenty, but presently only sixteen students attended classes.

Beth, also fourteen now, made sure to always sit in the desk beside Emmet. At lunch, she always made sure to sit with

Emmet and Ellis when they ate their sandwiches.

"Emmet, I think we should go fishing on Saturday," Beth said.

"Girls don't fish," Ellis said.

"Sure we do," Beth said. "I bet I fish better than you."

"Well I won't fish with no girl," Ellis said.

"Then Emmet and me will fish alone," Beth said.

"Go ahead, see if I care," Ellis said.

"Emmet, we'll fish at Johnson's creek on Saturday morning," Beth said.

"Come on, Ellis, it's just fishing," Emmet said. "We'll go after we do our chores."

"Alright, but we have to ask Pa," Ellis said.

"We'll ask him on the way home," Emmet said.

John worked the mill between the hours of eight and three-thirty. After school, Emmet and Ellis waited for him in the wagon.

"She's sweet on you," Ellis said.

"Beth?"

"Of course, Beth. Who else?"

"No matter."

"Are you sweet on her?"

"I don't know what it means exactly," Emmet said.

"It means do you like her?"

"Sure, but is that the same thing?"

"I don't know."

They waited until they were halfway home before Emmet said, "Pa, is it okay of we go fishing with Beth at Johnson's Creek on Saturday after we do our chores?"

"I don't see why not," John said.

"Thanks, Pa," Emmet said.

On Saturday morning, after completing all their chores, Emmet and Ellis, fishing poles in hand, set out for Johnson's Creek, located about a mile south of their farm. Emmet carried John's tackle box, Ellis carried John's storage box. A small, folding shovel was in the storage box as well as a lunch packed by Sarah in a paper bag.

Beth was already at the creek when they arrived. "I got two fish waiting on you," she said.

"Let me see?" Ellis said.

"In my storage box," Beth said.

Ellis opened her storage box. There were two white perch inside.

"Ain't much of a fish," he said.

"Let's dig for worms," Emmet said. He took the folding shovel from the storage and dug a hole near the bank of the creek and he an Ellis grabbed a dozen works.

Then they sat beside Beth, baited their

hooks and tossed in their lines. After ninety minutes of fishing, Emmet caught five fish, Ellis four and Beth another three.

They took a break to eat lunch. Emmet and Ellis had sandwiches of roast beef and apples for dessert. Beth had a chicken sandwich and an apple.

When they were done, Beth said, "Emmet, let's take a walk."

"Why?" Emmet said.

"Because I want to," Beth said. "Come on."

Ellis returned to fishing while Emmet and Beth took a walk along the creek. After about a quarter mile, Beth stopped under tall tree.

"Why did you stop?" Emmet said.

"Don't you know anything, Emmet Boyd?" Beth said.

"I don't know what you're talking about," Emmet said.

"You're supposed to kiss me, stupid," Beth said.

"Well, how am I supposed to know?" Emmet said.

"You're a boy, you're supposed to know."

"Well I don't."

"Oh, never mind," Beth said. "Let's go back."

"Wait, tell me what to do," Emmet said.

"You kiss me."

"Where?"

"On the lips."

"Well who starts?"

"The boy always starts."

"Okay."

Beth looked at Emmet. "Well, go ahead."

Emmet leaned forward and pecked Beth on the lips.

"Well that wasn't very much," Beth said.

Emmet looked at Beth and then grabbed her and kissed her full on the lips for twenty seconds. When they came apart, Beth was flushed and out of breath.

"Emmet," she said.

"I know," Emmet said.

"We better get back," Beth said. "Hold my hand."

Emmet took Beth's hand and they walked back to Ellis.

"We better not tell anybody about this," Beth said.

"Right."

When they neared Ellis, they separated hands.

"Where you been? I caught three more fish," Ellis said.

"Walking by the creek," Emmet said.

"Well come on, we can catch enough fish for Ma to fry up," Ellis said.

By four o'clock, Emmet and Ellis had fourteen fish and Beth had nine.

"See you in church tomorrow," Beth said.

"Hey, Beth, you fish real good," Ellis said. "For a girl."

In June, John took Sarah, Emmet and Ellis to Pepin for a checkup with Doctor Adams. After a careful examination, Adams estimated Sarah would give birth the first week of July.

"My opinion is the baby will arrive sometime during the first ten days of July," Adams said. "I'd like to propose something I often recommend to my patients who live ten or more miles away. I have an extra room in the back where Mrs. Boyd can stay before she goes into labor. There is a hotel in town where Mr. Boyd and the boys can stay until the baby arrives."

"A hotel?" John said.

"I'll be close to your wife for her delivery and you and your sons will be close to her when she delivers," Adams said. "Otherwise, you might have to ride ten miles to fetch me in the middle of the night."

"What do you think, hon?" John said to Sarah.

"It would be handy to have Doctor Adams at arm's reach," Sarah said.

"Alright, Doctor, we'll see you in early July," John said.

"A hotel?" Beth said when Emmet told her about the plans to stay in Pepin.

"I didn't know what it was either," Emmet said. "I had to look it up."

"I know what it is," Beth said. "I just never been to Pepin. Is it nice? Is it a big city?"

"It's not much bigger than here," Emmet said. "They got a restaurant and a doctor."

"You ate at the restaurant?"

"Twice."

"I'm jealous."

"Don't be. It was no big deal. It was like eating at home except somebody brings you the food and you don't have to wash dishes."

The teacher rang the bell for class to resume after lunch.

"We better go inside," Beth said.

"Yeah."

"We'll go fishing again on Saturday," Beth said. "You can kiss me again if you want to."

"Okay."

"Hold on a minute, son," John said when Emmet and Ellis were about to leave with their fishing poles.

"Yes, Pa," Emmet said.

"Ellis, you go ahead, I want to talk to Emmet," John said.

"Okay, Pa," Ellis said and headed out on his own.

"Did I do something wrong, Pa?" Emmet said.

"No, son. I just want to have a talk with you. Sit down."

John and Emmet took chairs.

"What is it, Pa? My chores?"

"No, son. It's your friend Beth Olson."

"Beth?"

"You see, son, you're fourteen now," John said. "At the age where you can't treat girls like you would your brother or another boy at school. Beth is a young lady and you have to be very respectful of her like you would your ma. Understand, son?"

"I would never disrespect Beth, Pa," Emmet said.

"Not on purpose," John said. "But without meaning to."

"I don't understand, Pa," Emmet said.

"I can see that," John said. "Say for instance, you try to steal a kiss and she doesn't want it, that's being disrespectful. Understand?"

"Yes sir, Pa," Emmet said. "And I would never do that."

"Good boy," John said. "Go catch your

brother."

"Okay, Pa," Emmet said. He left the porch and ran to catch up to Ellis.

"Did Pa scold you for something?" Ellis said.

"No. He just wanted to make sure I don't disrespect Beth," Emmet said.

"What does that mean?" Ellis said.

"I guess not to treat her like she's a boy," Emmet said.

"You mean don't punch her?"

"Something like that," Emmet said.

After an hour of fishing, Beth said, "Emmet, let's go for a walk."

Once they were far enough away from Ellis, Beth said, "Hold my hand."

"Are you sure?" Emmet said.

"Of course I'm sure. I just said so, didn't I?"

Emmet took Beth's hand and they continued walking until they reached the big tree.

"Okay, go ahead," Beth said.

"Go ahead what?" Emmet said.

"Kiss me, stupid."

"Are you sure?"

"What's the matter with you?"

"My pa said I shouldn't be disrespectful," Emmet said.

"It's not disrespectful if I ask you to," Beth

said. "Only if I don't."

"Okay," Emmet said and leaned in to kiss Beth. Her lips were soft and moist and the kiss seemed to go on forever, until breathless, Beth broke away.

"That's enough," she said.

Flushed in the face, Emmet said, "Okay."

"Emmet, I feel kind of funny," Beth said. "Like kind of warm."

"Me too."

"Do it again."

Emmet kissed Beth again and this time she held him closed and hugged him and he could feel her budding breasts against his chest.

Flushed and red in the face, Beth broke them apart.

"Emmet, something weird is happening," she said.

"Yeah."

"Is my face red?"

"Yes. Mine?"

"Yes."

"I don't think we're supposed to be doing this," Beth said. "Because we're not married yet."

"I think you're right," Emmet said.

"Just hand holding, okay?"

"Okay."

"Let's get back to fishing," Beth said.

■ ■ ■ ■

By mid-June, Sarah was all too ready to give birth. Her stomach was enormous and walking was an effort that left her winded and fatigued.

John, Emmet and Ellis got the crops as ready as possible and John went to see Jacob Toole, a farmer a mile north of the Boyd farm to make arrangements to have his son come twice a day to milk the cow and feed the chickens and hogs. They agreed upon the price of fifty cents a day for each day John and his family would be away from home.

On July 1st, at Sarah's instance, they packed up the wagon and headed for Pepin. By noon, they were in Doctor Adams' office. John, Emmet and Ellis waited in the waiting room while Adams examined Sarah.

It was the first time Emmet and Ellis had been inside a doctor's office.

After twenty minutes, Adams and Sarah entered the waiting room.

"My professional opinion is the baby is two, maybe three days away," Adams said. "I have the room ready for her down the hall. I suggest you register at the hotel and then come back and wait."

John, Emmet and Ellis found the hotel and got a room with two beds.

"We never been in a hotel before, Pa," Emmet said.

"It's been a long time for me, too," John said. "As a matter of fact, your ma and me spent our wedding night in a hotel back in Ohio."

"Pa, let's go see Ma," Emmet said.

Sarah was in the bedroom when John, Emmet and Ellis returned to the doctor's office. She had changed and was in a wide, comfortable bed.

"Ma, I never seen you in bed in the middle of the day before," Ellis said. "Are you sick?"

Sarah grinned. "No. I'm just resting. Doctor Adams, tell them."

"Tell us what, doctor?" John said.

"Well, after careful examination, it is my learned opinion that Sarah is going to have twins," Adams said.

"Twins?" John said.

"You mean two babies?" Ellis said.

"That's what he means, son," John said.

"Wow, two babies," Emmet said.

"Contractions have started," Adams said.

"Contractions, is that like arithmetic?" Ellis said.

"No, son. It means the babies will be coming soon," John said.

"Now, you three go about your business and I'll send for you when the time comes," Adams said.

John, coffee cup in hand, Emmet and Ellis sat in chairs on the porch of the hotel and watched the town go about its business.

Freight wagons were everywhere, some full, others empty.

"Pa, is Pepin a big city?" Ellis said.

"No, son," John said. "They have cities like New York, Boston and Philadelphia with hundreds of thousands of people living in them."

"I'm glad we don't live there," Emmet said.

"Me, too, son," John said.

"I'm hungry, Pa," Ellis said. "We missed lunch."

"Well, let's get some supper at the restaurant," John said.

The highlighted item on the menus was beefsteak. They ordered three and apple pie for dessert.

"Let's see how your ma is doing," John said after they left the restaurant.

"She's doing fine," Adams said. "The contractions are coming every five minutes now."

"What does that mean?" Emmet said.

"It means the babies will probably show up sometime tomorrow night," Adams said.

"Can we see her?" John said.

"Yes, but only for a few minutes," Adams said.

Sarah was in bed, propped up by two pillows. "John. My boys, what are you doing here?"

"We came to see how you're doing, Ma," Ellis said.

"I'm in good hands, boys," Sarah said. "And it will be a while, so why don't you go back to the hotel and get some sleep."

"My nurse will sit with her most of the night, so you might as well go to the hotel," Adams said.

Sarah didn't go into labor until two o'clock the following afternoon. Adams sent his nurse to find John, Emmet and Ellis and found them at the hotel.

"She's gone into labor, but this might take some time," Adams told John and the boys when they went to his office. "I advise you wait at the hotel and I'll send for you when the babies arrive."

John, Emmet and Ellis spent a restless, sleepless night waiting for news. At four in the afternoon the following day, Adams sent for them

"Your wife had a baby girl, six pounds and two ounces," Adams said. "The second one might take a while longer."

"Can we see the baby?" John said.

"My nurse has her, go through that door," Adams said and nodded to a door.

The nurse had the baby in a small crib, wrapped in a warm blanket.

"That's our sister?" Ellis said.

"She sure is," John said.

"Why is she all red and wrinkled?" Ellis said.

"She was just born," John said.

"What about the other one, Pa?" Emmet said.

"We'll just have to wait on her," John said.

Three hours later, the second baby, also a girl, was born.

Two days later, on July 4th, John loaded the twins, wrapped in blankets together in a crib into the back of the wagon and headed for home. Sarah rode in back with the twins, Emmet and Ellis rode with John.

"Pa, can we watch the fireworks tonight?" Emmet said.

"I think we all can, son," John said.

Sarah and John stayed with the wagon, each

holding a newborn. Emmet and Ellis went to the church to watch the fireworks from the steps.

The big news was the arrival of the twins and everyone stopped by the wagon to congratulate Sarah and John on their birth.

Beth came to the church and stood beside Emmet. "I saw the babies," she said.

"They look like a couple of grapes left out in the sun," Ellis said.

"Let's go up to the bell and watch the fireworks," Beth said.

Emmet and Beth entered the church and took the stairs up to the bell tower. It was dark and hot but had a great view of the night sky.

"You owe me a kiss," Beth said.

"We said we weren't going to do that anymore," Emmet said.

"Just one," Beth said.

Emmet held Beth and they kissed and Beth pressed her tiny breasts against Emmet and they both got flustered and dizzy.

"Emmet, did you feel that?" Beth said when they broke apart.

"I did," Emmet said. "I don't know what it was, but I did."

"I think it's love," Beth said. "Now hold my hand and let's watch the fireworks."

■ ■ ■ ■

The rest of the summer passed quickly. John worked at the mill and brought home enough lumber to build another room on the cabin. The babies grew quickly, although Sarah and John had difficulty giving them names.

One night after the fall harvest was complete, Sarah and John sat the family down at the table to decide on names.

"We need to name the girls," Sarah said. "Your father and I have had a difficult time and we need your help."

"I'm sort of used to baby one and baby two," Ellis said.

Sarah gave Ellis her look.

"Maybe not," Ellis said.

"We suggest we start with the letter A and go down the alphabet," John said.

The name picking went back and forth until the decision was made on Anna and Emma.

"Anna and Emma Boyd has a nice ring to it," John said.

"We need middle names," Sarah said.

"Elizabeth," Emmet said. "For both."

"Anna and Emma Elizabeth," John said. "What do you think, Sarah?"

"Has a nice ring to it," Sarah said.

"Which one is Anna and which one is Emma?" Ellis said.

"We'll decide that tomorrow," Sarah said.

On November 3rd, John loaded up the family and drove to Pepin to cast his vote for President.

The trip also gave Doctor Adams the opportunity to check Anna and Emma.

More than a thousand people swelled the streets of Pepin to cast their votes. John cast his ballot for John Freemont, fearing that Buchanan would do nothing to abolish slavery.

After he dropped his ballet, John went to Doctor Adams' office where Emmet and Ellis were in the waiting room.

Adams gave the twins a clean bill of health and afterward, John took the family to the restaurant for lunch.

Driving home, John feared that Buchanan would win the Presidency and slavery would continue to plague the nation for another four years.

Chapter Four: 1858–1859

Emmet was sixteen now and taller than John and just as stout. Ellis, fifteen, wasn't far behind. The twins, two-years-old, were walking and talking and laughed a great deal.

John's prediction came to pass. Buchanan had won the Presidency and under his leadership, the country was even more divided. The South threatened succession from the Union. The North had no real solution to the problem. There was even talk of war between the states.

Beth, also sixteen, was a young woman now and she and Emmet had serious talks about marriage. They knew they had to wait until they turned eighteen, but that didn't stop them from making plans.

They needed a house and at least one hundred acres of farmland, hogs, chickens and mules to start. They knew that both families would do whatever it took to ensure they had a good start to their married life.

Ellis had other ideas. He knew in his heart he didn't want to spend the rest of his life plowing fields and slopping hogs. The only place he had ever been to was Pepin and he wanted more. To see more, to go to more places, the places he read about in schoolbooks.

Exciting places like New York, Boston and Philadelphia.

He kept this ambition to himself for the time being as John needed all the help he could get to run the farm.

The talk of the summer, at least in the newspapers was the Lincoln-Douglas debates. Abraham Lincoln was running against Stephen Douglas for one of two senate seats. The debates began in August and ended in October.

While Douglas won the election, Lincoln won the hearts of the new Republican Party and it was clear the path he would take.

January of fifty-nine brought a massive snowstorm that dumped forty plus inches of snow on the ground.

John, Emmet and Ellis took two days to clear the house and barn and then a second storm saw another twenty-four inches of new snow.

After the second storm cleared, warmer weather followed and John, Emmet and Ellis were able to widen the paths to the barn and around the house. John decided to shovel off the roof and on the backside, he slipped on some ice and fell and broke two ribs.

The pain was excruciating and with the road to Pepin snowed in, there was nothing Sarah could do but wrap the ribs tight and put John to bed.

"It will be a month before your pa is up and around, boys," Sarah said. "The burden of work is up to you two."

"No problem, Ma," Emmet said.

On a bright, clear February morning, Emmet and Ellis set out with John's plains rifle to hunt for deer and turkey as they were low on meat.

Both were good shots, having been schooled on how to shoot by John the past several years.

Before they left the cabin, John, who was up and around, even if in some pain, gave Emmet his 1851 Navy Colt, extra powder, caps and ammunition.

Emmet remembered the Colt well. It was the gun his father used to kill the two men that morning who came for George and would have probably killed him and his father as well.

They left at dawn with a canteen of water and some food wrapped in brown paper in their gear bag and wearing snowshoes. Deer were plentiful in The Big Woods, but in winter and in heavy snow they were hard to find.

They headed for Johnson's Creek where deer gathered to eat bark off trees and drink water from parts of the creek that didn't freeze.

The walk through deep snow, even wearing snowshoes was long and tiresome, taking forty-five minutes to cover the one mile.

Then they found a large tree and climbed up to a sturdy branch to scout and wait.

They had four biscuits with bacon and ate two while sipping water. It took a while, but several deer came out of the woods and made their way through the snow to the creek. Emmet cocked the rifle and waited for the deer to come closer to the water.

One thing John taught both his sons was to never shoot the doe. Always shoot the buck. The does were needed to keep the population going, making the males expendable.

Emmet took careful aim on the big male. He had only one shot. If he missed it would take twenty seconds to reload and the deer would be long gone inside of three.

Emmet sighted, held his breath and fired. The bullet hit the mark and the buck fell dead from the wound in his neck. The doe and fawns crossed the creek and disappeared into the woods.

"Good shot, Emmet," Ellis said.

"Let's get to work." Emmet said.

They climbed down from the tree and ran to the buck. "I'll dress the deer, find some good branches," Emmet said.

While Emmet gutted the deer, Ellis cut two large branches from a pine tree to make a stretcher to carry the buck home.

Once the buck was gutted, there was a good eighty pounds of meat. They used rope from the gear bag to tie it by the legs to the two branches and they placed them on their shoulders so that each carried forty pounds.

They walked about a half mile in the snow before stopping to rest on a fallen log. They ate the second biscuit and bacon and drank some water.

The rabid wolf came out of nowhere, snarling and drooling white foam. Emmet hadn't reloaded the plains rifle and there wasn't time, so he grabbed the Navy Colt from his belt, cocked and fired.

The shot went wild, but the second and third shot brought the wolf down not ten feet from where they stood.

Emmet and Ellis walked to the wolf, which was still alive.

Emmet cocked the Navy Colt and put a bullet into its brain.

"Load the rifle and reload the Colt in case he's got any friends," Ellis said.

"Right," Emmet said.

March saw John regain most of his strength. As the snow melted and the ground became wet and muddy, he was itching to return to work plowing the fields.

On a trip to Noem's general store for supplies, John picked up a copy of the Milwaukee newspaper. Abraham Lincoln was emerging as the frontrunner to win the new Republican Party nomination for the Presidency.

Senators and governors in the South threatened succession from the Union if Lincoln won and tried to abolish slavery.

As John predicted, Buchanan was content to sit by and do nothing, hoping to pass the problem on to Lincoln.

Ellis, sixteen now, spent a great deal of time daydreaming about all the places in the world he'd like to visit and experience.

What was the point of learning about

places like Egypt and the pyramids, Rome and the works of art, India and its Taj Mahal if you never see them for yourself?

Staying on the farm and eking out a miserable existence seemed like a wasted life.

Ellis decided to wait until he turned eighteen to tell his parents the farm wasn't for him.

Emmet, seventeen now, stood several inches above John's height of five-foot-nine and was a broad as the front door. He worked tirelessly on the farm and saw it, along with Beth as his future.

On Sunday's after church, they would walk in the woods and along Johnson's creek, holding hands and talk about the place they would build and the kids they would have.

Politics and news of the world didn't interest Emmet. He felt that everything he needed was right here in The Big Woods of Wisconsin.

Sarah's hands were full with Anna and Emma, who were three-years-old now and into everything.

She enjoyed teaching them to add and multiply and it wouldn't be long before she would start them on the alphabet.

Mostly Sarah enjoyed watching them play outside. They had the energy of mountain goats and could play for hours rolling an old hoop or chasing butterflies.

John turned forty over the course of the summer. He completely forgot, but Sarah did not. The Sunday before his birthday, she had Emmet and Ellis invite most everybody in church to their home for a party.

John's birthday fell on a Thursday and she sent him to town for some items she needed for the twins to get him away from the house while everybody arrived and set up tables and barbequed beef and roasted corn.

When John returned. He was shocked to see thirty people at tables in his front yard.

It was the spirit of a small farming community come together and although John still hated crowds, he was also grateful to have such good friends.

Emmet and Beth sat at a table together and took some teasing about marriage and children, while Ellis daydreamed about faraway places.

Talk of politics and war were topics for another day.

Chapter Five: 1860–1861

By the spring of 1860, it was clear which way the political winds were blowing. Lincoln was the favorite to win the nomination and the South was in favor of succession.

Succession meant war between the states. For the South to preserve its way of life. For the North to preserve the Union and end slavery.

To Ellis, it all seemed so far away and unimportant. He dreamed of going west and seeing the country, maybe all the way to California and the ocean. There was so much to see, so much to do and the farm was like an anvil around his neck.

He loved his parents and Emmet and the twins, but life on the farm seemed more an end than a start on life.

Emmet turned eighteen and now stood inches above six-feet and weighed over two hundred pounds. He officially courted Beth and they made plans to homestead a good piece of land near the family farm.

Statewide, the talk was of succession, Lincoln and war. None of those things interested Emmet. His main focus was life with Beth.

In November, John took the entire family to Pepin, now a community of six hundred people, to cast his vote. The people of Wisconsin were very much against succession and slavery and made their voices known at the ballot box.

Winter blew in as usual, although the snowfall was lighter than most years. The twins were four-years-old now and able to appreciate the Christmas tree and understand the meaning of gift giving.

Emmet and Ellis went hunting twice, sometimes three times a week, although the plains rife had been retired and they used the new, single shot carbine that fired the self-contained cartridge. Like the plains rifle, it fired just one shot at a time, but you could reload in a matter of seconds and fire five shots to one in the plains rifle.

Emmet always carried the Navy Cold in his belt as a backup.

One February morning in 1861, after shooting a deer and two turkeys, Ellis confided in Emmet as they dressed the deer.

"Emmet, I have to get out of here," Ellis said.

"What are you talking about?" Emmet said.

"Here. These woods. The Farm," Ellis said. "I have to get away from it."

"I don't understand," Emmet said. "You mean leave Ma and Pa, the farm?"

"I can't do it," Ellis said. "Stay here my whole life and farm a patch of dirt, I'll go crazy. Plumb crazy."

"Well, what do you want to do?" Emmet said.

"Go places, see things, meet people," Ellis said. "Everything we read about in school books. Staying here is just nothing but plowing fields year after year. Not for me, Emmet. Not for me."

"Ellis, you're talking crazy," Emmet said. "You don't have the money for any of that. What do have saved, ten dollars?"

"And a bit," Ellis said. "But money doesn't have anything to do with it."

"Then what does?" Emmet said.

"Desire," Ellis said. "I'm an able person. I can work as I go along. I'm not saying it's gonna be easy, but if I put my mind to it I know I can do it."

"And what are you going to tell Ma and Pa?" Emmet said.

"I'm not eighteen for eleven more months," Ellis said. "I'll think of something."

"You'll think of something," Emmet said. "You're going to break their hearts is what you're going to do."

"Emmet, maybe working the fields is right for them and you, but doesn't everybody have the right to choose what they want out of life?" Ellis said. "Or is it chosen for you?"

"When you put it that way, yes, you have the right," Emmet said.

"Don't worry, I'll break it to them gentle," Ellis said.

"You better," Emmet said.

By March of 1861, Lincoln was the new President and Southern States were succeeding from the Union and establishing the Confederate States, electing Jefferson Davis as the President.

After a trip to Pepin in late March, John returned with the Milwaukee newspaper and read it on the porch.

War was almost a certainty.

Less than three weeks later, under the orders of Confederate President Jefferson Davis, Confederate Troops fired upon Fort Sumter and the War Between the States officially began.

By the end of the summer, nearly fifty thousand men from Wisconsin joined the Union Army, one of which was Emmet.

"Why, Emmet, why?" Sarah cried. "The war won't reach Wisconsin. There is no need for you to go join the Army."

"Ma, every man my age is joining to fight," Emmet said. "You and Pa didn't raise me to be a coward. I can't watch men going off to join up while I sit here on the farm and plow fields. That's not right."

"John, talk to him," Sarah said.

"He's right, hon," John said. "If I didn't have you and the girls to take care of, I'd join up myself."

"How could you say that, John?" Sarah said.

"Because it's true," John said. "This war, this cause is bigger than any one life. And we didn't raise Emmet to be a coward as he said. I expect next year for Ellis to join his brother."

"Oh dear God no," Sarah cried.

A week before he was scheduled to leave, Emmet took the wagon to Beth's family farm to talk to her.

She didn't take the news well.

On the front porch, she slapped Emmet

across the face.

"How could you do this to me?" Beth shouted.

"Beth, I . . ." Emmet said.

"After all the plans we made you up and join the Army," Beth said.

"A war started, Beth. What am I supposed to do, hide in the woods while other men go off to fight?" Emmet said.

"We were supposed to get married, Emmet," Beth said.

"We still will when I return," Emmet said.

"Not if you get yourself killed," Beth said. "Did you ever think of that?"

"Of course I thought of that," Emmet said. "Would you rather I hide behind your skirts? What kind of man would I be for you if I did that?"

"The alive kind," Beth said.

"You just have to believe I'll be back," Emmet said.

"It won't matter if you do, because I won't wait for you, Emmet," Beth said.

"Beth," Emmet said.

Beth turned and walked into the house, leaving Emmet alone on the porch. As he went down to the wagon, Beth's parents came out to the porch.

"She's just upset, Emmet," her father said. "Write her, son, she'll come around."

■ ■ ■ ■

"She's just upset at your leaving," John said. "She'll come around."

"That's what her father said," Emmet said.

Except she didn't come around and on the day the family drove Emmet to Pepin to join his regiment, Beth stayed home.

More than five hundred men between the ages of eighteen and thirty-five swelled the streets of Pepin, in addition to a dozen soldiers and several officers.

One of them enlisting was Doctor Adams.

"Doctor Adams, are you enlisting?" John said when he saw the doctor in a line.

"The Union will need surgeons," Adams said. "And that's what I am."

"Our boy is in good hands, now, Sarah," John said. "We best say our goodbyes."

Emmet kissed Sarah and the twins, shook hands with Ellis and John.

"I'll write as soon as I can," Emmet said.

"God be with you, son," Sarah said.

After the family left, Emmet stood in line and waited to hear his name called.

Chapter Six: The War Years

Just outside of Milwaukee, the training of the ninety thousand plus soldiers from Wisconsin took place.

For one month, Emmet drilled with thousands of others. Regular Army instructors taught proficiency with the new 1861 Springfield rifle, which fired a .58 caliber bullet. With proper training, a soldier could load and fire three shots in sixty seconds.

Besides the rifle training, which Emmet excelled at, there was drilling, marching and bayonet training.

Some soldiers were issued Colt 1851 revolvers, but Emmet brought his father's and he proved to be highly proficient with it.

Emmet wrote two letters per week, but with mail being carried by The Pont Express, he had no idea how long it would take them to arrive home. One letter was to the family, the second letter to Beth.

He doubted the letters written by his parents and Beth, if she did write, would ever reach him in the field.

In late September, the regiment traveled to Washington D.C. under the command of Brigadier General John Gibbon.

In Washington, the training continued for months as strategy was formulated by Lincoln and his generals.

While not training, there wasn't much to do except sleep in his tent, along with four other men and write letters home.

Most of the men were like Emmet, edgy and anxious to see battle and apprehensive at the same time as they had no idea how they would react under fire.

The job of the officers and instructors was to get the men ready for battle. During the day, makeshift battles were staged where the men loaded their riffles but without bullets.

The idea, Emmet wrote in a letter home, was to teach us so well that when battle happens we will know what to do by instinct. I pray this is the case.

After months of sitting around, training and waiting for orders, Emmet's brigade was finally called to action in August of sixty-two.

■ ■ ■ ■

During the six months that that Emmet had been away, Ellis and John worked the farm together and made the best of it. The work was harder with just the two plowing the fields and bringing in the harvest, but Ellis stepped up and they got the job done.

John made a trip to Pepin every two weeks to check the mail, hoping for a letter from Emmet. In six months they received four letters. As he stopped at the Pepin general store, which also served as the post office, a fifth letter from Emmet arrived.

John resisted the urge to open the letter, picked up some supplies and then rode home to read the letter with the family.

Before dinner, John read the letter on the porch with Sarah, Ellis and the twins. Anna and Emma were five now and understood a great deal about why Emmet was no longer at home.

The letter was dated two months ago. Emmet said his unit was moving to Washington DC. There was no word on why the move, but it could only be for combat reasons. Otherwise, he was well and healthy.

He did ask about Beth as she had yet to respond to any of his letters.

That night, after supper, the family wrote a letter to Emmet and even the twins had something to add. The next day, John rode to Pepin to deliver the letter.

Every letter Beth received went unanswered. She figured what was the point in corresponding with a man who would likely die in the war?

She was nineteen now and already was starting to think of herself as an old maid. Women married between the ages of sixteen and twenty and in another year she would be twenty and unmarried.

That was unacceptable.

She loved Emmet, or at least she thought she did, but maybe it was because he was the only eligible boy around that made him so attractable.

She had to get out of these woods or die choking to death on dust and dirt.

There seemed no way out. Emmet would probably die in battle and even if he didn't, who know how many years the war would take before it was over.

She needed a way out.

But there seemed no way out.

Every day was the same. Help ma with the cleaning and cooking, feeding chicken and hogs while Pa worked in the fields.

Day in, day out, it was always the same. Her hands were rough and chapped and her nails chipped. Her face was tan and leathery. She would never find a husband looking the way she did. She would be stuck here forever unless something changed and soon.

Her parents allowed her to travel to Pepin in the wagon when Noem was low on supplies. The war had made it difficult for him to stock his shelves.

When she arrived in Pepin, the small town was doing its best to stay alive. The war had taken the fighting age men and supplies were low because they were needed for the Army.

She was able to get flour, sugar, coffee and molasses and tobacco for her father's pipe and some ammunition for his hunting rifle. After the clerk loaded the supplies, Beth went to the restaurant for a piece of pie and coffee.

She entered the restaurant and took a vacant table and ordered apple pie and coffee. Before the pie and coffee arrived, a tall, rugged man of about twenty-five or so entered the restaurant. He was dressed as a cowboy and carried a Colt revolver in a holster on his right hip.

She looked at him as he approached her table.

"Excuse me, miss, but . . ." he said.
"Hat," Beth said.
"What?"
"Kindly remove your hat," Beth said.
He removed his hat. His longish, sandy-colored hair went well with his blue eyes.
"Better," Beth said. "Now, what is it you wanted to say?"
"I just rode in. May I sit at your table?"
"You may."
He pulled up a chair and said, "My name is Rip Taylor."
"Beth Olson."
"You live here?" Rip said.
"On a farm ten miles west," Beth said. "Where are you from?"
"Indiana," Rip said. "I was working a cattle spread in Michigan, but the war took most of the beef. I'm headed west."
"Why aren't you in the war?" Beth said.
"Opportunity," Rip said.
"I don't understand," Beth said.
"Simple, really," Rip said. "While millions of men are occupied with killing each other, opportunity awaits those smart enough to grab it."
"And you're smart enough?" Beth said.
"You don't see me in uniform, do you?" Rip said.
"What opportunity are you talking

about?" Beth said.

"Gold," Rip said.

"Gold?" Beth said.

"Colorado and California are rich in gold," Rip said. "While everybody else is off killing each other, I aim to go find some of it."

"And how do you plan to get there?" Beth said.

"I have a very able horse, three years' worth of wages and a brand new Henry Rifle that cost twenty-five dollars," Rip said.

"And you're just going to ride to Colorado?" Beth said. "What about Indians and such?"

"Stay on marked roads and trails and off their land and Indians won't be no problem at all," Rip said.

"You make it sound exciting, sir," Beth said.

"Well it won't be boring, that's for sure and while most men in the war will wind up dead or wounded or crippled, I plan on winding up rich," Rip said.

"How long do you plan to be in Pepin?" Beth said.

"Maybe two days to rest my horse," Rip said.

"How much does a horse cost?" Beth said.

"Forty dollars on average. Why?"

"I might like to accompany you," Beth said.

"You would?" Rip said.

"I am nineteen and I have no wish to spend the rest of my life on a farm, feeding hogs and chickens," Beth said. "I am an able person and can carry my own load."

"Can you ride?"

"I can ride."

"Have a stake?"

"If you mean money I have a life savings of two hundred dollars."

"Buy a horse at the livery and if you still want to go, we go in two days," Rip said. "But understand we have to ride hard to beat the winter."

Emmet's first taste of battle came in late August in the Second Battle of Bull Run in Prince William County in Virginia.

Lee led the Confederate Army, Major General Pope led the Union Army.

The fighting was fierce on both sides and once the first shot was fired, Emmet's fears vanished and he knew what to do and had no reservations doing it.

The battles raged in several locations and casualties were high on both sides.

Emmet's unit was defending Stony Ridge and the Confederate Amy led by General

Stonewall Jackson won the day and the victory as the Union Army was forced to retreat. Both sides were bloody and battered but the South claimed victory.

Afterward, Emmet took stock of his action under fire. He killed eleven Confederate Soldiers and proved himself to be battle-ready.

More important, he wasn't afraid.

After a few weeks of rest and planning, the next battle came.

Wearing riding pants and with a full satchel of clothes, Beth drove the wagon to Pepin and met Rip at the livery stables.

"I didn't think you'd show," Rip said.

"I said I would," Beth said. "I always do what I say."

"I picked out a horse," Rip said.

"Let me see," Beth said.

The horse was a painted bay, fifteen hands high and sturdy. The livery stable manager wanted forty dollars for the bay and twenty for a saddle. Beth paid for both.

"We need supplies," Rip said. "And you need a bedroll."

"I have one in the wagon," Beth said.

After getting supplies, Rip and Beth rode west out of Pepin.

Beth never looked back.

■ ■ ■ ■

Led by General George McClellan, on September 17th, 1862, the Union Army engaged Lee's Army in Sharpsburg, Maryland in the Battle of Antietam.

Emmet's unit, led by General Pope was absorbed into McClellan's Army and saw fierce fighting for ten consecutive hours. McClellan's objective was to stop Lee's advance into Maryland.

Emmet found himself fighting on a hill and then on a bridge. Three men in his unit were wounded and he carried them one at a time to the rear for medical attention. When he returned to the fighting, it had moved on to the Confederate line.

After three hours of non-stop fighting, Emmet's unit moved to Burnside Bridge, where he spent the remainder of the battle.

At 5:30 in the afternoon a truce was called for both sides to gather up their wounded and dead.

The carnage was high for North and South with a total of nearly four thousand dead, sixteen thousand wounded and eighteen hundred captured or missing.

The following morning, McClellan expected the Confederate Army to attack, but during the night, Lee retreated back across the Potomac to Virginia.

On September 22nd, Lincoln issued the preliminary to the Emancipation Proclamation and replaced McClellan after McClellan refused to pursue Lee across the Potomac.

Emmet's unit was sent in reserve to rest and recuperate.

For his bravery in saving the lives of three men under heavy fire, Emmet received a field promotion to corporal.

Beth's parents rode to the Boyd farm the day after Beth left home. Both distraught and Mrs. Olson cried in Sarah's arms on the porch.

"I don't understand it, John," Mr. Olson said as he showed John the note Beth left on her bed. "She's going to Colorado to look for gold."

"Gold?" John said.

"It just doesn't make any sense," Mr. Olson said.

Ellis understood. Beth was as miserable as he was with farm life. She was nineteen and wanted more than a plow, a roof, chickens and hogs. If Emmet wasn't off fighting, he would have left himself.

"She'll come back," Sarah said.

"No she won't," Mrs. Olson said. "I know my daughter."

While in Washington, Emmet went to an Army hospital to see some friends from his unit that were wounded.

He was surprised and happy to see Doctor Adams, a lieutenant colonel, was in charge of surgery.

"Emmet Boyd," Adams said. "You are a sight for tired old eyes."

"It's good to see you, Doctor," Emmet said.

"Have you news from home?" Adams said.

"Not much," Emmet said. "Mail is slow in the field."

"Have you seen much action?' Adams said.

"Bull Run and Antietam," Emmet said.

"I've operated on dozens of men from those battles," Adams said. "I'm afraid this war is going to drag on for years."

"I expect it will, Doctor," Emmet said.

"I'm due in surgery," Adams said. "Visit me again if you can."

Emmet went to a nearby mess tent and got a cup of coffee and sat at a table and wrote a letter home. He asked his parents for any information on Beth.

■ ■ ■ ■

"How far did we ride today you figure?" Beth said as she stirred a pot of stew.

"Forty miles," Rip said. "We could do fifty tomorrow with an early start."

"Colorado is a long way off, isn't it?" Beth said.

"Around eight hundred from here I reckon," Rip said.

"It should take two weeks then," Beth said.

"You have to account for the terrain, river crossings and such," Rip said. "More like three weeks."

"Where in Colorado?"

"Denver at first," Rip said. "Get the lay of the land and then find a claim and register it."

"You've studied on this a great deal," Beth said.

"For the last year or so," Rip said.

Beth filled two plates with stew and poured two cups of coffee. They ate with their backs against their saddles.

"You are probably going to want sex," Beth said. "I think it fair to tell you that I'm a virgin."

Rip looked at her. "Boy, you don't hold

back, do you?" he said.

"I don't see any point in holding back, as you put it," Beth said. "I'm almost twenty-years-old and have never laid with a man and in case you're wondering, I am quite open to the idea."

Rip stared at Beth.

"Quite open," Beth said.

After a day toiling in the fields, John and Ellis sat in chairs on the porch with cups of coffee.

"Son, I want to talk to you for a minute," John said.

"Sure, Pa," Ellis said.

"You're nineteen, soon to be twenty and you've grown to be quite a man," John said. "I expect you're giving thoughts to joining your brother in the war now."

"I've thought about it," Ellis said. "But I don't know what the right thing to do is. The Union Army has millions of men, but all you got is me. If Emmet gets killed and then I get killed, you and Ma got no one to help work the farm. Don't misunderstand, Pa, I don't like formwork and I want to see the world, but I can't abandon my folks when they need me."

"That's a very mature attitude, son," John said. "And I appreciate your honesty. And I agree that working a farm isn't for everyone. It suits me and your ma, but I didn't expect it to suit you boys. Especially you always being so restless and all."

"Pa, do you think Emmet is still alive?" Ellis said. "We ain't had a letter in a month."

"He's alive," John said.

"But how do you know?"

"Your mother wouldn't have it otherwise," John said.

It was the first time Beth stood naked before a man and the first time a naked man stood before her. She had many talks with her mother about the birds and the bees and sex, but seeing it in person was an entirely different matter.

Rip wanted to kiss and he put her hand on his bean and she had no idea what she was doing, but it was still fascinating. It hurt a bit when he put it inside her, but then it was pleasurable and nice.

Afterward they cuddled in their bedrolls and Rip fell asleep.

Beth stayed awake, wondering if it would have been the same had Emmet been her first.

Emmet, the jerk was probably dead by now or crippled. If he made it home he'd be useless, to her and himself.

■ ■ ■ ■

In late October, Emmet's regiment was on the move again. Under the command of General Burnside, over one hundred thousand men traveled to Fredericksburg, Virginia.

They stayed in the rear while battleplans were drawn and on December 11th, they engaged the Confederate Army General led by General Lee.

Once again the fighting was fierce and brutal on both sides with many casualties suffered.

On December 13th, on a field called Marye's, Heights Emmet heard a whizzing sound a second before he was struck on the side of the head.

"Two more days and we'll be in Denver," Rip said.

The night air was cold and Rip had to build a large fire for them to sleep beside. He proved handy with his Henry rifle and shot many a turkey and chicken. They stopped in a nice town called Sterling, that wasn't really a town but a settlement.

They had a small hotel and it was Beth's first bath since she left home. It was also the first time she stayed in a hotel room and had dinner in a real dining room. There was a laundry and she and Rip had all their dirty clothes washed.

It was also the first time she had sex in a real bed and the experience was quite pleasurable.

As they huddled under the bedrolls close to the fire, Beth could feel Rip's bean pressing up against her. She knew what he wanted.

"It's too cold," Beth said.

"Just open your pants buttons a bit, honey," Rip said. "That's all the room we need."

"You'll throw some more wood on the fire after?" Beth said.

"Promise," Rip said.

Emmet woke up several days after the battle in the hospital back in Washington where Adams was a surgeon.

He was in a bed in a room with twenty other wounded men.

He tried to sit up but a dizzy spell kicked in and he fell back in the bed.

The noise caught the attention of a young nurse on the other side of the room and she came to Emmet's bed.

"Welcome back," she said.

"Where have I been?" Emmet said.

"In that bed for three days," the nurse said.

"Three days? I have to get back to my unit," Emmet said.

"Relax, corporal. You're not going anywhere just yet."

"Is Doctor Adams around?" Emmet said.

"He's the one who bandaged your head."

"Could you get him for me?"

"Stay put."

The nurse left the room and returned a few minutes later with Doctor Adams.

"Emmet, you're awake," Adams said.

"What happened?" Why am I so dizzy?" Emmet said.

"Apparently a stray bullet struck you on the right side of your head and you have a concussion," Adams said. "You were unconscious for three days."

"That's what the nurse said," Emmet said. "I have to get back to my unit."

"Not for two weeks you're not," Adams said.

"Two weeks?"

"That's quite a serious dent you have in your head, Emmet," Adams said. "It's going to take some time to heal."

"That battle, who won?" Emmet said.

"I'm afraid the victory went to Lee," Adams said. “Now you stay put and I’ll have the nurse bring you some food.”

After Adams left, Emmet fell back asleep and woke a bit later when the nurse said, “Corporal Boyd?”

Emmet opened his eyes. There was a tray on the little table beside the bed.

“I have some beef broth with potatoes and carrots, some nice bread and coffee,” the nurse said. “Let me help you sit up.”

With some slow maneuvering, Emmet sat up in the bed. The nurse set the tray on his lap.

“What’s your name?” Emmet said.

“Rose.”

“Thank you, Rose,” Emmet said.

“Do you need help with that food?” Rose said.

“I can manage, thanks,” Emmet said.

“Alright then,” Rose said. I’ll be back.”

Emmet tasted the broth. At that moment, it was the best thing he ever tasted in his entire life. He broke off a piece of the crusty bread and dipped it into the broth and popped it into his mouth.

It reminded him of the bread Ma always made on Sunday. Good and fresh with hard crust and soft insides.

He ate all the broth and bread and then sipped the coffee.

Rose returned from the other side of the room. "All done?"

"Yes. Thank you."

"My pleasure, corporal," Rose said.

"My name is Emmet."

"Yes, I know," Rose said. "Try to get some rest now and maybe Doctor Adams will let you have some more food later."

"Wait, is it night or day outside?" Emmet said.

"It's night. Get some rest," Rose said.

After Rose left, Emmet closed his eyes and fell asleep, but the moans and groans of the wounded men woke him up. Several lanterns on the walls burned and Emmet could see well enough.

The man in the cot to his right looked at him. "Soldier, I'm going to die tonight," he said.

"How do you know that?" Emmet said.

"I can feel myself dying," the man said.

"Want me to get a doctor?" Emmet said.

"No," the man said. "Take my hand, say the Lord's Prayer with me until I pass."

Emmet took the man's hand. "Our father who are in heaven," the man said.

"Hallowed be thy name," Emmet said.

"Thy kingdom come, thy will be done, on earth as it is in heaven," the man said.

"Give us this day our daily bread and

forgive us our trespasses as we forgive those who trespass against us," Emmet said.

Emmet paused to look at the man. His eyes were open and blank. He was dead.

"And lead us not into temptation but deliver us from evil. For thine is the kingdom and the power and the glory forever and ever. Amen," Emmet said.

Emmet held the dead man's hand until he fell asleep.

Although Denver wasn't a big city by any means, its population of five thousand residents seemed to Beth as the largest, most congested place in the world as she and Rip rode down Main Street.

The streets were muddy, the buildings wood framed except for the church and jail and the streets were filled with people.

Six saloons lined Front Street and even though it was noon, piano music could be heard from several of them.

"I've heard about saloons, but I've never seen one," Beth said.

"Never mind that now," Rip said. "Let's find a hotel and the land office."

At the end of Front Street was the Denver Hotel. They dismounted, tied the horses to a hitching post and entered the lobby.

At the desk, Rip said, "We'd like a room, please."

"One or two?" the clerk said.

"One. We're married," Rip said.

"Sign the book. Two-fifty a day. Fifty cents for a bath. Fifty cents extra for a shave," the clerk said.

"Laundry service?" Rip said.

"Fifty cents."

Rip paid the clerk four dollars. "Where can we livery our horses?" he said.

"A block behind us in a livery," the clerk said.

"We'll be back," Rip said.

They walked the horses around the block to the livery and paid fifty cents each to board their horses and another fifty cents for grain.

Then they carried their saddlebags, satchel, rifle and bedrolls to the hotel and went to their room on the second floor. It had a balcony and Beth looked out while Rip went to the desk to order baths.

She found it odd how little she thought of home and her parents once she made the commitment to leave. She wasn't a cold, unfeeling person, she just needed to experience life before she dried up and blew away like dust.

■ ■ ■ ■

"How do you feel, Emmet?" Adams said.

"Much better," Emmet said.

Adams examined Emmet carefully while Rose stood in the background. "Your concussion is healing but I won't release you to your unit until it's a hundred percent," Adams said.

"How soon?" Emmet said.

"At least ten days."

"I feel well enough, can I get some real food?" Emmet said.

"Rose, walk Emmet to the mess hall," Adams said.

"Of course, doctor," Rose said.

Emmet stood up and waited for the slight dizziness to pass and then Rose helped him put on his robe and slippers. Then she took his right arm and walked with him to the mess hall at the other end of the hospital.

"Have you had lunch?" Emmet said.

"I have not," Rose said.

"Eat with me."

"I intend to in case you pass out."

They went to the serving line and got trays and then bowls of beef stew with bread, glasses of milk and apple pie, then found a table.

“So, corporal, Doctor Adams tells me you from his neck of the woods in Wisconsin,” Rose said.

“Yes. Could you call me Emmet?”

“I can if you call me Rose.”

“Deal.”

“So Emmet, what do you do in Wisconsin?” Rose said.

“Work the family farm,” Emmet said. “Where are you from?”

“Rhode Island.”

“You’re married,” Emmet said. “I see a wedding ring.”

“I was,” Rose said. “He was a lieutenant. He was killed at Belmont in sixty-one.”

“I’m sorry,” Emmet said.

“Me too. He was a good man and now I am a widow at the age of twenty-four,” Rose said. “What about you, do you have anybody?”

“I did but she decided not to wait for me,” Emmet said.

“She sounds like a very selfish girl,” Rose said.

“No matter,” Emmet said.

“It does matter a great deal,” Rose said.

“Maybe. How long were you married?” Emmet said.

“Three years.”

“Am I allowed to get more stew?”

"As much as you like," Rose said.

After a bath, Rip and Beth went to the claims office to request an application to file a claim.

"You have about a month before the weather turns nasty and the snow falls," the clerk said. "Until then, find your stake and file it with me when you get back."

They returned to the hotel and sat in chairs on the porch with cups of coffee. Rip rolled a cigarette and lit it with a match.

"Well, I got us to Denver," Rip said. "The rest is up to you."

"I don't understand. What is up to me?" Rose said.

"I'm going to find my claim," Rip said. "It's not going to be easy and there's only about a month, so it's up to you to come or not."

"I came this far, I can go the rest," Beth said.

"We'll need a tent, sleeping bags and supplies for a month," Rip said. "We can get all that tomorrow and a mule. Right now I'd like a steak."

"Me too," Beth said. "And if you're not too tired, maybe you'd like to wiggle your bean a little?"

"I'm never too tired for that," Rip said.

■ ■ ■ ■

Ellis raced the wagon home from Pepin with a letter from Emmet. Ma would be relieved. Every day, every week without a letter from Emmet she seemed to grow just a little bit older.

When Ellis arrived at the house, John said, "Son, these mules are in a lather."

"Sorry, Pa, but we got a letter from Emmet," Ellis said.

"Get your Ma," John said.

Sarah read the letter on the porch while John, Ellis and the twins, now six-years-old, listened.

"He was wounded at the Battle of Fredericksburg and is recovering at a hospital in Washington," Sarah said. "The wound is nothing more than a bump on the noggin and Doctor Adams, who is a Lieutenant Colonel has taken excellent care of me."

Sarah lowered the letter and started to cry.

John picked up the letter and finished reading.

"I love everyone and miss them and hopefully the war will be over soon," John said.

"How are you feeling today?" Rose said.

"Fine. No dizziness at all," Emmet said.

"Good. Let's get some lunch," Rose said.

Emmet reached for his robe.

"No, put your clothes on," Rose said. "I'll wait for you outside."

Emmet put on his uniform and went outside where Rose waited beside a buggy. "Get in, she said.

"Where are we going?" Emmet said.

"You'll see," Rose said.

Rose drove the buggy about a mile to a stone cottage nestled in the woods.

"You live here?" Emmet said.

"I do," Rose said.

She opened the door and said, "First order of business is you shave and take a bath."

"I don't have my razor," Emmet said.

"You'll find everything you need in the bathing room," Rose said. "I'll heat some water."

Thirty minutes later, after a shave and a bath, Rose walked into the bathing room as Emmet was dressing.

"Come with me," Rose said.

"I'm not dressed," Emmet said.

"Just come with me," Rose said.

She took his hand and led him to her bedroom. "My bed has been empty for three years," Rose said. "Lay with me, Emmet."

Emmet looked at Rose and she unbuttoned her blouse.

"I don't . . . I never have," Emmet said, feeling foolish.

"Oh dear," Rose said. "Well, do you know how to dance?"

"Not a step."

"Take my hand," Rose said. "I'll lead and you can follow. Okay?"

John and Ellis worked on building a third bedroom most of September into December and needed to get it finished before the first snowfall.

As they worked side-by-side, John could sense the pride Ellis felt in his work and when the roof was finished, they both felt a sense of accomplishment.

The harvest was good and most of it went to the Army and the family made over six hundred dollars for its toil.

John and Ellis went into the woods to cut down a tree for Christmas. They brought home a seven-foot-tall tree and spent Christmas Eve decorating it. Ellis lifted his sisters so they could reach the top and when it was done, it was the most beautiful tree ever, his sisters declared.

On Christmas Eve, Emmet left the hospital

and found a small store and bought Rose a gift, a silver crucifix on a silver chain.

That evening, she picked him up in her buggy.

Before dinner, they made love on the rug beside the fire. Making love with Rose was an amazing experience. Each time they laid together, Emmet learned something new about the experience and she seemed quite pleased.

After dinner, Emmet gave her the gift. She cried a bit as she opened it and immediately put it on. "I have something for you," she said.

It was a medal of Saint Christopher on a chain. "To protect you in battle," she said.

"I received my orders," Emmet said. "I'm to join General Grant's Army the first week in January,"

Rose cried again. "I knew I would fall in love with you," she said. "I should never have allowed this to happen."

Emmet held her close. "No, Rose, you're the best thing that ever happened to me," he said.

"Will you come back?" Rose said.

"Of course," Emmet said. "I love you. You couldn't keep me away if you wanted to."

"Please don't get killed," Rose said. "I

couldn't lose two men I love in the same war."

"I could use a bath," Beth said as she sponged herself with water warmed by the fire.

"Maybe so, honey, but this is our claim," Rip said.

"How much do you figure is in that preserve jar?" Beth said.

"The clerk in the claims office said the market price is almost nineteen dollars an ounce and that jar holds sixteen ounces," Rip said. "As soon as we fill it, that makes four jars and we head down to town before the snow locks us in for the winter."

"Four jars is a fortune," Beth said. "At least twelve hundred dollars."

"It's a good start for sure," Rip said.

Beth toweled dry and looked at Rip, who was already inside the sleeping bag. "I think I've lost some weight," she said.

"You look like what a real woman is supposed to look like," Rip said.

"You're just buttering me up because your bean wants some attention," Beth said as she got into the sleeping bag beside Rip.

"I don't deny that, but I also speak true," Rip said.

Beth took hold of his bean. "I guess so,"

she said.

Rose and Emmet spent New Year's Eve in his stone house in the woods. They built a fire and had a special dinner of steaks, which were very hard to come by during the war.

Rose managed to get a bottle of champagne and she poured two glasses to toast the New Year.

After Emmet took a sip, Rose said, "What do you think?"

"It's like vinegar with bubbles," Emmet said.

Rose laughed. "Yes, like vinegar with bubbles," she said.

After dinner, they made love in front of the fireplace.

In the morning, after breakfast, they took a long walk through the countryside. It was a bright, warm morning, around fifty-five degrees. The trees were bare. The creek that ran beside Rose's stone cottage was shallow and Emmet skipped some rocks across it.

They sat along the bank with the sun on their faces.

"Where are you going tomorrow?" Rose said.

"Richmond to join Grant's army," Emmet said.

"You will write me?"

"Every chance I get," Emmet said.

"After the war, what then?" Rose said.

"I'll come back, I promise."

"I'm older than you by a couple of years," Rose said.

"So what," Emmet said. "I don't see where that matters at all."

"Please don't die in the war," Rose said. "I couldn't bare it."

"It wouldn't do me any good either," Emmet said.

"Don't joke," Rose said.

"I'll come back. I promise," Emmet said.

The next day, Emmet was on a train to Richmond to join Grant's army in Culpepper. A thousand other soldiers were on the train with him. While some joked or played cards, most were silent or wrote letters.

In Culpepper, Grant's army amounted to three hundred thousand men and Emmet was thrown into the thick of several battles the minute he arrived. After Grant's victory at Chattanooga, Grant had Lee on the run and he wanted to break the spirit of the South.

There was a few weeks on downtime while Grant met with Lincoln in Washington.

Emmet wrote several letters home and to Rose.

In March, Lincoln promoted Grant to General of the Army, a position only George Washington had previously held.

A captain sent for Emmet one afternoon in late February and gave him sergeant stripes and told him he now commanded a platoon of men.

Emmet led that platoon in March as Grant and General Mead drove Lee out of Virginia.

Then came another month of inactivity as Grant again went to Washington to meet with Lincoln.

Grant now controlled an army of five hundred thousand men and he was determined to crush Lee and end the war and preserve the union.

The men were restless. They were battle-tested, hardened men, including Emmet and they wanted to end the war as badly as Lincoln and Grant.

They got their wish in May when Grant started the Overland Campaign, a series of brutal battles that went on for weeks. Grant in full uniform, sword in hand, led the charge and attacked Lee in the wilderness.

Battle after battle ensued until Grant led the Army to Petersburg, Virginia. The goal was to push Lee back and gain the railroad lines.

Emmet lost six members of his squad but they were quickly replaced.

Under Grant's leadership, Union forces captured Mobile Bay and Atlanta and controlled the Shenandoah Valley. Grant had Sherman march his Army to Savannah and he cut a path sixty miles to the sea.

By March of 1865, Lee was trapped. His Army was weakened and his soldiers were deserting at a high rate.

In April, Grant ordered a full assault on Lee's Army and took Petersburg and Richmond. Grant sent a dispatch to Lee requesting his surrender. On April 9th, Lee met Grant at the Appomattox Courthouse and war came to an end.

On April 14th, Lincoln was assassinated.

Beth came out of the creek after a bath and walked naked into the tent. Rip was at the table, weighing gold.

"How much you figure we got?" she said.

"Between this and back at the bank, maybe sixty-thousand," Rip said.

"We've been working almost three years now," Beth said. "We need another year to make our goal of a hundred thousand before we go to San Francisco."

"You're only twenty-four, hon," Rip said. "Another year and we can retire and live high off the hog the rest of our days."

"We should invest some of it in San Francisco," Beth said.

"I'm thinking a fancy saloon," Rip said. "You'll always make money with a saloon."

"I'm agreeable to that, but I want more," Beth said. "I want us to get married."

"Married?"

"We've been together three years, Rip. You tell me all the time you love me and a married couple is more apt to get things like a business and such in a big city like San Francisco," Beth said.

"Married, huh?" Rip said. "Well, they got a preacher in the church in Denver, why not?"

"One thing," Beth said. "I won't tolerate you tomcatting on me. You bring some saloon girl's pox home to our bed and I will kill you dead as last night's steak."

"I believe you," Rip said.

"Good, now quit fooling with that gold and come to bed," Beth said.

Ellis returned from Pepin with the newspaper and two letters from Emmet.

The family met him on the porch. Ellis held out the newspaper. "Two letters from

Emmet and the war is over," he said.

John took the newspaper and read the headline. "By God, it's over," he said.

Sarah read the letters. They were two months old when Emmet wrote them he had no idea the war would be ending just sixty days later.

"Is Emmet coming home," Anna said.

"Soon honey," Sarah said. "Very soon."

Emmet's latest letter came after Lincoln's assassination. He was well and being assigned to what Grant called the reconstruction of the South. He didn't know how long the assignment would last, maybe six months.

He would be allowed to have a week of free time and would come to Washington to see her.

Rose cried when she read the letter.

Cried because she was happy Emmet survived the war and broken hearted because the news that her husband who she believed dead was in Andersonville Camp as a prisoner of war for four years.

As they regularly did, Beth and Rip made a trip to Denver to deposit their gold and stock up on supplies.

They stayed overnight at the hotel and the

entire town was buzzing about the assassination of Lincoln.

At dinner, Beth said, "You were right all along, Rip."

"About what?'

"Skipping the war and coming here," Beth said. "You'd probably be one of a half million dead men instead of rich and prosperous. I would still be on the farm feeding hogs and chickens. I expect thousands will be coming this way to seek their fortune now."

"Let them come," Rip said. "We'll be in San Francisco by then. Right before we leave we can sell our stake to the highest bidder and make a tidy profit on it."

"Before we head back in the morning, let's talk to the preacher," Beth said.

"Since you brought up that idea, I must confess in the beginning marriage didn't interest me," Rip said. "But now I like the sound of it."

"Good," Beth said. "We'll go to San Francisco a wealthy, married couple."

Emmet arrived in Washington in early June and raced to the hospital with his heart pounding at the thought of seeing Rose again.

Since the day she gave him the Saint

Christopher medal, he had never taken it off.

He burst through the front door of the hospital and walked from ward to ward, looking for her until he spotted her in a room full of wounded men.

He opened the door and walked in and she saw him and her eyes went wide and she walked quickly to him and ushered him outside.

Emmet tried to kiss her but she pushed him away.

"What's wrong?" Emmet said.

Rose pointed to a sick soldier in a bed. "Do you see that man? He's been in a Confederate prison camp for four years," she said.

"I see him."

"He's my husband," Rose said.

"What?" Emmet said.

"My husband," Rose said. "He's been in a prisoner of war camp all this time. I'm still a married woman, Emmet."

Emmet stared at her. He was completely numb at the news.

"I don't know what to say," Rose said.

Emmet backed away. He removed the Saint Christopher medal from around his neck and placed it into her hands.

Rose closed her fist around the medal and

cried as Emmet walked out of her life.

Emmet, along with thousands of other soldiers were still on active duty in the South after Lincoln was assassinated for what Grant called the Reconstruction of the Southern States.

The Union Army was to keep law and order while the South rebuilt.

Emmet was promoted to First Sergeant and given a company of men to supervise. The job was difficult as the South resented their presence and the presence of freed slaves now walking about as free men and women.

Emmet, trying to forget Rose, threw himself into his work. The violence against the freed slaves was a daily occurrence and he didn't tolerate it and his company made many arrests during the first several months.

The task of cleaning up the mess left behind was monumental, especially in Atlanta, where Emmet was assigned.

In the deep south, groups opposed to the freed slaves formed an organization known as the Ku Klux Klan, a white supremacist group led by Confederate General Nathan Forest.

They wore white, hooded robes and staged midnight raids on defenseless black families, often hanging them and leaving burning crosses in the fields.

Emmet's company killed and arrested many members of the Klan during the six months he was assigned to Atlanta.

Late in sixty-five, Emmet was summoned to Washington by General Grant.

"Beth, honey, I think this is our last jar of gold," Rip said as he put a lid on the jar. "The price is over twenty dollars an ounce and we have a hundred thousand in the bank."

"We can sell our claim and head west," Beth said. "Right after we get married."

"Let's head to town, honey, we have a lot to do," Rip said.

After three years of living in Denver, Beth and Rip were well known to most residents. Tired of the hotel during the winter, they had a small cabin built on a back street where they stayed until spring.

At the bank, they got a final tally on their money. One hundred and three thousand dollars. They told the bank president they would wire the money to a bank in San Francisco when they got settled.

At the land office, they put their mine up for auction to the highest bidder. The mine fetched twenty-one thousand dollars.

Beth and Rip got married in the church and held a large reception at the hotel banquet hall. Hundreds of well-wishers attended.

As they went to bed afterward as husband and wife for the first time, Beth's past seemed like a faraway dream.

"Rip, honey, can I ask you for a favor?" Beth said.

"Sure."

"Before we leave Denver, can I wire my folks back some money?" Beth said.

"We certainly have enough to spare," Rip said.

"We certainly do," Rose said.

Emmet met with General Grant and a man named Thomas 'Doc' Durant in a hotel room near The White House.

"At ease, First Sergeant," Grant said when Emmet entered the room and stood at attention.

Emmet relaxed.

"Sergeant, this is Thomas Durant and he will be heading the transcendental railroad project from Iowa westward to join the Union Pacific Railroad, linking East to West for the first time in history," Grant said.

"Yes sir," Emmet said.

"This task will be monumental, requiring

thousands of men and take an estimated four years to complete," Grant said. "Sergeant, would you care for a drink?"

"No sir," Emmet said.

"Doc?" Grant said.

"Why not," Durant said.

Grant poured two drinks of bourbon and gave one to Durant.

"Now then, Sergeant," Grant said. "The task of joining the railroad is going to be a dangerous one from every prospective. From thieves to Indians, to bad weather and setbacks. Understand?"

"Yes sir," Emmet said.

"You were recommended to me by your commanding officer," Grant said. "The railroad will fall under the protection of the United States Army and you will be part of that. You will report in thirty days to the starting point in Iowa with the rank of Lieutenant and second in command of the twenty-four men assigned to the project."

"Thirty days, sir?" Emmet said.

"You spent four years in a war, I thought you might like to visit home for a bit," Grant said. "Just in time for Christmas."

"Thank you, sir," Emmet said.

"Relax tonight, Lieutenant," Grant said. "Tomorrow report to my stables and pick yourself out the best horse in the lot."

■ ■ ■ ■

It was one of those December afternoons where the temperature reached sixty degrees and the twins were playing outside, Ellis and John were working in the barn and Sarah baked fresh bread and pies for supper.

Suddenly Anna and Emma stopped playing and looked down the road and then ran into the house.

"Ma, there's a black man on a horse," Anna said.

"What?' Sarah said.

"A black man on a horse," Emma said.

They went to the porch. "Girls, go get your pa and Ellis," she said.

The twins ran to the barn and returned with John and Ellis. "Girls, get up on the porch with your ma," John said.

John and Ellis waited until the black man arrived. He wore a fine suit and tie and derby hat. He dismounted and looked at John.

"I'm a lawyer on my way to Atlanta to protect the rights of black folks," he said. "I just thought you might like to see what came of your investment."

"George?" John said.

George smiled broadly at John.

John went to George, hugged him and started crying.

"Ma. Pa is crying," Anna said.

"Because he's happy," Sarah said.

"But Pa's a man," Emma said.

"Men have tears same as girls," Sarah said.

Emmet did his best to resist going to the hospital when he left Grant, but in the end his desire to see Rose one more time won out.

He entered the hospital and went from ward to ward until he found her in a ward full of sick and injured soldiers.

Emmet entered the ward and she turned and looked at him. Her eyes closed for a moment and then she rushed to him and grabbed him in a hug.

"Outside," Rose said.

They left the hospital and stood beside the front door.

"Emmet, please don't hate me," Rose said.

"I could never hate you," Emmet said. "What happened isn't your fault. I'm glad he's alive even if it means losing you."

"Emmet, he's little more than a vegetable," Rose said. "They beat him severely as an officer. He has yet to open his eyes."

"I'm sorry," Emmet said.

"Me too."

"Can you have dinner with me tonight?"

"Dinner. Yes, please," Rose said. "I'll get someone to cover the rest of my shift."

"Another piece of apple pie, George?" Sarah said.

"I'm afraid I'm all out of room, Mrs. Boyd," George said.

"You'll stay the night," John said. "Emmet's bed is empty since he joined the Army."

"Please do," Sarah said.

"I'd be honored," George said.

"Why don't you men take coffee on the porch while the girls and I do the dishes," Sarah said.

John, Ellis and George went out to the porch with cups of coffee.

"Tell me about Canada," Ellis said.

"It's not much different than here," George said. "A lot of wide open country with a lot of farms and ranches. Cold winters and hot summers. I spent the last four years in Montreal going to school. I studied law and French."

"French?" Ellis said.

"They speak English and French in Canada," George said.

"And now you're going down south?" Ellis said.

"The people who were once slaves need help," George said. "I intend to give it to them."

"You must be very brave," Ellis said.

"Young man, if you want to see brave just take a look at your father," George said.

The second Emmet and Rose entered her stone cottage, Rose turned and kissed Emmet so hard he fell against the wall.

"Rose, this is wrong," Emmet said as he returned the kiss.

"I don't care," Rose said as she unbuttoned his uniform jacket.

"You're still married," Emmet said as he tore open Rose's blouse.

"I don't care," Rose said as she ripped at Emmet's belt.

"Rose, stop," Emmet said as he yanked her skirt down to the floor.

"I'll stop if you stop," Rose said as she pushed Emmet to the rug beside the fireplace.

Emmet kissed her and he got on top and Rose moaned loudly and dug her fingernails into his back when they came together.

■ ■ ■ ■

"Goodnight Mr. George," Anna said.

"Goodnight Mr. George," Emma said.

"Goodnight, girls," George said.

"We'll see you for breakfast," John said. "Ellis, don't keep George up too late, he's had a long trip."

"Yes, Pa," Ellis said.

Alone on the porch with George, Ellis said, "I'm not keeping you awake, am I?"

"Not at all, son," George said.

"Tell me more about Canada."

"First tell me about your brother Emmet," George said.

Emmet and Rose sat on the rug in front of the fireplace and drank coffee. Rose had a wrap over her shoulders.

"When you gave me back the medal I died inside," Rose said. "I cried for weeks from a broken heart."

"I gave it back because it belongs to your husband," Emmet said.

"You have to believe me that I didn't know he was still alive," Rose said.

"I believe you," Emmet said. "I saw thousands of men come home from prisoner camps that their families believed dead."

"I was feeling like a silly school girl when the war ended," Rose said. "Waiting for you to come back to me. I decided to ask you to marry me."

"The man usually does that," Emmet said.

"Would you have?"

"Yes."

"Where are you going next?"

"I've been sent by General Grant to act as security detail for the railroad."

"General Grant? You've done well for so young a man," Rose said. "When do you leave?"

"Tomorrow."

"Stay with me tonight," Rose said. "It may have to last me the rest of my life."

"Are you happy?" Beth said.

"We're rich and headed to San Francisco to become even richer and I'm married to a young, beautiful woman," Rip said.

"But are you happy?" Beth said.

They were in the bedroom of their small house in Denver. Beth was in the bed, Rip was at the desk against the wall. Reading a train schedule. In the past three years, the Union Pacific Railroad had come to Denver. They would take the train northwest into Idaho and west to San Francisco.

"We'll be in San Francisco for Christmas,"

Rip said.

"Rip, are you happy?" Beth said.

He looked at her. "I am," he said. "I truly am."

"With me or the money?" Beth said.

"You know something," Rip said. "The money wouldn't mean a thing without you, honey."

Beth patted the bed. "Come keep your wife warm," she said.

Emmet left before Rose woke up because he wouldn't be able to stand that kind of goodbye again. He left her a long letter on the kitchen table, then walked the mile back to Washington.

Grant had a stable of horses near his headquarters close to the White House. The stable manager was expecting him and said, "I was told a Lieutenant Boyd would be stopping by, not a Staff Sergeant," the manager said.

"I haven't received my bars yet," Emmet said.

"Well, let's go through the stock," the manager said.

Emmet inspected fifteen horses and chose a three-year-old Missouri Fox Trotter named Bull, a powerful horse that could cover long distances.

"How is he on trains?" Emmet said.

"How do you think he got here," the manager said. "Come on and get the saddle and Henry Rifle Grant left for you."

An hour later, Emmet loaded the horse, which was named Bull, into the boxcar of the train and then boarded and took a seat.

There was an overnight layover in Chicago before taking a train north to Milwaukee. He would be home in three days.

To keep his mind off Rose, he read a book by an English author named Lewis Carroll, titled Alice in Wonderland.

It was a very odd book about a young girl named Alice and her adventures in a fantasy place called Wonderland.

He finished the book before reaching Chicago and left it on the seat.

Although Chicago was a massive city of a hundred and fifty thousand residents, Emmet wasn't interested in seeing the sights and took a room at the railroad hotel, which also boarded horses.

Sleep was almost instant and filled with dreams of Rose and when he awoke, he was miserable and lonely.

He caught the train to Milwaukee and purchased supplies for a day's ride to The Big Woods.

■ ■ ■ ■

On the morning of December 23rd, John and Ellis went into the woods to cut down a tree for Christmas. Snow was lightly falling.

They had just returned and were met by the twins on the porch.

"Pa, a man is coming," Anna said.

John and Ellis went up to the porch for a better look. "Ellis, get you mother," John said.

Ellis went inside and returned with Sarah. "What is it, John?" she said.

"Company," John said.

They watched as Emmet arrived on Bull. At first, they just stared at him as he dismounted.

Then Emmet said, "Hello, Ma," and Sarah ran off the porch and threw herself into his arms and wept like a baby.

"Boy, everybody sure does cry a lot around here," Anna said.

Sarah served coffee in the kitchen and then said, "Come on girls, let's make a nice lunch for your brother's homecoming."

Anna pointed to Emmet's jacket that hung on the back of his chair. "What's all those decorations on your jacket?" she said.

"Those are medals, honey," John said. "Emmet won them in the war."

"Medals for what?" Emma said.

John looked at Emmet. "Bravery," he said. "Now go help your ma."

After the girls went to the cooking room, John said, "Tell us about this railroad assignment, Emmet?"

"I thought I'd be doing another year in the South for the reconstruction," Emmet said.

"How bad is it, son?" John said.

"Atlanta was destroyed by Sherman's Army," Emmet said. "It will take years to rebuild. Anyway, General Grant sent for me in Washington and . . ."

"General Grant? John said. "Sent for you personally?"

"Yes sir."

"Son, next to Lincoln, Grant is the most famous man in the world," John said.

"Pa, let him tell it," Ellis said.

"Go on, Emmet," John said.

"They're building the railroad to connect the East Coast to the West," Emmet said. "Grant picked me as second in command for the security detail to protect the workers. He gave me that horse."

"Grant gave you a horse?" John said.

"His name is Bull," Emmet said.

"Well I'll be damned," John said.

"Tell me all the places you been," Ellis said.

"Ohio, Pennsylvania, Virginia, Georgia, South Carolina and Washington DC," Emmet said.

"Were they wonderful?" Ellis said.

"No," Emmet said.

"Not even Washington?" Ellis said.

"Do you know what Washington smells like?" Emmet said.

"What?" Ellis said.

"The fields when we spread manure," Emmet said.

Ellis and John laughed.

"Son, are you going to stay in that uniform or are you going to change?" John said.

"Pa, all I have are uniforms," Emmet said.

"Come on," Ellis said.

Emmet carried his satchel to the bedroom he shared for most of his life with Ellis.

"Ma has washed all your clothes every month since you left," Ellis said.

Emmet opened his dresser and fished out a shirt and a pair of pants. "You did the right thing not joining up," Emmet said. "Six hundred thousand men died, Ellis. The odds are if not me, then you."

"I stayed because Pa needed the help and

with the twins, how could I have left him?" Ellis said.

Emmet hung his holster over the bedpost.

"So how many?" Ellis said.

"How many what?" Emmet said.

"Men did you kill?"

"I stopped counting after thirty," Emmet said.

Ellis stared at Emmet.

"Ellis, I hope you never have to find out what a man can do to another man," Emmet said.

"Let's go have lunch," Ellis said.

"I almost forgot," Emmet said and opened his satchel and dug out John's 1851 Navy Colt.

In the small dining room, Emmet handed John the Colt. "I carried it most of the war, Pa. It served me well," he said. "They gave me the new Colt 1860, so I thought you might want it back."

"Thank you, son," John said.

During lunch, the twins talked about school, John told Emmet about George's visit and Emmet told them about Doctor Adams.

"That old sawbones is a Colonel?" John said.

"I reckon he won't be home until next year sometime," Emmet said.

"Pa, let's go hunting tomorrow, the three of us," Ellis said.

"That's a fine idea, son," John said.

John and Ellis carried their single-shot carbine rifles, Emmet carried his Henry Rifle and his 1860 Navy Colt revolver in his Army holster.

"I read about that Henry Rifle," John said. "Never see one."

Emmet handed it to John. He looked it over. "Quite a rifle, son," he said and handed it back to Emmet.

There was just a moderate amount of snow on the ground and they spotted a flock of wild turkeys withing a half hour. Ellis and John each shot one.

"You didn't shoot, son," John said to Emmet.

"Pa, you hit a turkey with a Henry and there would be nothing left of it but feathers," Emmet said.

"Well, let's see if we can find us a deer," John said.

About an hour later, they spotted a large buck on a hill. Emmet cocked the lever of the Henry Rifle.

"Son, that's over four hundred yards away," John said.

"I know, Pa," Emmet said as he took aim.

He fired and the buck fell to the ground.

John and Ellis stared at Emmet.

"Was one of those medals for shooting?" Ellis said.

"Well, let's go get us some meat," John said.

After dinner, John, Emmet and Ellis put on their coats and took coffee on the porch.

"You didn't ask about Beth, son," John said.

"I didn't need to," Emmet said. "She never returned a letter so I stopped writing."

"She took off with some wandering cowboy three years ago and hasn't been heard from since, except two weeks ago when a letter from Denver, Colorado showed up," John said. "It contained a bank draft for five thousand dollars made out to her parents."

"No matter, Pa," Emmet said. "I forgot her a long time ago."

"It's getting cold, Pa, I better build a fire," Emmis said and went inside.

"I did meet a woman when I was in the hospital," Emmet said. "A beautiful nurse. Her husband died in the war, so we thought. We wanted to get married, Pa."

"What happened?" John said.

"Her husband was in a prisoner camp for

four years and came home," Emmet said.

John stared at Emmet. "Son, I . . ."

"It's alright, Pa," Emmet said. "I think I'll help Ellis with the fire."

"Ma, do you have an old tin pie plate I can have," Emmet said. "I want to teach Ellis how to shoot a revolver."

"I'd like to see that myself," John said.

"Can we watch?" Anna said.

"Grab a hammer and a nail," Emmet said.

Except for Sarah, everybody went to the backyard where a dusting of snow covered the ground.

"Pick out a tree, Ellis," Emmet said. "Then nail the pie plate to it."

Ellis selected a birch tree and nailed the pie plate to the trunk.

"Count out twenty-five feet," Emmet said.

Ellis walked to Emmet, counting out twenty-five paces.

Emmet drew his Colt, cocked it and more looked at the pie plate than aimed and fired six shots that formed a tight-knit group around the nail.

"By God, son," John said. "You really are a soldier."

Emmet handed the Colt to Ellis. "Load it," he said.

Ellis took the Colt to the picnic table

where the loading supplies were set out. He loaded powder, .44 caliber balls and caps and returned to Emmet.

"It's got a kick so don't let it scare you," Emmet said.

Ellis nodded, cocked the Colt, took careful aim, fired and missed the tree entirely. Then he fired five more shots and looked at Emmet.

"Not bad," Emmet said.

"Not bad? I never hit the tree once," Ellis said.

Reload," Emmet said.

Sarah washed and ironed Emmet's uniform a few days before he had to leave. He filled the weeks leading up to his departure with hunting with his father and Ellis, taking the twins for rides on Bull and target practicing with Ellis.

The night before he was to leave, Emmet called John to the bedroom.

"Pa, for four years I've been paid in script and have had very little to spend it on," Emmet said as he reached into his satchel for a money pouch. "This is for you and Ma," he said.

John took the pouch and looked inside. "Son, there must be a thousand dollars in here," he said.

"Ma deserves something nice and so do the twins," Emmet said. "Call it a Christmas present."

"Christmas was three days ago."

"So it's early for next year."

"But you . . ."

"I'm drawing Lieutenant's pay now, Pa," Emmet said. "And I won't have a thing to spend it on."

When Emmet walked Bull from the barn to the front porch, the family was waiting for him. John and Ellis shook his hand. Sarah smothered him in kisses. The twins hugged him and started to cry.

"I thought you two didn't believe in crying," Sarah said as they watched Emmet ride down the road.

Chapter Seven: 1866

On January 2nd, Beth and Rip woke up in a fine, San Francisco hotel. There was a cord beside the bed that summoned room service if you pulled it.

Rip pulled it. When an orderly arrived, Rip ordered a full breakfast for two.

While Beth brushed her hair, Rip rolled a cigarette and looked out the fourth floor window and the view of the bay. There was no doubt San Francisco was a big, beautiful town with a lot of promise.

He turned away from the window. "Beth, honey, I think there's a lot we can do here," he said.

"Besides open a saloon?" Beth said.

Rip nodded.

"Rip, honey, I've learned a lot the past three years, but I am still a girl from the woods, so you have to spell out what you mean," Beth said.

"You don't fool me, sweetheart," Rip said.

"You're as smart as they come and just as tough. After breakfast, we're going shopping for the best dresses for you and suits for me and then we're going to the bank."

"Maybe a shave and a bath is in order first," Beth said.

"Right."

"How do I look?" Beth said as she stood in front of the mirror in the hotel room.

"High society," Rip said.

"And you look very handsome in your new suit," Beth said.

"You don't suppose we can wiggle out of our new duds for a bit?" Rip said.

Beth knew his look when the mood struck Rip. "Later, honey, this dress and slip takes too long to get off," she said.

Rip sighed.

"Don't pout," Beth said. "You'll be taken care of later."

"Alright, let's go banking," Rip said.

"Now, how may I help you?" the bank president said after Beth and Rip took chairs in his office.

"We'd like to have an account opened here in your bank with a wire transfer from the Bank of Denver for one hundred thousand dollars," Rip said.

The bank president cleared his throat. "Do you have . . . ?" he said.

"Right here," Rip said and produced and envelope with the Denver bank information on it.

The bank president reviewed the documents. "First, let's open an account and then I'll wire for the funds," he said.

"Excellent," Rip said. "Now, if you could advise us on potential investments we might get involved with."

"Two things you might wish to invest in that bring solid yields," the bank president said. "Wine in the Napa Valley and gold in the northern goldfields. Both will do nicely for you if you invest wisely."

"Who do we see about investing?" Rip said.

"I suggest the San Francisco Chamber of Commerce as a starting place," the bank president said.

In Iowa, the starting point for the Union Pacific Railroad, Emmet reported to Captain Burke, his commanding officer for the project.

At a meeting, Emmet met Thomas Durant for the second time and chief engineer General Greenville Dodge, one of Grant's generals in the war.

The trainyard was immense and needed to be to house the large amount of trains and supplies needed to lay the track for the expansion west.

Greenville gave a basic outline of the plan to expand west. It would require eleven hundred miles of track to merge with the Central Pacific Railroad and thousands of workers, most of which would be Irish immigrants and veterans of the war and some freed slaves. The lay of the land would determine the course of direction. Black powder would be used to blast where necessary, otherwise workers would scale the terrain to make it fit for tracks.

The work would be done between April and the first snow. As track was laid, settlement camps would be established and workers who chose not to return home until spring could live in them.

They would travel with cattle and butchers and cooks and were authorized to buy cattle along the way when supplies were low.

There would be expected trouble from the Sioux, Arapaho and Cheyenne Indian tribes who would likely feel threatened.

There would be disharmony between white and black workers so soon after the war.

There would be brothels traveling with

the railroad as the men would need entertainment in the wilderness when none was available.

It was the Army's job to keep law and order and the peace.

Durant and Greenville would spend the winter ensuring there would be adequate supplies and recruiting qualified bridge engineers.

Captain Burke, Emmet and twenty-four soldiers would live in three separate living cars for the winter to protect the site from thieves and vandals.

Burke and Emmet established three, eight-hour shifts with eight men to a shift and they settled in for the winter.

Iowa was cold but no colder than Wisconsin and Emmet was used to that kind of climate.

There was little to do to occupy his time so Emmet always stood at least one shift per day and wrote letters home.

By early February, Beth and Rip had invested ten-thousand-dollars in a winery in the Napa Valley that guaranteed to yield a twenty-thousand-dollar return every year and invested another ten-thousand in a mining company that guaranteed a hefty return every year thereafter.

After that, they invested five thousand in an upscale saloon that featured gambling and live acts, mostly female singers.

By March they were quickly establishing themselves as part of the San Francisco elite in society circles.

They purchased a home in the neighborhood called Nob Hill for twenty-thousand-dollars and although it wasn't a mansion, it was still in Nob Hill.

One night, after returning from a dinner party at a neighbor's house, Rip brought up the topic of children.

"I'm thirty now, Beth," Rip said. "I would like a son."

Beth stared at Rip.

"Did you hear me, Beth?" Rip said.

"I hear you," Beth said.

"Well?"

Well what?"

"How do you feel about what I just said?"

"I've been trying to figure out how to tell you I'm two months pregnant," Beth said.

In early March, General Greenville arrived at the railroad camp to check conditions of the snow and terrain.

Burke and Emmet served Greenville coffee in their sleeping car.

"How was your winter, gentlemen?"

Greenville said.

"Not too bad, General," Burke said.

"Any problems?" Greenville said.

"Just boredom, General," Burke said.

"Captain, Lieutenant, I'm not here as a representative of the Army, that's why you're here," Greenville said. "I'm here as the chief engineer of this project. Mr. Greenville will do. Agreed?"

"Agreed," Burke said.

"Now I have some maps I would like you to look at," Greenville said. "Barring any more snow, I'd like to scout ahead a good forty miles and select a route in a few weeks."

"We'll be ready, Mr. Greenville," Burke said.

Spring came early to The Big Woods and the roads cleared by the third week of March. John and Ellis took the wagon to the settlement where John would put in a day's work at the mill, while Ellis went on to Pepin to pick up much needed supplies and any mail.

While in the general store, Ellis gathered up the supplies they needed and the mail, which was several letters from Emmet.

Ellis didn't dare open the letters, that right was reserved for Sarah. He was twenty-three-years-old and Sarah still thought of him as her baby. He supposed that would never change.

As he loaded the wagon with supplies, Ellis noticed a covered wagon across the street. Standing beside the wagon was a striking looking woman of about twenty. She had red hair and green eyes and was just about the most beautiful thing he'd ever seen.

She saw him and smiled and Ellis felt a charge of electricity run through his entire body. He wanted to speak to her but he felt clumsy and foolish, having no idea what to say to him.

She solved the problem for him when she crossed the street and said, "Excuse me, sir, do you live around here?"

Ellis cleared his throat. "Me?" he said.

"I'm looking right at you, aren't I?" she said.

"I live about ten miles west of here," Ellis said.

"Would that be the place they call The Big Woods?" she said.

"Yes, it is," Ellis said.

A burly man of about forty-five exited the general store and looked at the young woman.

"Pa, this man says The Big Woods is ten

miles west of here," she said.

The burly man looked at Ellis. "My daughter and I purchased a farm from the Olson family, are you familiar with them?" he said.

"I know them very well," Ellis said.

"That's where we're headed," the burly man said. "Ten miles west, you said."

"Ten miles west is a small settlement town," Ellis said. "A mile south of there is the Olson farm."

"Obliged," the burly man said.

"I'm headed back, you can follow me," Ellis said.

"We'll do that, thank you."

Several letters from Beth arrived within days of each other in February and when her father picked them up, he read them on the porch with his wife.

The first letter was an act of contrition, begging them for forgiveness at her leaving the way that she did. She explained that she felt that if she stayed on the farm she would have withered and died.

The second letter, Beth explained about the man she married and their good fortune they had in San Francisco.

The third letter contained a bank draft for five thousand and an invitation to live in

San Francisco with them as she was pregnant and they would want to be close to their grandchild.

The next day, they wrote a letter to Mr. Olson's cousin in Illinois and told him he could buy the farm for twelve hundred dollars.

John, Sarah, Ellis and the twins took the wagon to the Olson farm after Ellis came home with the news.

"John, this is my brother Lars Olson and his daughter Bettina," Mr. Olson said.

Ellis, star-struck as he looked at Bettina, nodded.

"Why didn't you tell us?" John said.

"It happened so fast there wasn't time," Mr. Olson said.

Bettina smiled at Ellis and Ellis felt as if he would throw up.

"Everybody on the porch, I made lemonade," Mrs. Olson said.

By the first of April, a hundred workers reported to the railroad yard, along with butchers, cattlemen, construction workers and carpenters.

Greenville and his crew of engineers and Thomas Durant also were on hand.

Greenville asked Emmet to pick four men

for a scouting detail and they rode out the next day. Greenville took a wagon and a soldier worked the reins. Every so often, Greenville made notes on a map.

After two days and forty miles, Greenville ordered the party to return to camp.

The first church gathering after mass saw a hundred or more people take coffee and doughnuts.

Ellis, as he had done a thousand times before, took a doughnut and coffee to the church steps. Thoughts of he, Emmet and Beth doing that very thing flashed through his mind.

"Are you always so clumsy around women?" Bettina said.

Ellis looked up at her. She had a doughnut and coffee and sat beside him.

"I don't get much practice with women," Ellis said. "Not around here."

Bettina looked at the crowd. "I can see why," she said. "I was chatting with your mother. She said your brother is in the Army."

"That's right," Ellis said.

"Why didn't you go?"

"Leave my father to work the farm with two young girls, I couldn't," Ellis said.

"My brother died in the war," Bettina

said. “It killed my mother.”

“I’m sorry to hear that,” Ellis said.

“So are you going to?” Bettina said.

“Am I going to what?” Ellis said.

“Court me or are you just going to sit there eating a doughnut and looking stupid?” Bettina said.

Beth and Rip met Beth’s parents at the railroad station in San Francisco. Her mother cried for twenty minutes. Her father shook Rip’s hand, kissed Beth and seemed genuinely confused.

“You have a great deal to explain,” Beth’s father said.

“Yes, I do,” Beth said. “And I will at home.”

“When is the baby due?” Beth’s mother said.

“Hopefully not before I finish explaining,” Beth said.

Greenville set a goal of three miles of track laid per day, six days a week. By July, thirty miles of new track were down and they were in Nebraska.

The work was back-breaking. Ground had to be graded before ties laid and then workers drove spikes through rails to secure track.

So close to Omaha, there was little concern for trouble from Indians, but Emmet and Burke took their responsibility seriously and kept armed guards escorting workers at all times.

While the starting point was still within easy reach, workers returned by train every night, but thirty miles out they established the first of many settlements they would build along the way.

Wood framed tents went up overnight, as well as saloons and even a brothel.

Emmet and his men kept the peace and there were few problems among the men as the Irish workers didn't socialize with the black workers when the sun went down.

Durant arrived and stayed with the project the rest of the way.

Beth and Rip had purchased a large piece of land in the Napa Valley near the winery and vineyards they owned. There was the main house for themselves and a second, smaller home for her parents.

Between the winery, vineyards, gold mine and saloon, Beth and Rip had an income of one hundred thousand a year, making them one wealthy couple. While her parents didn't quite understand it all, they were overjoyed when she gave birth to a healthy, baby boy in July.

By September, Greenville had led the Union Pacific some sixty miles from the starting point. His goal, weather permitting, was one hundred miles by snowfall.

In October, as they neared eighty miles of track, Emmet spotted the first real signs of trouble when a large group of Sioux warriors watched them from a ridge about three hundred yards away.

The Sioux were a fierce group of warriors, yet they did nothing except watch. At dusk they vanished.

Seeing the Sioux made the workers uneasy. Greenville and Durant met with Burke and Emmet in Durant's private car.

"We have one hundred Henry rifles and the like amount in Colt revolvers if it comes to that," Burke said. "Enough to arm every man in camp. Most of the men are war veterans and would have little trouble defending themselves."

"The point is to not have any distractions that would slow us down," Durant said. "Be it Indians or otherwise."

Emmet kept diligent watches with the men, often times until well into the night. He found that work was the best cure for what ailed him, namely he was still in love with Rose and he needed to keep her out of his thoughts.

On a sunny day in mid-November, Greenville halted work at noon to throw a small celebration at having reached one hundred miles of track.

"It's funny how things turn out," Ellis said. "When we were kids it was Emmett who was the one who wanted to stay on the farm and marry his girl Beth. I dreamed of traveling and seeing all the big cities and towns and it turned out just the opposite."

"Is that so terrible a thing?" Bettina said.

They were having coffee on the church steps after service on a bright, November Sunday morning.

"My father is forty-seven now," Ellis said. "In a few years he won't be able to work the fields alone anymore. He works the saw mill alright, but the work behind the plow is different. I'll be trapped here until I wind up like him, old and used up."

"Why don't we just leave?" Bettina said. "I'm twenty-one, we're both adults and entitled to our own lives."

"Go where? Do what?" Ellis said. "All I know how to do is farm."

"Alright, okay, but do we have to be farmers here?" Bettina said.

"What do you mean?" Ellis said.

"All you know is farming," Bettina said. "Same with your folks, same with my father. Why can't we move? Who says we have to farm here where its frozen half the year. We could sell the farms and move where it's warm and start over. It's been done you know."

"Like where?" Ellis said.

"California," Bettina said.

By the second week of December, most of the work force had returned home or lived in a settlement camp they built to wait out the winter.

They had laid over a hundred and twenty miles of track and constructed two bridges.

The settlement camp was constructed out of lumber and the buildings were quite sturdy, with wood floors and wood stoves for heat. The main source of activity for the men who stayed was gambling, drinking and visiting the brothel.

Emmet, Burke and the soldiers lived on the train and acted as peace officers in the settlement.

On Christmas Eve, while the men celebrated in the saloon, Emmet and his men were on watch and spotted a large group of Sioux warriors on a ridge.

Burke and Emmet watched them with their binoculars.

"What do you think?" Burke said.

"They're certainly interested in us," Emmet said.

"Is that war paint?" Burke said.

"I don't know, I've never seen war paint," Emmet said.

Burke looked to his left and right. All twenty-four men were prone on the roofs of the train, Henry rifles at the ready.

"Lieutenant, go get everybody and bring them into the cars," Burke said. "Give rifles to those that aren't drunk."

Emmet gathered up fifty men and armed them with rifles and placed them inside the trains. The prostitutes he locked away in a sleeper car.

"What do you think?" Burke said when Emmet returned to his side.

"See the one out front," Emmet said. "He the one to give the order to attack."

"Why?" Burke said.

"Well, Captain, they didn't exactly invite us here," Emmet said.

The Sioux warrior in front gave the signal to attack and fifty men on horseback, armed with bows and arrows and lances charged down the hill.

"On my order," Burke said.

When the warriors were fifty yards from the train, Burke yelled, "Fire at will men."

Seventy-five Henry rifles fired at the charging Sioux warriors and a dozen were killed before they retreated to the ridge.

"Are they leaving?" Burke said.

"Not without their dead," Emmet said.

After a quick regroup, the Sioux warriors mounted a second charge that resulted in another dozen dead and a second retreat.

"They don't have enough men for a third charge," Burke said.

"And they know it. Look," Emmet said.

At the top of the ridge, the leader held up his lance that had a white cloth tied to it.

"He wants a parlay," Burke said.

Emmet took off his neckerchief and tied it to the end of his rifle and waved it in the air. "I'll be back, Captain," he said.

"Lieutenant," Burke said.

"I'll be back," Emmet said and he climbed down to the ground.

There was very little snow on the frozen ground as Emmet walked up the side of the hill. The warrior rode down and they met halfway.

"Speak English?" Emmet said.

"Yes. And French and Spanish," the warrior said. "Learned from the traders."

"Why did you attack us?" Emmet said.

"We've done nothing to you."

"Your people have taken our land," the warrior said. "And this is our hunting ground."

"We are building a railroad and we won't disturb your hunting ground," Emmet said. "There are many more soldiers than your people. Your people don't have a chance as you saw today. We want peace and to hurt no one."

"I ask to gather my dead and to take them home."

"Go ahead," Emmet said.

"How are you called?"

"Emmet. You?"

"I am Crazy Horse."

"Go in peace, Crazy Horse," Emmet said.

The night of Christmas Eve, with the soldiers on watch, the men resumed their party inside the makeshift saloon.

Emmet and Burke were in their private car and Burke said, "Lieutenant, I need a drink. Please join me."

"Alright," Emmet said.

They left the train and went to the saloon. As soon as they entered, silence fell like an anvil to the floor.

Burke and Emmet walked to the bar. "Two whiskeys," Burke said and put a dollar on the bar.

"Pick it up, Captain," the bartender said. "The Lieutenant drinks free. tonight"

Burke and Emmet picked up their shot glasses. Burke tossed back his, Emmet took a small sip.

Then every man in the room erupted in loud applause.

On Christmas Eve, Bettina and her father came to dinner at the Boyd home. It started out a clear, crisp night, but after dinner, a sudden storm blew in and snow fell at the rate of two inches an hour.

"Mr. Olson, you can have Emmet's bed and the twins can double up and Bettina can have one of their beds," Ellis said.

"As we have no chance of making it home tonight, we accept your offer," Mr. Olson said.

After the twins went to bed, Bettina said, "Father, Mr. and Mrs. Boyd, Ellis and I would like to talk to you about California."

Chapter Eight: 1867–68

By April of 1867, work resumed. And track was laid at the rate of three plus miles a day, six days a week.

Durant and Greenville were pleased at the progress, but there was a long way to go to meet the Central Pacific in Utah. A final joining point had yet to be determined. Durant and Greenville studied every available map to find the right meeting place for the two railroads to come together.

Several bridges needed to be constructed and blasting of rock slowed the progress somewhat, but by July, they were in Wyoming Territory and established a large settlement they named Cheyenne, after the native tribe.

By November, they were one hundred miles west of Cheyenne and returned east to Cheyenne to spend the winter.

After a month, Cheyenne became more than a settlement, it became a town. People from Nebraska and Colorado showed up and Cheyenne, overnight, was a wild and lawless place. Outlaws, gamblers and rustlers flooded the town and Durant called upon his federal powers to appoint Burke, Emmet and the soldiers as the law.

"Cheyenne belongs to the railroad and as such is federal property," Durant said. "The Army is federal and I am appointing Captain Burke and Lieutenant Boyd as chief peacekeepers."

The job wasn't easy. Every night there was a drunken shooting, a rape a robbery or theft of a horse.

One night back in February, a drunk tried to murder a prostitute in the brothel because she giggled at his tiny bean. The prostitute ran naked into the freezing, snow-covered streets, followed by the drunk.

The drunk had a Bowie knife and grabbed the prostitute by the hair and dragged her through the streets.

"I gonna cut this whore bitch," the drunk screamed to all who watched. "And any man interferes gets the same."

Emmet was the first to arrive.

"Drop the knife, you're under arrest," Emmet said.

"Screw you, law dog," the drunk said.

"I won't say it again," Emmet said.

"I'm gonna gut her like a fish," the drunk said. He placed the knife against the prostitute's stomach and Emmet drew his Colt and shot the drunk dead on the spot.

"Get her inside and then everybody get the hell off the street," Emmet yelled.

Durant and Greenville were surveying maps in Durant's hotel room and witnessed the incident from a window. Durant sent for Emmet after the shooting.

Durant poured Emmet a drink of his best bourbon. "That was quite a display of courage, Lieutenant," Durant said.

"It doesn't take courage to shoot a man," Emmet said.

"None the less, you did what needed to be done and you didn't hesitate in doing it," Durant said. "A second's hesitation and that girl's insides would be all over the street."

Emmet took a sip of bourbon. It was a smooth, easy alcohol that didn't burn his throat.

"Lieutenant, I've seen your war record," Greenville said. "I understand why Grant picked you for this job."

"Are you a married man, Lieutenant?" Durant said.

"No sir," Emmet said.

"You should think about it," Durant said.

"I will," Emmet said.

In early May of 68, work was in full gear. After a full shift, Emmet and Burke were headed to their car when Burke said, "Let's get a drink, Lieutenant," he said.

"I'm not much of a drinking man, but I'll go with you," Emmet said.

When they entered the saloon, workers just off a shift were playing cards and drinking and some were in the back with the prostitutes.

"Bourbon," Burke said.

"Coffee," Emmet said.

"Want bourbon in it?" the bartender said.

"Just coffee."

The bartender poured a cup of coffee for Emmet from a pot resting on a woodstove.

"Let's get a table," Burke said.

Emmet and Burke found a vacant table and took chairs.

"Emmet, something I've been meaning to discuss with you," Burke said.

Emmet sipped coffee and waited.

"I'm resigning my commission," Burke said. "I've been away from home for six years and it's time."

"I understand," Emmet said. "I've been home once since sixty-one."

"This job is going to take another two

years, why not go?" Burke said.

"Funny thing, I got a letter from my folks back in Wisconsin not long ago," Emmet said. "They sold the farm and are moving to California. No word where yet, so I have no home to go back to at the moment."

"I'm recommending you to be promoted to Captain before I leave," Burke said.

"I appreciate that, Captain," Emmet said.

"I'm going to turn in," Burke said. "I'm not as young as I used to be."

"I won't be long," Emmet said.

"Mind if I sit with you?"

Emmet turned and looked at Eva. She was the madam at the brothel. A tall, striking woman of about thirty, she had auburn hair and green eyes.

"Sure," Emmet said.

Eva looked at the bartender. "Phil, a cup of coffee please," she said.

Phil brought a cup to Eva, who sat opposite Emmet. "You know, Lieutenant, you've been with us since 65 and not once have you visited my girls," she said. "Why is that?"

"I represent the Army, ma'am and the law," Emmet said. "It doesn't mix if one day I have to arrest you down the road."

"I see," Eva said. "Are you married, Lieutenant?"

"No, I'm not."

"How old are you if I may ask?"

"Twenty-six," Emmet said.

"Do you plan to spend your life in the Army?"

"No. I think when the job here is done, I'll be on my way," Emmet said.

"To where?"

"California, maybe."

"You know, Lieutenant, before you killed that drunk who was going to cut my girl, every man in camp respected you," Eva said. "Now every last damn one of them is afraid of you."

"I didn't realize that," Emmet said.

"Why are you wasting yourself?" Eva said. "My bed is empty. Come fill it."

"Not tonight, Eva," Emmet said. "I'm tired and need sleep."

"When this job is over, I'm going back to Cheyenne and open a real saloon. Why not go with me?"

"When this job is done, ask me then." Emmet said.

In June of 68, Captain Burke left the railroad and Greenville gave Emmet a field promotion to Captain will full authority concerning security on the project.

Durant was squabbling by telegram with

Charles Croker, head of the Pacific Railroad on where the two railroads would finally join. They argued that Salt Lake City should be the meeting place, but that was mostly to appease the Mormon leader Brigham Young, head of the Mormon Church who had built a large settlement in Salt Lake City.

With the aid of the invention of dynamite, the Union Pacific was able to blast through rock and build bridges quicker. As they reached Utah, General Grant came to camp in August to meet with Durant and Greenville.

Grant wanted a final meeting place established and he threatened withholding federal funds if one was not established within the month.

Greenville promised a final destination before the winter.

"I'm holding you to that, General," Grant said. "I'll expect a telegram before the winter."

Beth and Rip's primary residence was the large house in the Napa Valley near their winery. Beth's parents occupied the second house on the property where they doted on their one-year-old grandson Robert Junior, Rip's real name.

At breakfast one morning in late June, as he opened the mail, Rip said, "The bank in San Francisco needs our signatures on that money transfer from the mine."

"My parents can stay with the baby and I'll go with you," Beth said.

"We haven't done the town in a while, why not?" Rip said.

Sometimes Beth could hardly believe the good fortune she and Rip experienced. Had she stayed behind waiting for Emmet, she'd be an old woman by now with tanned skin and blistered hands and no future.

Rip was a good man and good to her and her parents and he loved the baby. They had wealth and good health and her parents forgave her for leaving them.

Still, every once in a while she thought of Emmet. Wondered where he was, what he was doing, if he was married with children, if he returned to the farm or struck out on his own.

Her parents told her he never returned to the farm, but since they've been with her, he could have, but she doubted it.

Thinking about him was a waste of time. He was not part of her life and hadn't been in seven years.

"We'll go tomorrow," Rip said.

■ ■ ■ ■

John, Ellis and Lars Olson walked out of the land office in Sacramento and walked across the street to the restaurant where Bettina, Sara, the twins and Bettina and Ellis's baby girl waited.

The trip to California wasn't easy. The two families had to sell their farms and scrape together every penny they could muster, but finally left The Big Woods with eight thousand dollars.

"Well?" Sarah said.

"We got our land," John said. "One thousand acres with room to build two houses."

"How much?" Sarah said.

"Four thousand," John said.

"Let's order lunch and go take a look," Sarah said.

The ride from stocking to the land they purchased took about an hour and they made the trip in two wagons.

Most of the farms in the valley grew melons and oranges and potatoes.

They decided on corn, which was in short supply in California and had to be imported.

"Corn will do just fine," John said as they inspected the rich topsoil. "And bring us a fair profit as they don't have winter here and we can grow two cycles a year."

"Pa, where do we go to school?" Anna said.

"Sacramento," John said. "It's only an hour away and I can take you and pick you every day."

"What do we do first?" Sarah said.

"Lars and I can get started on building the houses," John said.

"I can turn and plant, Pa," Ellis said.

"And I can help if Sarah can watch the baby," Bettina said.

"We can help," Anna said.

"Of course you can," Sarah said.

"That reminds me," John said. "We better write Emmet and let him know."

"We need to get back for the Fourth of July," Beth said. "We're hosting the barbeque this year."

"I know, hon, I'm doing most of the cooking," Rip said.

Beth squeezed his arm. "We've done well," she said.

"Because of you," Rip said.

"That's not true."

"Yes it is and you know it," Rip said. "Without you I probably would have squandered every penny."

They were in their carriage, on the way to Sacramento. The trip took about three hours each way. The plan was to stay overnight at the Sacramento Hotel, go to the bank in the morning and head home in the early afternoon.

As they rode by a grove of trees, two men on horseback rode out and blocked their path. Both men were armed with Colt revolvers.

"Such a nice day for a buggy ride," one of the men said.

Rip's first instinct was to reach for his gun, but Beth convinced him years ago not to carry one anymore.

"What do you men want?" Rip said.

"Everything you got," one of the men said and drew his Colt. "And maybe get her too."

Rip stood up in the buggy. "Over my dead body," he said.

"No problem," the man said and shot Rip in the chest and he fell to the ground.

Beth stood up and screamed.

"Shut her up," the other man said.

The first man rode to the buggy and smacked Beth in the head with the barrel of his Colt.

Before Grant left the railroad camp, he

called Emmet to his private car for dinner.

Grant's personal chef prepared baked chicken.

"Forgive my tardiness in presenting you your captain's bars," Grant said.

"Thank you, General," Emmet said.

"I'd like to ask a few things, Captain," Grant said.

Certainly, sir," Emmet said.

"It appears as if the railroad project will conclude next summer some time," Grant said. "What are your plans after that?"

"I don't know, sir," Emmet said. "My family sold their farm and moved away. I don't know where yet. "I suppose I'll go visit them when they do. After that I don't know."

"I'd like to propose something to you, Captain," Grant said. "And keep in mind you've more than proven yourself to me and the Army."

"Alright, General," Emmet said.

"The settlement Cheyenne is growing quickly," Grant said. "Talk is to connect to Montana and Colorado for the beef industry. But it's a lawless place as you know. Without law and order the cattle industry won't form a central hub. I'd like you to act as the law in Cheyenne and civilize the place. I know you can do it, hell you've already done it once before."

"For how long and what authority will I have?" Emmet said.

"A year and your authority is the Federal Government," Grant said. "You'll wear a badge but still be the rank of Captain and draw two hundred and fifty a month."

"I'll need deputies," Emmet said.

"Four to start," Grant said. "Pick your own men."

"Alright, General, as I have no other plans, I accept," Emmet said.

Beth opened her eyes in a bed in the hospital in Sacramento. For a few seconds, she had no idea where she was and then she sat up in bed and screamed.

A doctor and a nurse rushed into the room.

"Easy Mrs. Taylor," the doctor said.

"My husband?" Beth said.

"I'm sorry," the doctor said.

"They shot him for no reason," Beth said.

"Nurse, get a sedative and a glass of water," the doctor said.

"Right away, doctor," the nurse said.

"How did I get here?" Beth said.

"A man riding along came across your carriage," the doctor said. "He brought you in. The sheriff wants to talk to you but I told him it would have to wait."

"No. No, I'll see him now," Beth said.

Emmet left Grant and walked to his private car. The camp was alive with men singing in the saloon and others sitting in front of campfires.

Men nodded to Emmet as he walked past them until he reached the private car that was somewhat secluded.

As he took the first step, Eva came out of the shadows on the platform. "I've been waiting for you," she said.

"Why?" Emmet said.

"Let's go inside and I'll show you."

"Not a good idea," Emmet said.

"Relax, Captain," Eva said. "I'm the madam, not a whore. I choose who shares my bed, not who pays for it."

Eva opened the door. "You first," she said.

"We don't know who the two men are that shot your husband," the sheriff said. "Saddle tramps most likely. I have a posse out looking for them right now."

"Am I allowed to offer a reward for their capture?" Beth said.

"You are," the sheriff said.

"Do it. Make it ten thousand dollars," Beth said.

"Would you recognize the men if you saw

them again?" the sheriff said.

"I'll never forget them," Beth said.

"There's a man who sketches for the Sacramento Register," the sheriff said. "I'd like you to describe them to him and he'll make a sketch."

"Get him," Beth said.

Beth fell into a deep depression after Rip's death. For a month, she never left the house. Her parents took control of the baby while Beth took powders to sleep most of the day. She barely ate and lost considerable weight.

Concerned for her life, her parents sent for a doctor and paid him to live in the house.

She ignored the businesses and her parents did their best to understand the necessary paperwork required from the mine, the winery and the saloon and unable to execute what was needed, the sought the services of a lawyer in Stockton.

In September, the sheriff paid her a visit.

"The two men who murdered your husband were captured in San Diego, Mrs. Taylor," he said. "The trial is next week at the Stockton courthouse. Would you like to attend?"

"Not just the trial, but their hanging,"

Beth said.

By mid-September, the first crop of corn was close to harvest.

Ellis, John and Lars concentrated on building the first of two homes. As the property abutted a fresh creek, they knew water was underground and first installed two water pumps. The hardest part was digging the wells and installing the pipes and pumps. The house would be built around the pumps, with one being in the kitchen and the other outside near where a corral would be built.

They took several weeks off to harvest the corn and another two weeks to load both wagons and bring the corn to Stockton to market.

Their profit was considerable.

By late October, they were back to work on the construction of the first house. A second crop would be planted in December after the fields were enriched with manure.

After a week-long trial, the two men who murdered Rip were found guilty and sentenced to hang by the neck until dead.

The execution was scheduled to take place inside a barn and only the sheriff and his deputies, reporters and Beth and her parents and witnesses appointed by the court were allowed to attend.

It gave Beth great satisfaction to watch the two murderers cry like babies when they were led up the stairs to the gallows.

She stared at them as hoods were placed over their heads and her eyes never blinked as the hangman pulled the lever that dropped them to their death.

Only when they were cut down and their bodies removed did Beth turn and walk away.

Utah was a beautiful territory but cold. Wildlife was everywhere, even in the mountains. The Ute Indians were a fierce tribe but rarely showed themselves. Utah was also frigid during the winter months.

Construction shut down and another camp was established for the winter.

Durant and Greenville returned to Washington to report progress and secure funds for the coming spring, leaving Emmet literally in charge.

One bonus of the railroad expansion was that for each mile of track laid, telegraph poles were dug and wires strung, so that the camp was just a telegraph wire away from Washington.

Since the first time they slept together,

Eva didn't sleep with her girls in the tent. She spent her nights with Emmet in his private car.

No one objected. At twenty-six, Emmet was a commanding force and kept the peace and law and order and Eva was the envy of her girls.

After the first snowfall, the camp settled in to wait out the winter months.

Chapter Ten: 1869

Beth threw herself into running the companies she purchased with Rip. For years her interest was mild as he ran everything and took care of the paperwork as well as overseeing the daily operations.

She became so engrossed in the work, she left the baby in her parents care on a daily basis. Her parents didn't mind taking care of the baby, but they worried that Beth was neglecting her son in order to concentrate on business.

In early April, her father took Beth to Stockton to meet with the bank.

While Beth was in the bank, Ellis was loading a wagon with supplies at the general store across the street. Ellis happened to glance at the bank as Beth came out and he was nearly floored by the striking resemblance she bore to Beth Olson.

When Beth looked at Ellis and her face went white, Ellis realized that it was in fact

Beth. He ran across the street, dodging two horses and jumped onto the woos sidewalk in front of Beth.

"My God, it is you," Ellis said.

"Ellis," Beth said. "What are you doing here?"

"I live here," Ellis said. "North of here on a farm. With Ma and Pa, the twins, my wife and baby girl."

"Oh my God," Beth said.

"So this is where you went?" Ellis said.

"Not at first," Beth said.

"You look fine and prosperous," Ellis said.

"And you look like you've done well, too," Beth said.

"Wait until I tell everybody," Ellis said.

"We have a great deal to catch up on," Beth said. "Come to the house on Saturday and bring everybody."

"Where do you live?"

Beth opened her handbag and reached for a pad and pencil. "I'll write it down for you," she said. "Come around one."

In late March the snow melted. Durant and Greenville returned from Washington and by early April, construction resumed.

One night after work, while Emmet and Eva were having dinner in his private car, Emmet said, "Remember the talk we had about Cheyenne?"

"I remember," Eva said.

"I will be going to Cheyenne after this job is done," Emmet said. "General Grant has asked me to be the law in Cheyenne for a period of one year."

"That's wonderful, Emmet," Eva said. "I can make a lot of money in Cheyenne with my girls and with you keeping the peace, it should be easy."

"We've gotten close, haven't we?" Emmet said.

"You knot head, I love you," Eva said.

"I believe I feel the same way, so this is difficult," Emmet said.

"What is difficult?" Eva said.

"Being the law while you run a brothel," Emmet said.

"I don't sleep with . . ."

"I know you don't," Emmet said. "But if Grant orders me to shut down and arrest the girls, I don't want to be caught in the middle."

"I see," Eva said. "Well, would he shut down a legitimate saloon?"

"No, he wouldn't," Emmet said. "Is that what you're thinking?"

"For months now me and the ladies have been discussing what to do after the railroad is complete," Eva said. "I have enough money squirreled away to open a saloon and furnish it with whiskey and tables. My girls will handle all the gambling and one sings like you never heard."

"Lady gamblers?" Emmet said.

"Dealers," Eva said. "Poker, blackjack, pharaoh, dice, think of the crowds women dealers will draw. Two girls will work the bar, one singer and I'm the owner. What do you think?"

"I think you'll make a fortune," Emmet said. "One thing you'll need is qualified men working for you to keep the peace."

"Bouncers is what they call them back east," Eva said.

"Whatever they call them, you'll need them," Emmet said. "Gambling, drinking cowboys will want whores and when they can't get them they'll get mean."

"You'll help me with that, right?" Eva said.

"I'll enforce the law, but you'll still need two qualified men and you'll have to pay them decent," Emmet said.

"When do you think the railroad will be finished?" Eva said.

"A month," Emmet said.

"That quickly?"

"The Union Pacific is so close I can ride to it in a day," Emmet said.

■ ■ ■ ■

John, Sarah, and the twins rode three plus hours to reach Beth's home in the valley. Lars, Ellis, Bettina and the baby followed in a second wagon.

When they reached Beth's home, John said, "Will you look at this."

"She's done well," Sarah said.

"That is an understatement," John said.

When both wagons arrived, they were met on the porch by Beth and her parents.

"By God," Lars said when he shook his brother's hand.

Beth had a fulltime cook and housekeeper and lunch was served in the main dining room. Talk was of Beth's adventures with Rip and how she came to her wealth and his untimely murder.

"I read the story in the paper but didn't connect it to you," John said.

"They used my married name so there was no reason you should," Beth said.

"I can't get over this," John said. "Half a country away and here we all are again."

"After lunch, let's take a ride through the vineyards," Beth suggested.

Durant, Greenville, Emmet and four of

Emmet's men rode west to meet with Charles Croaker, the head of the Central Pacific project.

The day before, Emmet sent a rider to request Croaker meet half way.

They met Croaker in a field where a large table with chairs waited. A gallon coffee pot rested in a campfire.

Durant and Greenville sat with Croaker. Emmet and his men and Croaker's men stood watch in the background.

"Brigham Young has a pretty good grouch on about the railroad missing Salt Lake City," Croaker said.

"The railroad, not to mention the federal government isn't in the habit of promoting religious cults," Durant said.

"Nonetheless, he can make trouble for us in Washington seeing as how you promised him in return for services and lumber the railroad would stop in Salt Lake City," Croaker said.

"Considered, not promised," Durant said.

"Gentlemen, we have sixty miles of track on the Union Pacific side and the like amount from the west," Greenville said. "We can link the two in as early as twenty days if we decide on the place to do so. Grant is awaiting our answer."

"Let's look at the map," Croaker said.

After an hour or so of back and forth, all agreed on Promontory Point as the joining location of the two railroads.

When Durant, Greenville and Emmet returned to camp, Durant sent a telegram to Washington with the news.

While getting supplies in Stockton, Ellis checked the mail and there was a letter from Emmet. As usual, he didn't open it and left it for Sarah to read later tonight.

As he returned to the wagon, he spotted Beth coming out of the bank with her father. He crossed the street and met them at their buggy.

"Beth, Mr. Olson, how are you?" Ellis said.

"Just fine, Ellis," Mr. Olson said. "How is the baby?"

"Growing like a weed," Ellis said.

"Honey, I have some shopping to do at the general store, why don't you catch up with Ellis?" Mr. Olson said.

Ellis and Beth went to the coffee shop.

"Ellis, at dinner the other night we talked about everything except Emmet," Beth said.

"Ma thought it best not to bring him up unless you did," Ellis said.

"I'm twenty-seven-years old, a widow, a mother and control three business, I'm not going to fall apart at the mention of his name," Beth said.

"I expect not," Ellis said.

"So tell me about him," Beth said.

"He came home from the war a Lieutenant," Ellis said. "Changed some, but I expect war changes a man."

"How?"

"More quiet. Like he had things he could never talk about," Ellis said. "He said he was asked by General Grant to . . ."

"General Grant?" Beth said.

Ellis nodded. "General Grant asked him to work as the security for the railroad expansion," he said. "He's now a Captain."

"A Captain? You mean he's been with the railroad all this time?"

"The last four years."

"The newspapers say the railroad will be complete in a month," Beth said. "Will he be coming to visit?"

"I expect so," Ellis said.

"Would you let me know?"

Ellis looked at her.

"Please," Beth said.

On May 9th, on Promontory Point, about a thousand people gathered in anticipation of the joining of the railroad.

Hundreds of reporters from around the

country gathered with Washington officials and diplomats. The atmosphere was charged and circus-like.

Emmet and his men were on high alert for any signs of trouble.

That night, the swelled camp was like one giant party. He had dinner with Eva in his private car and then returned to duty until after two in the morning and found her waiting up for him.

"I can't sleep without you anymore," she said.

"Tomorrow all this nonsense is over," Emmet said.

"And then we go to Cheyenne?" Eva said.

"I want to visit my parents first," Emmet said. "Will you go with me?"

"I don't think so, Emmet. Not right now," Eva said.

"Why not?"

"Let's just say I don't think your parents are quite ready to meet me," Eva said. "Go on and I'll wait for you in Cheyenne."

"Alright," Emmet said.

The next day, at 12:47 in the afternoon, the final rail was laid and Durant drove in the Golden Spike to complete the Transcontinental Railroad.

After receiving Emmett's telegram that he

would be in Sacramento on May 14th, the entire family waited at the railroad station for his westbound train to arrive.

When the train arrived at the station, Sarah could barely contain herself and John had to hold her arm.

Hundreds of passengers exited the train and flooded the platform. Some were reporters, some were railroad executives, others came from New York, Boston and Philadelphia just to ride across the country in five days.

Then, from behind the crowd, Sarah spotted Emmet as he walked with his horse Bull, She watched in awe at the sight of her son as people parted to make way for him.

Unable to contain themselves, Anna and Emma, now thirteen broke free and ran to Emmet.

They hugged him and Emmet said, "You two are young ladies now."

He lifted both onto the saddle and walked the rest of the platform to Sarah, John, Ellis, Bettina and the baby.

Emmet smiled. "Hello, Ma," he said.

"Welcome home," Sarah said. "Captain."

Emmet, after changing clothes, sat with Ellis at a picnic table in the backyard of the house he shared with Bettina and the baby.

Each had a cup of coffee.

"I don't really see any point in seeing Beth, Ellis," Emmet said. "Whatever we had was a long time ago in the past and from what you told me, she's done alright."

"More than alright," Ellis said. "She's the richest woman in the entire valley."

"I'm happy for her, but I came to see my family, not her," Emmet said. "And I'm only going to be here for a short time."

Bettina rang the dinner bell on the front porch.

"She's a hell of a cook, come on," Ellis said.

At the dinner table, talk was of the railroad and Emmet told them of his appointment by Grant as federal peace officer for Cheyenne.

"Is that what you want, son?" John said.

"I don't know what I want, Pa," Emmet said. "I'm not needed here but I am needed there and Cheyenne is now less than three days away on the train."

"Why don't you see Beth?" Sarah said. "Make peace with her before you go."

"I'm not angry with her Ma," Emmet said. "We were little more than kids back then. She has the right to her own life, as do I."

Sarah stared at Emmet.

Emmet sighed. "Alright, I'll go see her," he said.

Emmet wore his full uniform when he set out on Bull to Beth's house in the valley. The ride took about three hours. He didn't mind. It was a very pretty ride and after so much cold weather a little sun on his face was more than welcome.

As he rode up to Beth's massive house, her father was on the porch. He stood and looked at Emmet in disbelief. "Beth, you better get out here," he said.

Beth came out to the porch and her face registered her shock at seeing Emmet atop his tall horse.

As he dismounted, Beth fought the urge to run and hug him. Instead she said, "Emmet, what a lovely surprise."

"Hello Beth, Mr. Olson," Emmet said.

"Come on up, I'll get you something cool to drink," Mr. Olson said.

"Father, ask Ma to pack a picnic basket," Beth said. "I'll take Emmet for a ride through the groves."

"Have you ever seen orange groves before?" Beth said.

"No," Emmet said.

"We have orange groves here and on the

other side is a vineyard for wine," Beth said.

"Your husband must have been a sharp businessman," Emmet said.

"He was," Beth said. "He was a lot of things. Some good and some bad like all men."

"Your son is how old?"

"Twenty six months."

"You've done well," Emmet said.

"So have you," Beth said. "There's a good spot in that clearing."

Emmet drove the buggy to the clearing and helped Beth down. Then they spread out a large blanked and unpacked the basket.

Beth's cook had made fried chicken and the bottle of wine was made from the grapes at the vineyard.

"What do you think of the wine we make?" Beth said.

"I'm not much for drinking, but it's pretty good," Emmet said.

"What are your plans?" Beth said.

"Well, it's back to Cheyenne for at least a year," Emmet said.

"Why?"

"General Grant asked me to," Emmet said.

"General Grant? Personally?"

"Yes."

"What is Cheyenne?" Beth said.

"As the railroad moved west it built settlements along the way," Emmet said. "Cheyenne is a settlement that has become a town. It's now a major hub for the beef industry coming out of Montana and Colorado. Grant has appointed me a federal marshal to keep the peace."

"You have done well," Beth said.

"Could I ask a small favor?" Emmet said.

"Sure."

"May I have a few bottles of this wine to give to Grant?" Emmet said.

"Of course," Beth said. "You know, Emmet, you don't have to be so polite to me. After all, I wasn't very nice to you when you joined the Army."

"We were kids and it was a long time ago," Emmet said.

"I need to ask you for forgiveness," Beth said.

"There is nothing to forgive," Emmet said. "Like I said, we were just kids."

"We can be friends, can't we?" Beth said.

"When did we stop?" Emmet said.

A week later, when the family saw Emmet to the train, he left with a case of Beth's wine for Grant.

Emmet didn't bother getting a sleeper car.

The ride to Cheyenne was just sixteen hours and he spent most of the time looking out the window at the scenery. The countryside was beautiful and each state and territory was unique to itself.

Nevada was mountains and pine trees. Utah was beautiful mountains and rough terrain. Idaho was also mountain and valleys and Wyoming was a combination of all three.

It was a strange experience seeing Beth after eight years. He still didn't know how he felt about it. She was still pretty, but more woman than girl now. In a way she reminded him of Eva in that regard. A woman's face and body rather than a young girl.

Beth will remarry. She was too wealthy not to. Some businessman will come to town and their marriage will be more of a merger than a union of two people.

Around six o'clock, Emmet went to the dining car for dinner. He ordered a steak with rice and carrots and it was surprisingly good.

By eight o'clock, Emmet was back in his seat. Night had taken the view and there was nothing to do but wait.

It occurred to him that he had no idea where Eva would be in Cheyenne. Not that with a thousand residents it was that big, but she could be anywhere.

He wasn't worried about the family. Everyone was well and they were prosperous and even Ellis seemed content with his wife and baby.

For some reason that escaped him, Emmet thought of Rose. He wondered how she was doing, if her husband recovered and if she was happy.

He hoped that she was. Happy. She deserved a happy life.

The train arrived in Cheyenne just after midnight. He retrieved Bull and carried the crate of wine from the station to the center of town and walked along Front Street.

The saloons were alive with music and laughter.

He needed a place to sleep and board Bull for the night. As he walked along, he noted the many changes that took place since the railroad had established Cheyenne as a settlement. Most of the buildings were made of wood, but a few were constructed of brick. Grant was president now and appointed John Campbell as the governor of Wyoming Territory and as governor, Campbell would be located somewhere in Cheyenne.

"You, soldier," a man called from above.

Emmet paused and looked up. On the second floor balcony of a hotel, John Campbell looked down.

"I was told to expect Captain Emmet Boyd, would you be him?" Campbell said.

"I am," Emmet said.

"Come on up," Campbell said.

"I need to board my horse," Emmet said.

"The hotel has a livery," Campbell said. "Get a room and then meet me in number twelve."

After getting a room, Emmet knocked on Campbell's door. He answered with a drink in his right hand and a cigar in his left.

"Captain Boyd, welcome," Campbell said. "President Grant sent me your file. Most impressive. Care for a drink?"

"Not tonight, Governor," Emmet said. "I'm looking forward to a bed after sixteen hours on the train."

"Understandable," Campbell said. "Let's meet for breakfast in the lobby at eight tomorrow morning. After that I'll show you the brand-new sheriff's office and your living quarters."

"Grant has promised me I can pick my own deputies," Emmet said.

"He told me," Campbell said. "Believe me I have no intentions of interfering with your duties, Captain."

"Thank you, Governor," Emmet said. "I'll see you for breakfast."

Wearing civilian clothes, including a vest and his Colt sidearm, Emmet entered the hotel dining room where Campbell was at a table.

"Good morning, Captain," Campbell said. "Sleep well?"

"Very," Emmet said as he took a chair.

Campbell motioned to a waiter who brought Emmet coffee.

"First order of business," Campbell said and slid a marshal's badge across the table. "From President Grant."

Emmet pinned the badge to his vest.

"Cheyenne has growing pains," Campbell said. "In less than a year from now it will be connected to Montana and Colorado by the railroad and will become a hub for the beef industry. The problem is it needs law and order to prosper. That's where you come in, Marshal."

"I sent for four men I want as my deputies," Emmet said.

"Fine."

"They need a place to live."

"Taken care of," Campbell said. "I'll show you after breakfast."

■ ■ ■ ■

The sheriff's office and jail was constructed of brick and had four cells, a desk, a rack of Henry Rifles and a spare cot. Emmet took the keys and locked the door on the way out.

At the end of Front Street, down a side street stood a small, wood frame house. Campbell handed Emmet the key. "This one is yours," he said.

"My deputies?" Emmet said.

"That two-story house across the street is theirs," Campbell said.

"Grant has been most generous," Emmet said.

"Grant expects a lot in return. I'll tell you what I expect," Campbell said. "I expect you and your men to enforce the law to the letter. Now I realize that men, especially cowboys off a drive need their fun, but I will not tolerate a brothel inside the town limits. One hundred yards off the town limits and they must build it themselves. No tents."

"Are there any in town right now?" Emmet said.

"Two and I want them both closed and moved as soon as they build a structure one hundred yards beyond the town limits," Campbell said. "The Gay Lady and the Cowboy Tavern,"

"I'll speak with them today," Emmet said.

"The other thing," Campbell said. "I've been here five weeks and there has been eleven shootings. It is within my power to enact a no firearms inside the town limits ordinance, which I will do when your deputies arrive."

"I expect them any day and we will enforce it," Emmet said. "Is there a print shop in town?"

"A newspaper."

"That will do."

"I'll have signs made for you to post," Campbell said.

"I'm going over to the office, then I'll speak to the brothels," Emmet said. "Oh, Governor, before I forget, my lady friend from the railroad has this crazy idea of opening a saloon with all women dealers and bartenders."

"Oh yes, she saw me," Campbell said. "Two days ago. I told her to get a license from the town clerk and wished her luck. You'll find her on Main Street at the center of the block."

"Thanks, Governor," Emmet said.

After leaving Campbell, Emmet took a

walk through town. The streets were muddy but wood sidewalks helped people come and go without too much trouble. The town had a general store, seven saloons, a freight company, two livery stables, a post office, a telegraph office, a town hall and a half dozen more buildings were under construction.

Close to the railroad, cattle pens were being built.

Across the street from the hotel, a building was being constructed for the Stock Grower's Association.

Emmet went into the general store. The man behind the counter looked at Emmet's badge. "About goddamn time," he said. "I'm Greenly, owner of this establishment."

"Emmet Boyd and I'm the new marshal," Emmet said.

"What can I do for you, Marshal?" Greenly said.

"Do you have the conversion kits for my Colt?" Emmet said.

"I do. Is yours a .44?"

"It is."

"The kit is fifteen dollars, but for twenty-five you can buy a factory made Colt chambered in the new .44 self-contained cartridge," Greenly said.

"Let me see the Colt," Emmet said.

Greenly unlocked a case and placed a brand new Colt revolver on the counter. Emmet picked it up. It was nearly identical to the Colt he'd carried the past five years, except it was chambered for the new self-contained cartridge instead of cap and ball.

"I'll take the Colt, a conversion kit and a couple of bricks of ammunition," Emmet said.

"President Grant has allowed two hundred dollars a month for expenses for the sheriff's department, so I'll just add this to the tab," Greenly said. "Oh, you'll want a new holster that holds eighteen rounds."

"Thank you," Emmet said.

After leaving the general store, Emmet went to his office and loaded the new Colt, added eighteen rounds to the holster and put it on. Then he locked the office door and walked to the Main Street to a building that was being converted to a saloon.

He opened the door and walked in. Eva's girls were busy cleaning and building and several men were hammering and sawing.

One of the girls stopped what she was doing and walked to Emmet. "Eva is at the freight office," she said. "We're expecting some furniture and fixings."

"Where have you girls been staying?" Emmet said.

"Eva rented a house at the end of the block," she said. "If you want to wait we have some coffee."

"I have some things to do," Emmet said. "Tell her I'll be back."

Closest was the Cowboy Tavern and Emmet stopped there first. Although it was just eleven o'clock in the morning, thirty men were at tables and the bar. The bartender looked at Emmet's badge. "I heard we were getting the law," he said.

"Who owns this place?" Emmet said.

"See that rather large man at the table there? Him. Name is Corker," the bartender said.

Emmet walked to the table. "Corker?" he said.

Corker looked at Emmet's badge. "Heard Campbell was expecting a marshal. Sit down, have a drink," he said.

Emmet took a chair. Corker had a shot of whiskey and a cup of coffee in front of him.

"Governor Campbell wants you to move your brothel outside the town limits," Emmet said.

"That's crazy," Croker said "I got eight girls working here and . . ."

"And they can continue to work outside the town limits," Emmet said. "Build them a house and it's business as usual."

"And who pays for it?"

"What do you charge?"

"Five dollars for a straight, extra for an extra," Croker said.

"Put in a nice bar for your customers, a bath tub and have your ladies trained in haircuts and shaving and up your prices and you'll make a fortune," Emmet said.

Croker looked at Emmet.

"And obey the no firearms ordinance and you won't have any trouble," Emmet said.

"What firearm ordinance?"

"The one Governor Campbell is enacting."

"Can he do that?"

"He was appointed by President Grant, he can do it," Emmet said. "Look at it this way, if nobody is armed, nobody in your place gets shot."

"Can you enforce it?" Croker said.

"I'll enforce it," Emmet said. "And build your brothel on the west side of town a hundred yards away," Emmet said. "I'll have the Gay Lady do the same on the east. That way you'll get your fair share of business without stepping on each other's toes."

"Marshal, I have the feeling you're going to do just fine here in Cheyenne," Croker said.

Emmer crossed the street and spoke to

the owner of the Gay Lady, a man named Pike.

"Croker agree to this?" Pike said.

"He saw the wisdom of expanding his business," Emmet said. "I hope you do the same."

"East side of town, huh?"

"A hundred yards out," Emmet said.

"I can live with it," Pike said.

"Good," Emmet said.

Emmet returned to Main Street where Eva was waiting for him in front of the saloon she was building with her girls.

Eva's face lit up as she hugged him. "I am so glad to see you, Emmet," she said.

"Same here," Emmet said.

"Come inside for some coffee," Eva said.

Emmet went in with her and Eva said, "Girls, take a break."

Eva's eight girls came to the table, bringing a pot of coffee and cups.

"Did you see Campbell?" Eva said.

"I did," Emmet said.

"He thinks we're crazy," Eva said. "But you just wait until we open."

"What about two men for bouncers?" Emmet said.

"I thought I'd leave that to you," Eva said.

"I'll see what I can do," Emmet said.

"Right now I have more work to do."

"Come get me when you're done," Eva said.

Emmet found Campbell at the hotel in the lobby.

"My house is ready but my office isn't," Campbell said. "So I run the state from the lobby of this hotel."

"I spoke with Croker and Pike and both have agreed to your plan," Emmet said.

"Any trouble?"

"None."

"Good. I asked the newspaper to print up a hundred fliers about the no guns in town policy," Campbell said. "He said two days."

"My deputies will be here tomorrow," Emmet said. "As soon as the fliers are ready we'll post them all over town."

"Marshal, I don't invite violence but don't let anybody buffalo you when it comes to enforcing the policy," Campbell said.

"We won't," Emmet said.

"I see you changed out your sidearm," Campbell said.

"Yes and if you hear shooting tomorrow it's me and my men practicing outside of town," Emmet said.

"Where are we going?" Eva said.

"I'm hungry," Emmet said. "I thought we'd get something to eat at the restaurant in the hotel before going to my house."

"You got a house?" Eva said.

"It comes with the job," Emmet said.

"Don't go getting yourself killed," Eva said. "I like it here."

Emmet met the four men he selected as deputies at the railroad station. They had served with him for years on the railroad project and they were good men.

Each had their own guns and horse and had proven themselves many times during the railroad expansion.

Cody was twenty-eight, Flint a year younger, Younger was twenty-nine and Lynn, at twenty-seven was Emmet's age. All were sergeants in Emmet's command.

After a tour of the town and jail, Emmet took them to their house and then to the general store to trade in their cap and all Colts for the new, self-contained models. With several bricks of .44 ammunition, Emmet and his men rode a half miles outside of town to practice.

Emmet was the best shot, but his men were nearly as good.

After firing off several bricks of ammunition, they returned to town to the office.

"We'll work a similar schedule to how we worked the railroad. Two men on at all times," Emmet said. "And always carry a Henry rifle. Once the town is used to no firearms, things should get easier."

"It's going to take some doing convincing cowboys to surrender their guns," Cody said.

"Not if we do it right," Emmet said. "Tomorrow we hang posters and put everyone on notice that the policy goes into effect in twenty-four hours."

Emmet and his four deputies hung one hundred posters on buildings all across Cheyenne. Campbell accompanied Emmet as Emmet nailed posters to answer questions.

"How's a man supposed to defend himself?" a cowboy asked.

"If nobody is armed except the law, defend himself against what?" Campbell said.

"A man has a right to own a gun," another cowboy said.

"And nobody is taking that right away from you," Campbell said. "The procedure is simple. If you ride into town with a gun, you check it at the marshal's office and then pick it up on your way out."

"And if we refuse?" the cowboy said.

"I'll arrest you," Emmet said. "And you'll sit in jail until you pay a fine."

"Fair warning," Campbell said. "Anyone caught wearing a firearm after six o'clock tonight will be arrested."

"We'll see," the cowboy said.

"Don't test me," Emmet said. "Or my deputies."

The first night, five men were arrested. Three came peacefully, two put up a fight. Emmet used his Colt to buffalo the man, the other required two deputies to restrain him.

By midnight, the entire town was disarmed.

Emmet sat behind his desk amid a pile of handguns and drank a cup of coffee. His four deputies were with him.

"I hate having to buffalo a man," Emmet said.

"He gave you no choice," Cobb said. "He was going to pull on you and you would have killed him for sure. A headache is better than dead."

Emmet thought for a moment. "Anybody remember that game they used to play during the war? The one with the stick and the ball?"

"Baseball," Flint said.

"Yeah, baseball," Emmet said.

"What about it?" Flint said.

"What did they call the stick?" Emmet said.

"A baseball bat," Flint said.

"Yeah, a baseball bat," Emmet said.

When Emmet entered Eva's saloon, she greeted him with a kiss.

"What's that they're building?" he said.

"It's a runway," Eva said.

"What's it for?"

"Oh you poor uneducated man," Eva said. "So the singer can stand on it and sing to the audience from a higher viewpoint and resonate her voice."

"What's his name, that carpenter building the . . . ?" Emmet said.

"Runway and his name is George."

"Hey, George, can I see you for a minute?" Emmet said.

George came to the table. "What do you need, Marshal?"

Emmet removed a folded piece of paper and handed it George. "This," he said.

George looked at Emmet's sketch of a baseball bat. The dimensions were eighteen inches long with the handle narrower than the two and a half in diameter head. A hole was near the end of the bat with the end being nubbed.

"A nice looking club," George said. "What's the hole for?"

"A strip of leather," Emmet said. "What's the hardest wood you have?"

"Oak."

"Make eight of them with oak," Emmet said.

"Take me a week," George said. "I got to finish here during the day."

"I'll give you two dollars each if you rush it," Emmet said.

Three days later, Emmet presented each of his deputies with a mini baseball bat, complete with a leather strap tied through the hole.

"Carry it through the leather strap in your left hand so you gun hand is always free," Emmet said. "As hard as oak is it's not iron."

"Emmet, we open for business in two nights," Eva said. "I need two reliable men as bouncers."

"I sent for two more railroad men," Emmet said. "But you got to pay them well."

"How much do your deputies make?"

"One-fifty a month."

"Three hundred a month for two, we can

handle it."

"You can't expect them to work seven days," Emmet said. "Six at most so I'll ask my deputies if they want to be fill-ins. They won't mind making extra money."

They were in the kitchen, Eva was cooking breakfast. She looked over her shoulder at Emmet. "Are you ever going to ask me?" she said.

"Ask you what?" Emmet said.

"Never mind," Eva said. "Come get your breakfast."

Eva and her girls tossed names into a hat to pick a name for the saloon before opening night. They had six gaming tables, two bartenders, a piano and player, two full-time bouncers armed with clubs Emmet had made for them and sidearms with permission from Campbell, a healthy supply of liquor and all that was lacking was a name.

One hour before Eva unlocked the front doors, George was putting the finishing touches on the runway. Emmet and Eva were having coffee at a table as her girls did a mad scramble to clean and polish everything.

Emmet said, "Hey, George, I need to pay for the extra clubs you made."

"Be right with you, Marshal," George

said. "As soon as I finish Eva's runway."

"That's it," Eva said. "That's the name."

"What?"

"Eva's Runway," Eva said.

Opening night was a big success. Emmet posted two deputies outside to check any firearms. Emmet sat with Campbell at a table. Campbell drank bourbon, Emmet coffee. Crowds were gathered as each table as Eva's ladies were not only excellent dealers but they were damn good to look at.

There were twenty-four tables with six chairs and every one was occupied. The bar held fifty standing and it was elbow-to-elbow.

At the center of it all, Eva was the ring master. Every thirty minutes, she came out on the runway and called one or two girls to the runway to sing. Most couldn't hold a tune, but they were nice to look at and showed considerable leg wrapped in fishnet tights and they got loud applause.

Even Campbell got in on the fun and sang along with one of the girls.

On opening night, Eva made back enough cash to cover her entire expenses.

A few weeks later, as Emmet and Eva were having dinner at the restaurant in the hotel when several gunshots sounded from the brothel on the eastside outside of town.

Emmet raced outside and crossed the street to where his horse was tethered to the post outside his office, mounted and ran the horse to the brothel.

Although it was after dark, the brothel was well lit and Emmet was there in a matter of seconds. He jumped down, drew his Colt and opened the door and rushed inside.

Several of the ladies and some cowboys were in the lobby.

"Who fired that shot?" Emmet said.

"Cowboy in room seven shot little Gloria," a girl said.

"Where's your bouncer?" Emmet said.

"He shot him too."

"Everybody stay put," Emmet said.

He took the stairs and walked to room seven. The door was open. Emmet entered. Colt cocked and ready.

The bouncer was on the floor, bleeding out from a bullet to the stomach. Little Gloria was on the bed, bleeding from a bullet to her right shoulder.

The cowboy, wearing his long underwear, sat in a chair, a two-shot derringer in his right hand and he was talking to himself.

"She robbed me," he said. "The bitch cleaned me out, the stinking whore."

"I didn't goddamn rob you, you stupid

cow puncher," little Gloria said. "Marshal, I didn't goddamn rob him."

"Be quiet," Emmet said. "Cowboy, give me the derringer."

"She robbed me, the bitch," the cowboy said.

"I didn't rob you, goddammit," little Gloria said. "Marshal, he fell asleep drunk. I was putting my clothes on, he waked up and shoots me. Ralph charges in and he shot him, too."

"Cowboy, give me the gun," Emmet said.

The cowboy looked at Emmet. "I kilt that bouncer, didn't I?" he said.

"Looks like it," Emmet said.

"I ain't gonna hang on account of no whore," the cowboy said.

"Give me the gun, cowboy," Emmet said.

The cowboy cocked the derringer.

"Don't do it, cowboy," Emmet said.

The cowboy aimed the derringer at Emmet. "I ain't gonna hang for no whore," he said.

Just before he pulled the trigger, Emmet shot the cowboy dead center in his chest.

"Goddammit," Emmet said.

"I didn't goddamn rob him," little Gloria said.

Emmet walked out of the room and looked down at the gathering crowd that included two of his deputies. "Get the doctor," he said.

Campbell entered Emmet's office and sat in the chair opposite the desk.

"Coffee?" Emmet said.

"Please," Campbell said.

Emmet stood, went to the woodstove, filled two cups, handed one to Campbell and then returned to his chair.

"The bouncer died," Campbell said. "The doc said the girl will be okay."

Emmet nodded.

"You did what you had to do," Campbell said.

"I know," Emmet said.

"Well, thanks for the coffee," Campbell said. "I'm off to bed. I suggest you do the same."

At one am, Eva locked the doors and waited for Emmet to pick her up. A few minutes later, he knocked on the door.

She took his arm and they walked home on the streets that were lined with mounted lanterns.

"Are you okay?" Eva said.

"Stupid cowboy didn't have to die," Emmet said.

"From what I heard it was him or you,"

Eva said. "You made the right choice."

"Yeah," Emmet said.

New Year's Eve brought a cold front and a blizzard. The saloons, including Eva's Runway, rang in the new year with laughter, songs, food and plenty to drink.

Emmet picked her up at one in the morning and they walked home in a snowstorm.

"I stopped by the house and made a fire," Emmet said.

"Thank you, hon," Eva said.

When they reached home, Eva sat in front of the fireplace. Emmet poured two small drinks of bourbon and sat beside her.

"Remember last week when I told you your Christmas gift would be late?" Emmet said.

"I remember," Eva said.

"It arrived," Emmet said and handed her a ring box.

Chapter Eleven: 1870

John and Ellis walked through a field of freshly planted corn.

"Ellis, we've made enough profit the last three season's to buy another two hundred acres," John said.

"Pa, before you go off half-cocked to the bank, we best talk to the women least we get our heads chewed off," Ellis said.

"I know that, son," John said. "I haven't made it to my fifties without knowing that. The point is to build up as much of what they call equity to leave the women when we die."

"Here come the girls," Ellis said.

Anna and Emma were fourteen now, both budding young women who caught the attention of every young man when they walked by.

"Ma says to hurry up," Anna said.

"She means it, too," Emma said.

"Tell her we'll be right there," John said.

After Anna and Emma left, John said, "Son, you're twenty-six now, so you must have figured out by now we men only pretend we're in charge."

Ellis smiled "Yeah, Pa, I figured it out."

Ellis rode with Bettina, their daughter and the twins, while John, Lars and Sarah rode in a separate carriage to Stockton.

Bettina was pregnant with their second child and she was scheduled to see the doctor. While Ellis and Bettina visited the doctor, everyone else went shopping for supplies. Anna and Emma took charge of the baby.

The checkup went well, the baby was due in early fall. As Ellis and Bettina left the doctor's office, Ellis spotted Beth across the street in front of the bank.

"I want to see Beth for a minute," Ellis said.

Betting kissed him. "Don't take too long," she said.

Ellis crossed the street. "Hello, Beth," he said.

"Ellis, nice to see you," she said.

"Beth, I just thought maybe you should know that Emmet is getting married," Ellis said.

Beth looked at Ellis and for a moment he saw coldness in her eyes. Then her face softened and she smiled. “That’s wonderful,” she said. “When?”

“Late summer.”

“I’m very happy for him,” Beth said. “Give him my best.”

“The price per acre is four dollars,” John said. “Between the three of us we can easily afford an additional two hundred acres.”

“That’s a little more than two hundred and fifty from each of us,” Lars said.

“Sarah?” John said.

After shopping for supplies, they went for lunch at a restaurant in Stockton before returning home.

Sarah looked at Bettina.

“What?” John said.

“John, you and Lars are in your fifties now,” Sarah said. “That’s another two hundred acres of land to be plowed and harvested twice a year. Who is going to do all this extra work. Bettina is pregnant, the girls are in school and Ellis is overtaxed as it is.”

John smiled.

“What?” Sarah said.

“Ma, we hire a sharecropper to work the extra two hundred acres and pay him half the profits for his work,” Ellis said. “We don’t have to work the field and it’s an extra third of the profit for the three farms."

"Sarah?" John said.

"Honey?" Elis said to Bettina.

"The bank should still be open by the time we finish lunch," Sarah said.

Halfway home, as she passed a creek, Beth stopped her buggy beside the creek and stepped down to the soft grass. She removed her shoes and stockings and sat down and put her feet in the cool water.

She was surprised at how hard the news of Emmet's pending marriage hit her. Although she had no right to feel so, she felt resentment at the news. Why, she didn't understand.

Emmet had the right to live and marry as he saw fit, same as any other man.

As did she. And she certainly had no problem exercising her right to do so.

So why the sick feeling in her stomach?

Beth looked at her reflection in the water. The answer was in her own eyes.

Campbell was a bit surprised when he received a telegram from President Grant telling him he was coming for a visit the first week in May,

Grant requested that he tell no one, not even Emmet.

Campbell wondered why the secrecy. Perhaps it was because he granted women the right to vote in Wyoming Territory?

Except that Grant approved of the move, so it couldn't be that.

Well, he'll just have to wait a week and find out.

As was their usual custom, Emmet walked Eva to Eva's Runway at six o'clock, right after they had dinner together.

Emmet, the most respected man in Cheyenne naturally made Eva the most respected woman in Cheyenne. Whenever she walked alone, men tipped their hats to her and women always said, good day.

When she worked, everybody was always respectful to her and never got out of line.

Because nobody in town wanted to deal with Emmet if they did.

As they walked the street to Eva's Runway, she clutched his arm and said, "Emmet, are you sure you want to have the wedding at your parent's in California?"

"Sure," Emmet said.

"I'm . . . well, sort of worried," Eva said.

"We've been over that a hundred times already," Emmet said. "My parents will love you like a daughter, so quit worrying about it."

They reached Eva's Runway.

"There's still the other thing," Eva said.

"We'll talk about that later," Emmet said.

"Alright," Eva said. She gave Emmet a quick kiss and pushed in the swinging doors.

"What is the matter. Honey?" Beth's mother said.

"I'm fine, Ma," Beth said.

"You're not fine," Mrs. Olson said. "You've been moping around the house for a week now. You didn't even want to go riding with your father. Now what is it?"

"I'm twenty-eight, a widow, a mother and a wealthy woman and live a life of luxury and I feel like . . . like my life is empty," Beth said.

"You're missing your husband," Mrs. Olson said. "Give it more time, Beth."

"Yes, you're probably right, mother," Beth said. "I'm just missing Rip."

"Of course I am," Mrs. Olson said.

Campbell met President Grant on Grant's private train at the Cheyenne station. Six soldiers were on the train with Grant and they kept watch while Campbell and Grant had coffee together.

"Governor, you're probably wondering

what the nature of my visit is," Grant said.

"Naturally, I'm curious sir," Campbell said.

"It's about Emmet Boyd," Grant said. "I'm going to steal him from you, or at least attempt to."

"You mean offer him a new position?" Campbell said.

"If he'll have it," Grant said. "Can you send for him?"

Emmet was having breakfast with Eva when Flint knocked on the front door.

"Marshal, President Grant is at the railroad station," Flint said. "He wants to see you right away."

Emmet already had his horse saddled outside, so he rode Bull to the train.

Grant and Campbell were having coffee when Emmet entered the private car.

"Marshal, grab a cup and have a seat," Grant said.

Emmet took a cup and sat next to Campbell.

"Marshal, you've done exactly the kind of job in Cheyenne as I knew you would," Grant said. "So, I'll come right to the point. I'm organizing a new division in Washington called the Secret Service and their job is to provide protection to the President so that we never have another Lincoln assassination on our hands. I would like you to be part of the team."

"I would have to live in Washington?" Emmet said.

"I'm afraid so," Grant said. "Now the Governor tells me you're getting married, so talk it over with her and bring me an answer in the morning."

"Yes sir," Emmet said.

"Washington DC?" Eva said.

"I don't have to take the job," Emmet said. "I can stay right here."

"Emmet, when the President of the United States asks you to do something, you do it."

Emmet looked at Eva. "But?" he said.

"I'm scared to death to meet your family and now I have to fit into Washington society," Eva said. "Emmet, I was a . . ."

"And I was a farm boy," Emmet said. "Eva, it doesn't matter what we were, it only matters what we are and we're going to get married no matter what."

"I'll need new clothes," Eva said.

"Me too," Emmet said.

"What about the saloon?"

"Hire one of the girls to manage it and send you your end every month, or sell it outright," Emmet said.

Eva sighed. "Tell Mr. Grant you'll take the job. Provided we can go to California for the wedding."

Emmet and Eva had dinner with Grant in his private train.

"I'm told you created and run the best saloon in Cheyenne," Grant said to Eva.

Eva looked at Grant.

"It takes a lot of intelligence and dedication to create and run a successful business," Grant said. "Emmet, I hope you appreciate that."

"I do, sir," Emmet said.

"Good. When is the wedding?" Grant said.

"Late July at my parents farm in California," Emmet said.

"Would September first be too soon to report to your new position in Washington?" Grant said.

Emmet looked at Eva and she nodded.

"That would be fine, sir," Emmet said.

"Excellent," Grant said. "Send me an invite. My schedule allowing, I'd like to attend."

"Emmet, what if he actually shows up at our wedding?" Eva said.

"Quit worrying," Emmet said.

"What if your parents . . ." Eva said.

"That settles it," Emmet said. "We're going to California this weekend so they can meet you and you can stop all this nonsense."

"This weekend?"

"Yes. I'll wire my parents to pick us up at the station," Emmet said.

"I'll need some dresses for the trip," Eva said. "And you'll need a suit or do you plan on getting married in you cowboy boots, six-gun and hat?"

"I'll get some clothes in Sacramento," Emmet said. "I'll need them for the new job."

When Emmet and Eva stepped off the train, they were met by the entire family. Anna and Emma hugged Emmet. Ellis, Lars and John shook his hand. Sarah kissed Emmet on the cheek and then stepped back and looked at Eva.

"Emmet, she's absolutely lovely," Sarah said.

"Thank you," Eva said.

"Let's get home and feed you two some lunch," Sarah said.

While the ladies took coffee in the living room, Emmet, Ellis, John and Lars took theirs on the porch.

"I've never heard of a Secret Service before," John said.

"It's something Grant just created," Emmet said. "Protection against assassination like with Lincoln."

"And you'd have to live in Washington?" Ellis said.

"Yes, but it would give you someplace new to visit," Emmet said.

"This new job sounds dangerous," John said.

"Dad, Emmet fought in the war, then protected the railroad and is now a Marshal," Ellis said. "Everything he's done so far has been dangerous."

"Ellis, why don't you and Bettina come back with us for a few days?" Emmet said. "We have plenty of room and it will do you good to get away."

"Go, Ellis. Take Bettina and have a good time," John said. "The work will be here when you get back."

"I need a suit," Emmet said. "Let's go to town tomorrow and have lunch. My treat."

"All of us?" John said. "Son, that's expensive."

"Pa, don't worry about it," Emmet said.

"She's a lovely girl, Emmet," John said. "Both my sons have done well."

■ ■ ■ ■

While all the women went to the ladies dress shop, the men visited the men's tailor on the next block. Eva purchased three dresses suited for Washington and Emmet got three suits for his new position.

Afterward, they met at the restaurant on Front Street for lunch, across the street from the bank.

Beth, coming out of the bank, recognized the two buggies parked in front of the restaurant and she looked into the window and saw Emmet seated with his family and a woman that had to be his future wife.

She reentered the bank and stood by the window and waited.

Fifteen minutes later, the entire family came out and Beth took a good look at his future wife. She was tall and striking looking and walked with an air of confidence.

"Well, good for you Emmet," she said aloud. "Good for you."

Ellis and Bettina left with Emmet and Eva when they took the ten o'clock train east to Cheyenne. The nine-hundred-mile long journey, with several stops in major cities and towns would take about twenty-four hours.

Just ten years ago, such a trip could take months by horse or wagon.

They had lunch at one o'clock and dinner at seven and in between they talked and watched the scenery roll by at fifty-miles per hour. It was the first time Ellis had slept in a sleeper car aboard a train.

Ellis was particularly excited to see Cheyenne. Stockton was a big, prosperous town, but it wasn't part of what was considered the wild west.

Eva and Bettina hit it off from the beginning and by the time the train arrived at ten the next morning, they were chatting like old friends or sisters.

Cheyenne was everything Ellis hoped it would be. Wet, muddy streets, wood plank sidewalks, saloons and cowboys.

As they walked to Emmet and Eva's house, packages in arms, everyone in the street nodded or tipped their hats to Emmet.

At his office, Emmet said, "I need to check in. I'll be along directly."

Eva led Ellis and Bettina to the house and showed them the second bedroom. "Get settled and I'll show you around town," Eva said.

Emmet spent the morning catching up

with his deputies and on paperwork. Eva, Ellis and Bettina came by around one o'clock and they went to lunch at the restaurant across the street.

"Emmet, what is that building outside of town?" Ellis said.

"That is a brothel," Emmet said. "The governor doesn't allow them inside the town limits."

"A brothel?" Ellis said.

"Never you mind," Bettina said.

"After lunch, I have to see the governor," Emmet said.

Campbell's office was completed and he moved from the hotel into the new building on Main Street, where Emmet met him after lunch.

"Emmet, have you given any thought as to your replacement?" Campbell said.

"Any one of my four can step up," Emmet said.

"And there lies the problem," Campbell said.

"How do you mean?"

"When you have four men equal to the task and one is selected over the other three, it always leads to resentment," Campbell said. "That's why I've asked President Grant to select your replacement."

"Understood."

"I would appreciate this if you didn't mention it to your men," Campbell said. "I'll do that after you leave for Washington."

"Understood."

"Your brother and his wife are in town," Campbell said.

"A quick visit," Emmet said.

"Bring them to dinner tonight, say seven o'clock," Campbell said.

"With the governor?" Bettina said. "What do I wear?"

"What you have is fine," Eva said.

"No, I didn't bring anything appropriate for dinner with a governor," Bettina said.

"We're about the same size," Eva said. "Let's go through my closets."

While Eva and Bettina went through Eva's clothes, Emmet and Ellis took coffee on the porch of the house.

"Emmet, I can't have dinner with the governor looking like a farm boy," Ellis said.

"Wear something of mine," Emmet said.

"You're five inches taller and got fifty pounds on me," Ellis said.

"Alright, let's go to the tailor on Front Street and see what he's got," Emmet said.

"Expensive?" Ellis said.

Emmet grinned. "Come on," he said.

■ ■ ■ ■

As they walked to Campbell's residence, Ellis said, "Emmet, do you ever take that gun off?"

"To sleep," Emmet said.

"Sometimes not even then," Eva said.

Leaving Campbell's residence around ten o'clock, Eve said, "Well they might as well know, Emmet."

"Know what?" Ellis said.

They reached Eva's Runway and Eva said, "Well, let's go in."

"I can't go into a saloon," Bettina said.

"Of course you can," Eva said. "The owner is a woman."

Eva was greeted by everyone in the saloon as she burst through the swinging doors, followed by Emmet, Ellis and Bettina.

One of Eva's girls said, "Table for the marshal."

After being seated, Ellis and Bettina looked at the bar, the runway, the gaming tables and at Eva, who was on the runway, introducing one of the girls.

"You mean Eva owns this place?" Ellis said.

"She built it from the ground up,"

Emmet said.

"I'll be damned," Ellis said.

One of the girls brought three beers to the table. Bettina looked at it.

"It's okay, honey," Ellis said.

"If Pa could see me now," Bettina said as she picked up the glass.

About an hour later, Flint entered the saloon and found Emmet. "Trouble," he said. "Two cowboys refuse to surrender their guns."

"I'll be back," Emmet said. "Wait here."

Emmet and Flint rushed out and ran to the Gay Lady Saloon where Cody, Younger and Lynn were in the street with two armed cowboys.

"What's the problem, boys?" Emmet said.

"These two refuse to check their guns," Lynn said.

"Is that right, you won't surrender your guns?" Emmet said.

"You got no right to take a man's guns," a cowboy said.

"I have every right," Emmet said. "It's a town ordinance and I'm the Marshal."

"You want them, come get them," the other cowboy said.

"Everybody off the street. Now," Emmet said.

Twenty feet behind Emmet, Ellis got up

onto the sidewalk.

"Cowboys, last warning," Emmet said.

"Screw you, law dog," a cowboy said and grabbed for his gun.

Before he cleared leather, Emmet drew and shot him in the arm. Then Emmet cocked his Colt again and looked at the second cowboy. "Want to try your luck?" he said.

The cowboy shook his head.

"Lock them up. Get the doc for his arm," Emmet said.

Ellis stood almost hypnotized at seeing his brother in action. Emmet seemed without fear at facing two armed men and it was obvious he could have killed both and chose not to do so.

Emmet turned and walked to Ellis. "I told you to wait in the saloon," he said.

"Who's talking to me, my brother or the Marshal?" Ellis said.

"Both, you knot head," Emmet said. "Come on."

When they returned to Eva's Runway, everybody was outside with Eva and Bettina front and center.

"This doesn't bother you, him running off like that?" Bettina said.

"I have been watching him do this very thing since sixty-six," Eva said.

"You alright, Marshal?" a man in the crowd said.

"Fine," Emmet said. "Everybody go on and have a good time. I have to write a report and see to the prisoners."

After Emmet left, everybody went back into Eva's Runway and Eva sat with Ellis and Bettina.

"What happened out there?" Bettina said.

"My brother is a very dangerous man," Ellis said.

"You just found that out," Eva said.

"I don't think I'll mention this to our parents," Ellis said.

While Eva and Bettina hugged, Emmet and Ellis shook hands.

"See you at the wedding," Emmet said.

After the train left, Emmet and Eva walked through town. Flint waved them down. "Marshal, the Governor wants to see you," he said.

"Would you walk Eva home?" Emmet said.

"Sure," Flint said.

Emmet walked to Campbell's office where he was behind his desk. "Emmet, come in," he said when Emmet knocked on the door.

"You wanted to see me, John?" Emmet said.

"Cowboys on a drive from Montana will be arriving tomorrow sometime," Campbell said. "Twenty drovers and a foreman and two thousand head. You know the drill. Have your boys at the pens to confiscate guns."

"We'll handle it, John," Emmet said. "But there's something I've been meaning to talk to you about. The way Cheyenne is growing and with more drives coming through, you might need two extra deputies."

"It's within my power to appoint deputies," Campbell said. "I'll discuss it with your replacement when he arrives. And that reminds me, you'll be leaving soon."

"Couple of weeks," Emmet said.

"I've been meaning to ask you when you plan to do with the saloon," Campbell said.

"Eva hasn't decided yet," Emmet said. "She could sell it outright or have her girls manage it in exchange for a share in the profits."

"She is soul owner?" Campbell said.

"She is."

"I'd like to propose a deal to her," Campbell said. "May I call upon you tonight?"

"Come for dinner," Emmet said. "We generally eat at six."

"I'll be there," Campbell said.

■ ■ ■ ■

"I have to admit that you two will be missed around here," Campbell said as Eva served after dinner coffee.

"Governor, you are taking the very long way around the barn," Eva said as she took a chair.

"You're right, I am," Campbell said. "Here's my offer. I wish to buy you outright and am willing to go as high as twenty-five-thousand for Eva's Runway."

"Twenty-five-thousand?" Eva said.

"Emmet is in a risky business," Campbell said. "Something could happen to him at any time. You'll need a comfortable nest egg to fall back on if something should happen."

Eva looked at Campbell.

"It's your business, honey," Emmet said.

"Can I sleep on it, Governor?" Eva said.

"I expect you to," Campbell said.

"Give me a few days," Eva said.

Eva and Campbell reached an agreement and she sold the saloon to him for twenty-five-thousand dollars that was deposited into the Bank of Cheyenne. She would transfer the money when she and Emmet reached Washington.

Their wedding took place in the backyard of the family farm and true to his word, Grant did attend, causing quite the stir in town.

Reporters attempted to crash the wedding, but Grant's Secret Servicemen kept them at bay. After the wedding, Grant left to meet with the Governor of California.

Beth received an invitation from the family, but she declined.

One month later, Emmet reported to Grant to assume his new duties.

Chapter Twelve: 1871

By April, Emmet had settled into a comfortable routine at The White House as a member of Grant's security team.

There were twenty agents total, but the number would grow shortly as Grant envisioned the Secret Service as having added duties. Lincoln had established the service to fight the large amount of counterfeit money in circulation, but they didn't provide protection at that time. As the Service was part of the Justice Department, Grant could use them as he saw fit and he assigned the twenty to protect The White House.

Emmet and Eva purchased a small home ten miles south of Washington. The ride to work took just thirty minutes each way on Bull.

Eva was trying her best to have a baby and when she was unable to get pregnant, she and Emmet saw a doctor in Washington. After a thorough examination, Eva was given a clean bill of health with advice to just keep trying.

In June, Grant called Emmet to the White House Oval Office.

"The Klan has become very active again, especially in Tennessee, Mississippi and Georgia and South Carolina," Grant said. "Now that Congress has passed the Klan Act, I am free to do something about this scourge on society on a federal level. Emmet, I want you and nine men to head to South Carolina and put a stop to the Klan. You'll have to infiltrate, arrest and destroy the Klan for good."

"Any of the men from the South that fought for the North?" Emmet said.

Grant smiled. "It takes a southern boy to catch one, is that it?" he said.

"They'll know as soon as I open my mouth I'm northern," Emmet said. "I can make up a story I'm a northern investor looking to invest in southern interests, but I'll never be able to get close to the Klan without southern boys."

"I figured you say that, Emmet, so I already went through records of the men," Grant said. "You know them and have worked with them for months now."

"Good, at least that part will be easy," Emmet said.

"Emmet, this job could take months," Grant said. "Maybe Eva could go to California and stay with your parents until you return?"

"I'll mention it to her," Emmet said.

"Go home and talk it over with her tonight," Grant said. "We'll have a meeting tomorrow with the nine men you'll be commanding tomorrow."

"The Klan?" Eva said.

"It's something that has to be done, honey," Emmet said. "They're murdering freed slaves in the night, burning houses and crosses. They've got to be stopped."

"And as always, it's you," Eva said.

"Eva, it's my job to . . ." Emmet said.

"I know," Eva said. "And if you want me to go stay with your family while you're away, I'll do it. But I won't like it."

"I don't like it either, but I'd feel better knowing you were safe with my family," Emmet said.

"When?"

"I don't know yet," Emmet said. "I'm meeting with Grant in the morning."

The nine men selected were from Georgia, South Carolina, Tennessee and Virginia. They met with Emmet and Grant in The

Oval Office at nine o'clock.

"The mission of this expedition to put an end to the Klan," Grant said. "And I want that son of a bitch Nathan Forrest brought before a senate hearing. Understood? Emmet, you have the floor."

"I will be a northern investor looking to invest in the local economy," Emmet said. "I'll headquarter in Atlanta and Agent Forrest will be my partner, selected because he's from Atlanta and can help me fit into the city. The rest of you will act the part of bigots and racists and gain as much information as possible. We will never meet in person unless absolutely necessary. We will communicate through hand written notes only. Where we will determine upon arrival. Questions?"

"Do we arrest?" an agent said.

Emmet looked at Grant. "Sir?"

"No," Grant said. "You give the information to Emmet, who takes it to the Army. They will do the arresting."

"Any move on our part to arrest and detain only blows our cover," Emmet said.

"When do we leave, sir?" Forest said.

"One week from today Emmet and Forest will leave and establish their cover," Grant said. "They will wire me using a portable telegraph box when it is safe for the rest of you to travel."

"We will be able to carry a sidearm?" another agent said.

"Shoulder holster rigs under your suit jackets," Emmet said. "No open carry for obvious reasons. The South isn't the West."

"The goal is to locate the Klan and expose them for what they are," Grant said. "The Army will take care of the rest."

"What about expenses, sir?" Emmet said. "We'll need to put on a good show?"

"Indeed you will," Grant said. "And I'll take care of that end before you leave. Emmet, Forest, I suggest you take a few days off and go be with your family."

"How long do you think you'll be gone?" Eva said.

"I'm guessing three months," Emmet said.

"I don't like it here," Eva said. "All these snobby Washington women with their snooty airs. I prefer Cheyenne, with all of its danger and lack of society. A person can breathe in a place like Cheyenne."

"I promised Grant a year," Emmet said. "After that we can move to Stockton if you'd like."

Eva grinned. "Go back to being a farm boy?" she said.

"I didn't say that," Emmet said. "Between

the two of us we have quite a nest egg saved up. We can open a business and invest in something for the future."

"I can look around while I'm there," Eva said.

"Sure you can," Emmet said. "Think of it as a scouting expedition."

Eva pushed her empty dinner plate away and stood up. She took Emmet's hand. "Come do some scouting of your own and see if we can make a baby," she said.

From Washington to Stockton would take four and a half days on the train. After Emmet brought Eva's luggage to her sleeper car, they hugged, kissed and said their good-byes.

"They'll pick you at the station," Emmet said. "Wire me right away because I'll be leaving the next day for Atlanta."

"Whatever you do, don't go get yourself killed," Eva said.

"After Cheyenne, Atlanta will be a picnic," Emmet said.

Beth had just finished some shopping with her father and left him to go to the post office when she spotted John and Sarah riding by in their buggy. They didn't see her and headed to the railroad station.

Maybe Emmet was coming for a visit?

Beth entered the post office and after getting her mail, she stood by the window and watched. Twenty minutes later, John drove the buggy past the post office. Emmet's wife Eva sat between John and Sarah.

Beth waited until they had turned the corner to leave the post office.

As Emmet and Forest walked the main thoroughfare of Atlanta, Emmet said, "The last time I was here the place was still on fire."

"It still is," Forest said. "Under the surface."

"And that's why we're here," Emmet said. "Let's find a hotel, get settled and look around."

They checked into the Hotel Atlanta, requesting a room with two beds. After packing away their luggage, Emmet said, "Let's get a feel for things, walk the streets."

Atlanta was a sprawling town of twenty-thousand people and it seemed as if every single one of them was on the streets.

While most of the city had been rebuilt, there was still a ways to go and buildings were under construction everywhere.

Freed slaves worked side-by-side with whites in construction projects under the watchful eyes of mounted Union soldiers.

Many freed slaves walked the streets dressed in fine suits.

"Let's grab a bite to eat," Emmet said.

They found a restaurant a few blocks away. A sign in the window read **No Negros Allowed,** even though the cook was a black man.

As they ate a full lunch, Emmet said, "We need to scout around and find some potential businessmen with ties to the Klan."

"After walking these streets, I think I can spit and hit one of them."

"We'll start the charade at the bank in the morning after we deposit our money." Emmet said.

"You were with Grant?" Forest said.

"From sixty-three to sixty-five and then was detached to the railroad until sixty-nine," Emmet said. "I spent a year as marshal in Cheyenne before he recruited me to the Secret Service."

"I have to tell you something," Forest said. "I was born south of Athens, Georgia in forty-two. I grew up in a slave culture and thought the whole world was like us. It wasn't until my father sent me to Boston to study agriculture did I see the horrors of slavery. Black men and women in Boston enjoying the same freedom I had. After three years in Boston, when the war broke out I enlisted for the Union."

"And your family?" Emmet said.

"My father died in the war," Forest said. "My mother died a few years ago in a hospital."

"Even those who lived died a little bit in that war," Emmet said.

Forest nodded. "I guess that's why we're here," he said.

After a week living with Emmet's parents and the twins, Eva felt more at home that at any time in her life.

Anna and Emma, when they weren't in school, were working the fields with John, Lars and Ellis. Sarah and Bettina spent most of their time in the kitchen, despite Bettina having a two-year-old and another one on the way.

Eva was never one for cooking, but she learned a great deal from Sarah and Bettina about how to navigate a kitchen.

Saturdays, Ellis hitched up the wagon and he took her, Sarah, Bettina and the twins to town to do the weekly shopping.

The Boyd family had become a fixture in Stockton and everybody knew them. After shopping, they always treated themselves to lunch at a small restaurant across the street from the bank.

After lunch, as they returned to the wagon, Eva said, "Would you mind waiting a moment, I want to run into the bank."

Eva entered the bank and bumped into Beth, who was just leaving.

"You must be Eva, Emmet's wife," Beth said.

"I am and who are you?" Eva said.

"I am the woman who was stupid enough to turn her back on him," Beth said and walked out of the bank.

Eve made an appointment with the bank president and then returned to the wagon. "I bumped into a woman who knew me and said she was stupid enough to turn her back on Emmet," she said. "Do you know her?"

"Oh dear," Sarah said.

Emmet and Forest met with the president of the First Georgia Bank, requesting to open an account in the amount of twenty-five-thousand dollars.

"We'd like to invest locally," Emmet said. "Perhaps you can suggest who we should see in that regard?"

"That Atlanta Chamber of Commerce would be where I would start," the bank president said. "They meet every Wednesday for lunch at the Squire Restaurant. I myself attend."

"Perhaps we may accompany you to the meeting and you can introduce us?" Emmet said.

"I don't see why not," the bank president said.

"Excellent," Emmet said. "And is there a livery we may rent horses for the day? We'd like to see your beautiful countryside."

Riding rented horses, Emmet and Forest rode south out of town and followed the railroad tracks for about five miles.

"What do you think?" Forest said.

"Let's find where the telegraph lines head to the west away from the tracks," Emmet said.

They rode several more miles until they reached the spot where telegraph lines went west. They dismounted and Emmet removed his shoulder bag.

"Ever climb a telegraph pole?" Emmet said.

"No, but I've seen it done," Forest said.

"It's easy once you do it," Emmet said. He opened his shoulder bag and removed the portable telegraph box, climbing spikes and harness.

After he climbed the pole and hooked the wire over the lines, Emmet tossed the box down to Forest, then shimmed down.

The telegram Emmet sent to Grant was brief. **Have established contact. Send additional funds.**

"Ma, Eva's sick," Anna said as she entered the kitchen.

"Sick how?" Sarah said.

"To her stomach," Anna said.

"Watch the bacon," Sarah said.

Sarah went into the bedroom Eva was staying in and she was bent over a large basin while Emma stood in the background.

"Eva, what is it?" Sarah said.

"I don't know," Eva said. "The last few days I've been nauseous in the morning. It will pass in a while."

"Oh dear," Sarah said.

"What is it?" Eva said.

"Emma, would you tell your brother to hit up the buggy, we're going to town after breakfast," Sarah said.

After shaving, Emmet and Forest soaked in tubs in the hotel bathing room.

"I'll speak first to let everyone know I'm a Yankee," Emmet said. "They you speak to put everybody at ease."

"What do I say?"

"Talk about coming home to Georgia,

growing up in Athens, stuff like that," Emmet said. "Make them feel like you're one of them."

"What time are meeting that banker?" Forest said.

"Noon," Emmet said. "We better go get dressed."

Sarah, Bettina and Ellis waited in the doctor's waiting room while he examined Eva. The examination seemed to take forever, but was only about thirty minutes.

"Is she sick?" Ellis said.

"No, silly, she's pregnant," Bettina said.

"Well, how do you know?" Ellis said.

Sarah and Bettina burst into laughter.

"What's funny?" Ellis said.

"Ellis, you don't have to wait," Sarah said. "You needed a few things at the general store anyway."

"I'll be back," Ellis said.

After he left, Sarah and Bettina burst into a second round of laughter.

Fifteen minutes later, Eva and the doctor entered the waiting room.

"Well, Bettina, seven months after I deliver yours I'll be delivering hers," the doctor said.

The bank president stood at the long dining

table in the private room at the Squire Restaurant and tapped his water glass with a knife.

"Gentlemen if you please," he said. "I have brought two guests with me who are interested in investing locally. Can you give them a few minutes of your time?"

Emmet stood up. "My name is Emmet Boyd and as you might gather from my accent, I am a Yankee," he said. "Wisconsin born but I made my money in Colorado gold. My partner and I are interested in investing locally and would appreciate guidance in our choices. Mr. Forest, please introduce yourself."

Forest stood up and Emmet sat down. "My name is Beauregard Forest and I hail from Athens," he said. "After the war, no need to tell you which side I was on, I set out to Colorado to seek my fortune and met Mr. Boyd. We struck up a friendship and made a fair amount of money. When it came time to figure out what to do with it, I suggested we go home to my place of birth and invest in the rise of the south."

"Let's welcome them both," the bank president said.

After the meeting, Emmet and Forest mingled with members of the Chamber of Commerce.

"I see darkies walking around wearing suits like white men," Emmet said.

"Pay them no mind," a member of the Chamber of Commerce said.

"How do you stand it?" Emmet said.

"My father would be rolling around in his grave if he saw this," Forest said.

"Don't let it upset you, Gentlemen," the bank president said. "It's a hardship forced upon us by Lincoln, but we deal with it."

"Never mention Lincoln to me again," Forest said. "Hearing it turns my stomach."

"Let's talk about what you wish to invest in, shall we," the bank president said.

"A baby?" Emma said. "So you're not sick?"

"No, honey, I'm just fine," Eva said.

"We have no way of notifying Emmet," Sarah said.

"Maybe we could get word to President Grant?" John said.

"No, please don't," Eva said.

"But . . ." John said.

"Emmet is on a secret mission for President Grant," Eva said. "I don't want him distracted in any way. He needs to keep his mind on his work and I don't want to give him any reason to get careless."

"She's right, John," Sarah said. "The news can wait."

■ ■ ■ ■

Emmet and Forest sat in chairs on the front porch of their hotel and drank coffee.

"What do you think?" Forest said.

"I think we made a fine first impression," Emmet said.

"If you mean we posed as a pair of racist bigots, I have to agree," Forest said.

"Don't let it get to you," Emmet said. "Remember why we're here."

"Hey, isn't that one of the men from the meeting?" Forest said.

"Sure is and he's headed this way," Emmet said.

The man approached the porch and climbed the steps. "Mr. Boyd, Mr. Johnson, my name is Chester Bodine and I own the largest general store in town," he said. "May I have a word with you?"

"Pull up a chair," Emmet said.

Bodine sat in a chair. "Well now, gentlemen," he said. "I would like to extend an invitation to you both to attend a private meeting at my store at ten o'clock tonight."

"What kind of meeting?" Emmet said.

"A meeting of like minds," Bodine said. "Where we discuss the topics of the day."

"Sounds interesting," Emmet said. "We'll

be there."

"Good," Bodine said and stood up. "Until tonight then."

Eva and Bettina shared cups of coffee on the front porch and watched the sun go down.

"They're so different, Emmet and Ellis," Eva said. "Emmet is like a piece of iron and when he sets his mind to something he never looks back. Like what you saw in Cheyenne that time."

"In his own way, Ellis is just as stubborn," Bettina said. "He spent nearly a year getting rid of a giant tree stump using just an ax. Every morning and every night, he'd spend a half hour fighting with it until one day when it was nearly free I told him to hitch up the team. He said he started it alone he would finish it alone."

"Both are good men," Eva said.

"I've got to see to my little girl," Bettina said.

"I'll go with you," Eva said. "And get some practice."

Bodine opened the front door to his store to allow Emmet and Forest entrance. "This way, gentlemen," he said.

A large storeroom was the site of the

secret meeting. Six members of the Chamber of Commerce, including the bank president were included in a group of twelve.

"For those not at the meeting this afternoon, this is Mr. Boyd and Mr. Forest," Bodine said. "They are new to Atlanta, but they share our values."

"I don't trust newcomers," a man said.

"Gentlemen, they deposited twenty-five-thousand in my bank and are looking to invest in Atlanta, let's not discourage them," the bank president said.

"What say you Mr. Boyd?" Bodine said.

"Mr. Forest and I have a great deal more than twenty-five-thousand to invest, but we don't like what we see around here," Emmet said. "Uppity darkies wearing suits like they were white men, it sickens my heart."

"Are you willing to do anything about it?" Bodine said.

"Like what?" Emmet said.

"There's an uppity lawyer named George," Bodine said. "He's got the darkies all riled up about their rights. Says he's going to march them to the ballet box this November."

"That's all we need, coloreds who can't read voting," the bank president said.

"What are you going to do about it?" Emmet said.

"He lives in a cabin about ten miles south of town," Bodine said. "We're going to pay him a visit, him and that uppity wife of his."

Emmet looked at Foster. "What do you say Mr. Foster, want to put an uppity darkie in his place?"

"Sounds like a good time," Foster said.

"Friday night we meet south of town," Bodine said. "Be ready to ride hard and fast and if you own guns, bring them."

"Jesus Christ Emmet, what do we do?" Forest said.

"I know this man George," Emmet said. "I've known him since I was eleven-years-old. I'm going to warn him."

"When?"

"Tonight."

"We'll have to rent horses again."

"No. I'll go. Get to the Army and speak to whoever is in charge," Emmet said. "Tell him to meet me at George's house ten miles to the south."

"Be careful," Foster said.

"You too and take your Colt," Emmet said.

The moon was nearly full and the ride south was a fairly easy one. George's cabin, barn and corral was the lone residence in an otherwise empty field. Emmet could see smoke rising up from the chimney against the strong moonlight.

He dismounted at the porch, tied the horse, went up and banged on the door. "George, wake up. It's Emmet Boyd. George."

A lantern lit in a window. Emmet stepped back. The door opened and George appeared. "Emmet?" George said. "What in blazes are you . . ."

"Inside, George. Hurry," Emmet said.

"George, what is it?" a woman's voice said/

"It's alright, honey," George said. "It's an old friend."

"Secret Service, you've come far, Emmet," George said.

"More coffee?" Mary, George's wife said.

"Thanks," Emmet said.

"Major?" Mary said.

"Yes ma'am," the Major said.

Mary filled cups.

"Major, how many men can you spare Friday night?" Emmet said.

"As many as are needed," the Major said. "What are you thinking?"

"Hide twenty behind the house," Emmet said. "And twenty behind them in the field where they can't see you. When you show yourself from the front, the other men cut them off from behind."

"You served with Grant, didn't you?" the Major said.

"My partner and I will be with the Klan riders, so don't shoot us," Emmet said.

"I expect these cowards to run," the Major said. "When they do, you and your partner stay put and we'll know it's you."

"Write down their names in case any get away," Emmet said.

"What about us?" George said.

"Major, I think George and Mary should wait behind the house with your men," Emmet said.

"Good idea," the Major said. "George, stay out of town until Friday. I'll send a couple of men in the morning to stay with you."

"Alright, Major," George said.

"Goodnight."

After the Major left, George said, "How's the family, Emmet?"

Emmet checked his Colt before putting it in his shoulder holster. "Are you ready?" he said.

"I'm ready," Forest said.

"Let's go," Emmet said.

Emmet and Forest left the hotel and mounted the rented horses they tied out front. They rode to the south of town where are group of twenty men waited.

Bodine was in charge. "Alright men, put on your spook hats," he said.

"You didn't say anything about spook hats," Emmet said.

"We have some extras," Bodine said.

Once every rider had a spook hat on, which was a cloth bag with two holes for the eyes, Bodine said, "Let's ride."

They rode south until Bodine stopped them a hundred yards from George's house. "Light the torches, men," Bodine said.

Emmet and Forest didn't have torches but nobody noticed.

"Now ride hard and scare this black bastard out of his bed," Bodine said.

They charged the house but before they could do any damage, twenty soldiers armed with Henry rifles came out from behind the house.

"It's a trap," Bodine yelled. "Run."

The Major and another twenty soldiers on horseback charged from the rear, locking Bodine and the riders in his web.

"Nobody moves and nobody gets shot," the Major said.

■ ■ ■ ■

After breakfast, Emmet and Forest went to see the Major and use his telegraph to wire Grant. Grant's reply was to head to Mississippi where the Klan had a powerful influence.

"Every last one of them will be charged and brought to Washington," the Major said. "And every last one of them will talk to save their hide. Great work Emmet, Forest."

Before leaving Atlanta, Emmet visited George at his office, which was located in the black section of town.

People on the street thought it odd that a well-dressed white man would be visiting George, but no one said anything.

Emmet and George took coffee at George's desk.

"How's your Pa?" George said.

"Fine. He'd be proud of you, George," Emmet said.

"You know, not all the white folks around here are like Bodine," George said. "Many will march with us when we turn out to vote in November."

"Things will change, George," Emmet said. "It's just going to take some time."

“Where are you off to next?” George said.

“Grant wants us to go to Mississippi,” Emmet said.

“Good luck, my best to your family,” George said.

“George, why not come for a visit?” Emmet said. “It’s only five days on the train. They’d love to see you.”

“After the election,” George said.

Emmet and George shook hands, then Emmet headed back to the hotel.

After a month in Mississippi, especially Mobile and Biloxi, Emmet, Forest, the nine Secret Service Agents and the US Army had arrested more than forty Klan members and squashed their movement.

By October, Emmet was ready to go home to Washington and make a final report to Grant on the Klan activities and their demise.

Ellis took Bettina and Eva to Stockton for a checkup with the doctor. Bettina was due in November sometime and Eva in January.

While the women were with the doctor, Ellis went to the post office for the mail and found a telegram from Emmet waiting. It was addressed to Eva and he rushed back to the doctor’s office and gave it to Eva when she and Bettina came out.

Eva tore open the telegram and read it quickly. "Emmet has finished the assignment and will be in Stockton in one week," she said.

"Let's get home and tell everybody the news," Ellis said.

Two miles from home, the rear left wheel on the buggy cracked. Ellis stopped to inspect the wheel. It needed to be replaced. Under the buggy was a spare wheel and a pot of grease.

"I guess I better get dirty," Ellis said.

Bettina and Eva watched as Ellis got under the buggy to remove the spare wheel and grease pot.

While under the buggy, three men on horseback rode to the buggy from the north.

"Ellis," Bettina said. "Rider's coming."

Covered in grease, Ellis got up from under the buggy and looked at the three men. They had the look of bad men about them. All were armed with sidearms and rifles. They were scruffy and unkept.

"Help you gents?" Ellis said.

"Sure can," the rider in the middle said. "You can give us all your money."

"Now see here," Ellis said.

The man in the middle drew his Colt and aimed it at Ellis. "Fancy rig, two fancy women, you got money. Hand it over."

"Better do as he says, Ellis," Bettina said. "They have guns."

"Smart lady," the man in the middle said.

"Hey Suggs, I know that woman," the man on the left said.

"Shut up, Swann," Suggs said.

"That's the railroad madam," Swann said.

"He's right, Suggs," the man on the right said.

Eva tucked the telegram into Bettina's skirt pocket.

Suggs dismounted, aiming his Colt at Ellis as he looked at Eva. "By God it is," he said.

"We'll give you our money, just leave her alone," Ellis said.

"She's a little plump, but she's still a looker," Suggs said.

"She's pregnant, you moron," Ellis said.

Suggs smacked Ellis on the side of his head with the Colt and as Ellis hit the buggy, Suggs clubbed him on the back of the head.

Bettina screamed and Suggs cracked her with the Colt.

"Boys, let's teach the madam some hospitality," Suggs said.

Bettina woke up next to Ellis, who was still unconscious. She was overcome with dizziness and vomited. Then she tried to stand up and was hit with vertigo and fell against the buggy.

"Help," she cried. "Somebody please help."

Bettina stood beside Ellis for what seemed like forever before a family riding by in a wagon stopped.

"That's Ellis Boyd and his wife," a man said.

"Help us," Bettina said.

"We better get you to the doctor," the man said.

"Eva's missing," Bettina said.

"We'll look for her later," the man said.

The sheriff of Stockton, Tom Barclay, who was also the county sheriff spoke to the doctor privately in the doctor's office.

"How is she?" Barclay said.

"Mrs. Boyd has a mild concussion," the doctor said. "She'll recover in a few days."

"Ellis?" Barclay said.

"He has a fractured skull," the doctor said. "He'll be in bed a month or more."

"I sent a deputy to the Boyd place," Barclay said. "Tell them I'll be with six deputies looking for Eva."

"You men have done a fine job," Grant said.

"You busted the back of the Klan and we have Nathan Forest in custody."

"Sir, I'm going home to California to see Eva and my family," Emmet said.

"And I know what's on your mind, son," Grant said. "The year you promised me is nearly up."

"It is on my mind, sir," Emmet said.

"Would the rest of you men excuse us for a moment," Grant said.

After they were alone, Grant said, "I want to give you something to think about while you're home, Emmet," Grant said. "I'd like to appoint you to the number one position in the Secret Service."

"That's quite an honor, sir," Emmet said.

"Give it some thought," Grant said.

"I will."

In the doctor's waiting room, Ann and Emma cried as the doctor gave the family the news. John, in shock, slumped into a chair.

"Who would do such a thing?" John said.

"Where is Eva?" Sarah said.

"Sheriff Barclay is out looking for her right now," the doctor said.

"I want to see my son right now," Sarah said.

"He's unconscious," the doctor said.

"Bettina?" Sarah said.

"She's awake," the doctor said.

Sarah and the twins followed the doctor to a bedroom where Bettina was conscious. John stayed in the waiting room with the baby.

"Mom, those men, they . . ." Bettina said and burst into tears.

Sarah hugged her and said, "Everything will be alright."

"Ellis is badly hurt and Eva is missing," Bettina said.

"The sheriff will find her," Sarah said.

Sheriff Barclay and his six deputies found Eva's body a hundred yards from the wagon beside a creek.

Eva's skirt was ripped off and her neck was broken.

"Cover her up," Barclay said. "Gently."

"What kind of monsters would do such a thing?" John said.

"Eva's dead?" Anna said. She and Emma burst into tears.

"Girls, stop your crying," Sarah said. "Sheriff, Bettina can identify these men. She told me so."

"Where is she?" Barclay said.

"With the doctor," Sarah said.

Sarah led Barclay into the bedroom where the doctor was checking Bettina's eyes.

"Can she talk?" Barclay said.

"Yes, but not too long," the doctor said.

"Bettina, can you identify the men who did this?" Barclay said.

Bettina nodded. "Yes," she said.

"Can you describe their faces?"

"I'll never forget them," Bettina said. "Or their names."

"You know their names?" Barclay said.

"One was called Suggs. The other was called Swann," Bettina said. "I don't know the third man's name. Doctor, I have a terrible headache."

"That's enough for now," the doctor said. "Bettina, I'm going to give you something to make you sleep."

"Wait," Bettina said and took the telegram from her skirt pocket and handed it to Sarah. "Eva gave me this to hold for you."

In the waiting room, Sarah read the telegram. "Oh my God," she said.

"What is it?" John said.

"Emmet is coming home," Sarah said.

"My God," John said.

"John, go home and get Lars. He doesn't know yet," Sarah said. "Anna, Emma, you look after the baby. I'll be getting a room at the hotel down the street."

■ ■ ■ ■

Rose watched as her husband took his final breath in his hospital bed. He never regained consciousness and died peacefully.

She left the room and went outside and stood on the front steps of the hospital. The air had a bit of a chill to it, but it felt good and clean and alive.

As she stood on the steps of the hospital, she could see the crowded street and thoroughfare across the street. Horse and buggies, men and women walking and in the background was The White House.

For a fleeting moment, she saw a man who looked like Emmet. He wore a gray suit and walked with a commanding presence.

Then she realized it was Emmet and she was frozen in place from the shock at seeing him again after so many years.

"Emmet, wait," she said, softly, but of course he couldn't hear her.

Rose raced the hundred feet to the gate, opened it and ran to the street, but Emmet was gone, lost in a crowd of faces.

Maybe she just imagined it. Emmet had been in her thoughts every day for six years while she nursed her husband and now that he finally died, she saw a stranger on the street who resembled Emmet and she thought it was him.

Her eyes deceived her. It was that simple and nothing more. She turned and went back to the hospital.

"John, I am so sorry," Lars said. "I don't know what to say."

"There is nothing to say," John said.

The doctor entered the waiting room. "She asleep," he said. "Come back tomorrow."

"Ellis?" John said.

"He's young and he's strong," the doctor said. "He has a good chance of recovering fully."

"Thank God for that," John said.

"Go home. Come back tomorrow," the doctor said.

John and Lars stopped by the hotel to see Sarah.

"John, the girls and the baby need you home," Sarah said. "Come back tomorrow and bring me clothes for a week."

"A week?" John said.

"I'll not leave my son or his wife in such a condition," Sarah said.

"Alright," John said, knowing that when Sarah made up her mind there was no changing it.

■ ■ ■ ■

"How is she this morning?" Sarah said as she entered the doctor's office.

"I think you can take her home," the doctor said. "But she must rest as much as possible. Her concussion still isn't fully healed yet."

"Ellis?"

The doctor smiled. "Come with me," he said.

Sarah followed the doctor into the room where Ellis was staying and he was awake and Bettina was standing beside him, holding his hand.

"Hi, Ma," Ellis said.

"Anna, Emma, you stay with Bettina night and day and take care of the baby," Sarah said. "Lars, you're welcome to stay in Emmet's room until he arrives. John, you can bring Bettina to visit Ellis tomorrow."

"Alright, honey," John said.

After they left in the wagon, Sarah returned to the doctor's office.

"Mrs. Boyd, I wonder if you wouldn't mind bringing this beef broth to Ellis?" the doctor said.

"Of course," Sarah said. She took a tray

with a bowl of beef broth into Ellis's room where he was awake in bed.

"I brought you some broth," Sarah said. "Can you sit up?"

After Sarah went to the hotel to take a bath and change, Ellis was dozing in bed when the doctor came in and said, "Ellis, are you up for a visitor?"

"Sure, Doc," Ellis said.

Beth entered the room and smiled. "Hi, Ellis," she said.

"Beth," Ellis said.

She walked to the bed and took his hand. "Ellis, I am so sorry," she said.

Bettina sat in a chair in Barclay's office after visiting Ellis.

"Now Bettina, this man is the sketch artist for the Stockton Gazette newspaper," Barclay said. "He is going to draw a sketch of the three men based upon your descriptions. If you get tired, just let us know."

The sketch artist opened his pad and held a sketching pencil. "Are you ready?" he said.

Bettina nodded.

When Emmet walked Bull along the platform, he expected to see his family. Ellis was missing, so was Eva and they all looked miserable.

As he neared them, Anna and Ella started to cry.

Emmet walked to Sarah. "What's happened?" he said.

"I couldn't stop them, Emmet. I'm sorry," Ellis said and started to cry as he told Emmet what happened.

Emmet took his hand. "Three armed men, no," Emmet said. "It's a miracle you and Bettina are alive."

"I told them she was pregnant, but they didn't care," Ellis said.

Emmet looked at Ellis. "Eva was pregnant?" he said.

"She didn't want you to know until you got home," Ellis said.

The doctor came in and said, "That's enough for today, Emmet."

"The doctor said he will release the . . . her body anytime you want," John said.

Emmet nodded. "Tomorrow I'll dig a grave," he said. "I'd appreciate it, Pa, if you went to town tomorrow and ordered a marker and ask the preacher if he'd come say a few words."

"Sure, son," John said. "Dammit, son, I have no words."

"Nobody does, Pa," Emmet said. "Mind if I pick out a place to bury her?"

"Go right ahead, son," John said.

Emmet left the porch and walked around to the rear of the house. He walked to a large oak tree about a hundred yards away and decided this would be Eva's resting point.

Emmet wrote his letter of resignation to Grant and asked John to mail it for him when John left to retrieve Eva's body. He gave John money for a coffin and then went to the oak tree with a pick ax and shovel and got to work digging a grave.

Around one in the afternoon, Anna and Emma brought him lunch.

"Are you going to live with us now?" Anna said.

"We want you to," Emma said.

"I don't know, girls," Emmet said. "I have something to do first."

They stayed with him while he ate and then took the basket back to the house.

Emmet continued digging until dark and was satisfied the grave was ready.

As he washed up at the pump beside the barn, John came to him and said, "She in the wagon in the barn. The preacher said he'd be here around ten in the morning."

"Thanks, Pa," Emmet said.
"Come to supper," John said.

Besides the family and the preacher, Sheriff Barclay and Beth and her parents were at the service for Eva. Ellis also came with the doctor.

Emmet, John, Lars and Barclay lowered the casket into the grave.

Then Emmet grabbed a shovel.

"We can help," Barclay said.

"No, I'll do it alone," Emmet said.

"Everybody in the house for cake and coffee," Sarah said.

Alone, Emmet got to work burying the casket. It took about two hours and then he went and sat on the porch.

Beth came out with a cup of coffee and a piece of cake and gave it to Emmet.

"Thanks," Emmet said.

"Mind if I sit?" Beth said.

"Sure," Emmet said.

Beth took the chair beside Emmet.

"Emmet, I really am sorry about Eva," Beth said. "I didn't know her but if you married her I'm sure she was a wonderful woman."

"Thanks."

"Emmet, what I did when you left for the war, I was wrong," Beth said.

"It was eleven years ago, Beth," Emmet said. "We were just kids back then."

"What . . . what are you going to do now?" Beth said. "Are you staying?"

"I honestly don't know what I'm going to do," Emmet said.

"I guess I'll be heading home now," Beth said.

"Thanks for coming," Emmet said.

After Beth and her parents left, Sheriff Barclay joined Emmet on the porch. "If now is not a good time to talk I'll understand," Barclay said.

"No, it's alright," Emmet said.

"Bettina was able to provide an excellent likeness of the three men to the sketch artist at the newspaper," Barclay said. "She even provided the names of two of them."

"Let me see," Emmet said.

Barclay removed three sheets of paper from his pocket, unfolded them and passed them to Emmet. "The first is named Suggs. The second is Swann. We don't know the third," he said.

"Frog," Emmet said.

"What?"

"I don't remember his real name, but the men called him Frog on account of his bulging eyes," Emmet said.

"You know these men?"

"They laid track on the railroad," Emmet said. "I saw them every day for four years."

"It makes sense now."

"What?"

"Bettina said they recognized Eva," Barclay said.

"Eva worked on the railroad," Emmet said. "It's where we met."

"I'm having these posters printed up," Barclay said. "By next week every sheriff west of the Mississippi will have them."

"You'll let me know if something turns up," Emmet said.

"Sure, Emmet. Sure."

For a month, Emmet worked sunup to sundown, plowing, chopping, repairing, planting, clearing brush and helping Lars with his fields.

One afternoon, Sarah, Ellis and Bettina sat on the porch and watched Emmet plow a field.

"He's going to work himself to death," Ellis said.

"No, he's fine," Sarah said.

"I should be out there with him," Ellis said.

"Not until the doctor says so," Bettina said.

"By then they'll be nothing left for me to

do," Ellis said.

"Ellis, don't you know what your brother is doing?" Sarah said.

"Yeah, working harder than the mule," Ellis said.

"No, Ellis," Bettina said. "He's grieving."

One November morning, Emmet saddled Bull after breakfast and rode into Stockton and stopped by the bank to see the president.

"My wife deposited twenty-five-thousand into your bank," Emmet said.

"It's all here plus interest, ready for you to draw on," the bank president said.

Emmet set his bank information from Washington on the bank president's desk. "I have twelve thousand dollars in this bank," he said. "I'd like you to wire transfer them to your bank as soon as possible."

"Of course, Mr. Boyd," the bank president said. "I'll send the wire today."

By December, Ellis was well enough to work the farm, although he wasn't at full strength and tired easily.

The day after Christmas, Emmet, Sarah and John took coffee after dinner on the porch.

"Ma, I'll be leaving soon," Emmet said.

"Where are you going, son?" John said.

"Wherever those three men went," Emmet said.

"Revenge, son?" John said.

"No, Pa, justice," Emmet said.

"Son, don't harden your heart over this," John said.

"No, Emmet, that's exactly what you need to do," Sarah said.

"Sarah," John said.

"Those three men murdered his wife and baby, nearly killed Ellis and Bettina and justice won't be served by the weak," Sarah said. "Emmet, you will never know another moment of peace as long as these men are free."

"Don't worry, Ma, I won't rest until the three of them are caught and hung, or killed by my own hand," Emmet said.

In early January, Emmet went to see Sheriff Barclay.

"I wish I had news for you, Emmet, but I don't," Barclay said.

"I know. If you had, you would have told me by now," Emmet said. "What I wanted to ask you is to post a ten thousand dollar reward for information leading to their capture."

"Who's posting the money?" Barclay said.

"I am," Emmet said.

At the bank, Emmet withdrew twenty-five-hundred dollars and then rode home.

The following morning, Emmet said goodbye to his family and rode Bull south.

Chapter Thirteen: 1872

San Diego was a port town of about three-thousand people. Most of the men Emmet saw as he rode Bull down Main Street were unarmed and they watched him with mild curiosity as he dismounted at the sheriff's office.

The sheriff, a man named Broussard, was at his desk when Emmet entered the office. Broussard looked at the Colt on Emmet's right hip before he stood up from the desk.

"Can I help you?" Broussard said.

"My name is Emmet Boyd," Emmet said. "I was the US Marshal out of Cheyenne before I went to work for President Grant in the Secret Service."

"What are you now?" Broussard said.

"Looking," Emmet said.

"For?"

"Three men," Emmet said. He removed the posters from his shirt pocket, unfolded them and handed them to Broussard.

"I got these posters two months ago," Broussard said. "A month after they were here."

"So they were here?" Emmet said.

"Three months ago," Broussard said. "Are you a bounty hunter now?"

"No. I'm the husband of the woman they murdered," Emmet said.

"I see," Broussard said. "Well, it's nearly suppertime. Let's go over to the cantina. I assume you want a place for the night."

"I do," Emmet said.

"Let's get you situated," Broussard said.

The Casa Hotel across the street was a three-story building with balconies on the second and third floor. Emmet got a room on the third floor and boarded Blue in their livery. After dropping off his gear and rifle in the room, Emmet and Broussard went to the cantina down the block.

Although California became a state in 1850, its roots were Mexican and it's Spanish origins were evident everywhere, including the food.

In the cantina, Emmet and Broussard ordered tortillas with beans and rice.

"The posters say there is a ten-thousand-dollar reward for these three," Broussard said.

"That's right," Emmet said.

"See that old man behind the counter? That's Jose, the owner," Broussard said as he waved to Jose.

Jose came out from behind the counter and walked to the table.

"What I do?" Jose said in a thick, Spanish accent.

"Nothing. Have a seat for a moment," Broussard said.

Jose took a chair. "What I do?" he said.

"Just want to ask you a question," Broussard said.

"I'm looking for three men," Emmet said and put the posters on the table. "These three men."

Jose picked up the posters and looked at them. "Si, they eat here," he said. "Maybe three months ago."

"You can remember three faces from three months ago?" Emmet said.

"I remember these three," Jose said. "They bother my daughter. I get the sheriff to throw them out."

"I remember that," Broussard said. "Thank you, Jose."

Jose returned to the counter.

"They were pestering his daughter Maria," Broussard said. "I had to ask them to leave. At the time I didn't know they were wanted."

"Do you know where they stayed?" Emmet said.

"Same place you are, although they spent most of their time at Lucia's place," Broussard said.

"A brothel?" Emmet said.

"Only one in town," Broussard said.

Lucia employed a dozen girls and they all lived in a two-story home at the far edge of town. Lucia, a native Californian was born when Mexico still ruled the territory.

"What did I do?" Lucia said when Broussard knocked on the door.

"We just need to talk," Broussard said.

"Talk? Men no come here to talk," Lucia said.

"I have a few questions," Emmet said.

Lucia looked at Emmet. "Oh, he a dangerous one, this one," she said.

"Let's go in the parlor," Broussard said.

Lucia led them to the parlor where several of her girls were lounging around.

"Can you get all your ladies together?" Emmet said.

"Ladies," Lucia giggled. "That's a good one. Ladies."

Three of the twelve women employed by Lucia were occupied, the other nine gathered around Lucia in the parlor.

"Girls, this man wants to talk to you," Lucia said.

"We're not paid to talk," one of the women said.

"You'll talk or I'll close this place down and you can all live on the street," Broussard said.

"So talk," Lucia said.

"I'm looking for three men who are wanted for murder," Emmet said. "I need you to take a look at them."

Emmet passed out the posters. "Yeah, I see them here, two, three times," Lucia said. "I forget who handles them."

"This one, I know this one," one of the girls said.

The woman identified Swann. "You sure?" Emmet said.

"I sure," the woman said. "I remember because he like to talk. All the time talk, talk, talk."

"About what?" Emmet said.

"Who listens?" the woman said. "Wait, he talk about getting rich in Colorado. He say when he get rich he come back and make me his woman. He full of shit, that one."

"Did he say where in Colorado?" Emmet said.

"He say he have family in Denver and would go to the place they call Boulder," the woman said.

"And the other two men?" Emmet said.

"I had this one," another woman said.

"What's your name?" Emmet said.

"Josie."

"Josie did he tell you his name?" Emmet said.

"No, but his friend called him the frog," Josie said.

"And the third?" Emmet said, holding the poster of Suggs.

"That one, he mean," another of the women said. "Very rough with his hands."

Emmet took one hundred dollars from his wallet and gave it to Lucia. "For their time," he said.

"The question is did they ride to Colorado or take the train?" Emmet said.

"If they went to Colorado at all," Broussard said.

"They went," Emmet said.

"How can you be so sure?" Broussard said.

"Men bragging to whores is nothing new," Emmet said. "On the railroad, the men told the prostitutes all their little secrets. These three are no different. When their pants are down their mouths open."

"The train depot doesn't open until eight

tomorrow morning, you can talk to the ticket agent then," Broussard said.

Emmet and Broussard were having coffee in the cantina.

"Why not join me for breakfast around seven?" Emmet said. "We can walk to the depot together."

"They serve a decent breakfast right here," Broussard said.

"I'll meet you here at seven," Emmet said.

Before going to bed, Emmet stripped down, poured a glass of water from the pitcher and opened the balcony for some fresh air.

He looked at the dark, nearly deserted streets below.

After riding over six hundred miles over several months and stopping in dozens of towns, including the big town of Los Angeles, he finally had a legitimate lead to go on.

Emmet closed the balcony doors, got into bed and fell asleep within minutes.

Breakfast was beans over rice with three fried eggs and a side of bacon and strong, black coffee.

From the cantina, Emmet and Broussard walked to the edge of town to the railroad depot.

"This here is Moses, but we just call him

Mos," Broussard said. "He runs the depot."

Mos looked at Emmet from behind the ticket window. "Ticket, mister?" he said.

"I'm looking for three men," Emmet said. "They may have taken the train from here."

Emmet slipped the three posters under the ticket window. Mos picked them up and looked at each of the three.

"Him," Mos said. "I remember him."

Mos identified Suggs.

"You sure?" Emmet said.

"Only reason I remember is because he complained about having to pay a boarding fee for his horse to use the box car," Mos said.

"The other two?" Emmet said.

"Only saw him," Mos said. "But he bought three tickets. Denver I believe."

"When is the next train east to Denver?" Emmet said.

"Noon tomorrow."

"Give me one ticket and boarding for my horse," Emmet said.

As they left the depot, Emmet said, "Where is the telegraph office?"

Ellis and John inspected the crop of corn that was planted on the additional two hundred acres of land they purchased along with Lars a year ago.

The man they hired, Thad Proctor, owned his own farm a few miles west, but it was small and he was happy to have an extra three-hundred-dollars in his pocket for his work.

"Pa, we're doing well, aren't we?" Ellis said.

"Better than I ever hoped. Why?" John said.

"The other day in Stockton when I was picking up the mail, I ran into Beth," Ellis said. "We got to talking about her orange groves. She told me there's a new kind of orange tree that she's buying called a Naval Orange. I think we should buy another fifty acres and plant orange trees."

"Fifty acres is five hundred dollars at today's market," John said.

"We got what, twelve thousand in the bank?" Ellis said. "We can afford five hundred dollars."

"But the buying and planting and harvesting, we know nothing about that," John said.

"No, but Beth does and she's offered to sell us twenty-five trees to start," Ellis said. "Pa, you have two sixteen-year-old daughters who could use a solid future and . . ."

"Okay, son, we'll go talk to Beth," John said.

■ ■ ■ ■

Rose entered the hospital's chief of staff's office, dressed in civilian clothing.

He looked up from the paperwork on his desk. "Rose, why aren't you ready for your shift?" he said.

She set an envelope on the desk. "My resignation, sir," she said.

"What?" the chief of staff said.

"I've been here for ten years," Rose said. "Now that my husband is dead there is nothing holding me here. I want to go where nurses are really needed. Here I'm just another nurse on a ward. I hope you understand, sir."

"Actually, I do. Best of luck to you, Rose."

Beth sold her house to a young doctor just starting out and kept only her clothes and medical equipment that belonged to her. Before resigning and selling the house, she did a search through medical journals to find where nurses were needed most.

Several locations expressed a need for nurses. A hospital in Minnesota called the Mayo Clinic, but didn't want to leave one hospital for another where she would be just another face in a ward.

Another response came from Chicago and

she crossed that out for the same reasons.

Another came from Cincinnati in Ohio and another from Boston. Those too were out as well.

Then she received a letter from the Governor of Wyoming, John Campbell about a hospital that was being built in Fort Laramie. She replied that she would be there within a week.

After a restless night sleep at a Washington hotel, Rose caught the train to Cheyenne, Wyoming to meet Governor Campbell.

She booked a sleeper car for the three-day journey.

Once she had put her bags in the sleeper car and the train started moving, Rose felt excitement and fear in her stomach.

Excitement at an unknown future.

Fear for the same reason.

For the thirty-six-hour ride to Denver, Emmet booked a sleeper car for himself and a box car for Bull.

There was very little to do on a long train ride except eat, sleep and look out the window or read. As was his habit, Emmet chose to read. He had a hard back copy of Twenty Thousand Leagues Under the Sea by Jules Vern.

Except for lunch, dinner and breakfast,

Emmet stayed locked away in his sleeper car, reading about the exploits of Captain Nemo and his ship The Nautilus.

It was a far-fetched story, but exciting and enjoyable.

Denver was a muddy, wild town of four thousand residents and every one of them appeared to have gold fever.

Emmet never knew the full story of Beth and her husband, but apparently they struck it rich mining in the hills during the war.

As he walked Bull through the crowded streets to the sheriff's office, Emmet had the feeling the only people getting rich in Denver these days were the hardware stores selling mining equipment to new residents.

He found the sheriff's office, tethered Bull to the hitching post and went inside where the sheriff was behind his desk.

"Help you?" he said.

"Are you the sheriff?" Emmet said.

"I am. Name is Asper. What can I do for you?"

"I'm looking for three wanted men," Emmet said and took out the posters from his pocket and set them on the desk.

Asper looked at them. "Yeah, I got these a few weeks ago," he said. "Are you a bounty hunter?"

"No," Emmet said. "The woman they murdered was my wife."

"I see," Asper said. "What's your name?"

"Emmet Boyd."

"Any relation to the marshal they had in Cheyenne a few years ago?" Asper said.

"I was the marshal in Cheyenne until President Grant asked me to be on his Secret Service detail," Emmet said.

"I see," Asper said. "My condolences. But what makes you think they're in Denver?"

"Swann supposedly had family in the area, possibly Boulder," Emmet said.

"Boulder's a day's ride south of here or an hour on the railroad," Asper said. "Maybe they went straight there without stopping because I sure haven't seen them."

"Are they gold mining in Boulder?" Emmet said.

"Gold?" Asper said. "It's where they're building the University of Colorado they approved back in sixty-one."

"If he has family there, he might be holed up there," Emmet said. "When is the next train to Boulder?"

"Ten o'clock tomorrow morning," Asper said. "Maybe I'll go with you."

"Can you recommend a hotel?"

"The Denver House," Asper said. "I'll

walk over with you. It's near suppertime anyway."

The Denver House was a nice, four-story hotel on Main Street that had a restaurant and it's on livery stable.

After getting a room and boarding Bull, Emmet and Asper got a table in the restaurant and ordered steaks.

"You were the first marshal in Cheyenne, correct?" Asper said.

"Appointed by Grant," Emmet said.

"Not that Denver is tame, but that's one wild town," Asper said.

"It had its fair share of trouble, but it's not a bad place to set roots," Emmet said. "How long have you been sheriff in Denver?"

"Since sixty-nine," Asper said. "Before that I was a deputy in Topeka."

"Why did they pick Boulder to build the college?" Emmet said. "I would think Denver would be the place."

"I honestly don't know," Asper said. "Ideal location, I suppose. Like I said, I was a deputy in Topeka at the time."

After dinner, Emmet and Asper took coffee to the front porch.

"Denver seems quiet enough," Emmet said.

"I have eight full-time deputies to make sure it stays that way," Asper said.

"People got rich in those mountains," Emmet said.

"Some got lucky and made a fortune," Asper said. "Not so much now, but they still dream. Our stores sell more pick axes and tin pans than anything else."

"I doubt the likes of Swann is interested in breaking his back," Emmet said. "If anything, he's looking for a place to hole up since these posters have been circulated."

"The ten-thousand reward, who posted that?" Asper said.

"I did," Emmet said.

"Look, Marshal . . ." Asper said.

"I'm not a Marshal anymore, or a Secret Service Agent," Emmet said.

"What I meant is, what is your intention?" Asper said.

"I intend to return them to Stockton to stand trial for murder," Emmet said.

"So you don't plan to kill him?"

"That will depend upon him," Emmet said. "The warrant says dead or alive. I'd rather alive and see him hang."

"Well, I guess I'll see you in the morning," Asper said.

"Let's meet for breakfast at eight," Emmet said.

■ ■ ■ ■

Rose looked out the window of her sleeper car. Even at night she could feel the speed of the train looking out at the blackness.

In twelve hours she would be in Cheyenne and hopefully employed at the brand new hospital in Fort Laramie.

She fell asleep as she had for the past seven years, thinking about Emmet, wondering where he was, if he was well, married with children, whatever.

That man she saw in Washington the day he husband passed, it was silly to think it really was him from a fleeting glance a hundred feet away.

She closed her eyes.

She just wanted him to be happy.

Emmet and Asper walked their horses to the railroad station after breakfast. They purchased roundtrip tickets and boxcar tickets for their horses.

According to the schedule, the would arrive in Boulder at ten-forty-five.

Barely time to get a cup of coffee.

Rose left her luggage at the train depot in Cheyenne and walked into town not knowing what to expect.

The streets were muddy, the sidewalks full and the air seemed full of excitement and danger and uncertainty.

Some people watched her as she walked along the wood sidewalks. She spotted a post office, went in and asked where she might find Governor Campbell. She was told where his office was located and continued walking.

The streets were alive with shops, stores, people and cowboys. She passed the sheriff's office and a saloon called Eva's Runway until she located the governor's office. It was a nice, brick building with flowers out front.

Rose knocked on the door. A woman dressed as a maid answered. "Yes?" she said.

"I'm here to see Governor Campbell," Rose said.

"Do you have an appointment?"

"No, but I have this," Rose said and handed Campbell's letter of invitation to the maid.

"Come in," the maid said.

Rose followed the maid to a closed, office door. The maid knocked, opened the door and stepped inside and closed the door. She returned a few seconds later and said, "The Governor will see you now."

Campbell was standing behind his desk when Rose entered the office.

"Please, have a seat," Campbell said. "May I offer you some coffee?"

"I would like some, thank you," Rose said.

Campbell had the maid bring in a pot of coffee and two cups. Campbell told Rose about Fort Laramie and the two hundred soldiers stationed there and the new hospital built to service the fort but also civilians from Laramie and the surrounding area.

The brand new hospital had twelve rooms, two recovery rooms, one surgeon, one general practitioner and three nurses and needed a fourth, a nurse with experience in assisting a surgeon.

"When you wrote seeking employment, I decided to hold that fourth position for you based upon your years as a surgical nurse in Washington," Campbell said. "May I ask why you decided to leave Washington?"

"After my husband died I decided I needed a change," Rose said.

"I'm sorry to hear that," Campbell said. "And I understand."

"He was sick for a long time, since the war," Rose said. "But let me ask you, when can I go to the hospital?"

"Tomorrow morning on my private train," Campbell said. "Have you a place to stay for tonight?"

"Not yet, Governor," Rose said.

"My wife and I have plenty of room, stay with us and we'll get an early start in the morning," Campbell said.

"My bags are at the station," Rose said.

"I'll send for them," Campbell said. "Right now, let me walk you over to my house."

As they walked their horses from the railroad depot to Boulder, it seemed construction was underway everywhere.

"That's where the college is being built," Asper said.

Buildings were being erected outside the town limits. Like the entire town, it was surrounded by mountains and hills.

"They got a sheriff?" Emmet said.

"Name is Jasper Moon," Asper said.

"Let's find him," Emmet said.

Moon's office was in the center of town, a wood structure with two cells. Moon had one deputy, his son, Jed.

Emmet and Asper tied the horses to the hitching post and entered the office. "Moon was behind a desk, Jed was cleaning a Henry rifle.

"Why, Dale Asper, what brings you to Boulder?" Moon said.

"Business, I'm afraid, Jasper," Asper said.

"Jed, pour a cup of coffee for the sheriff and his deputy," Moon said.

"He's not my deputy. He used to be the marshal up in Cheyenne," Asper said.

"Not the one they called Emmet Boyd?" Moon said. "Are you Emmet Boyd, mister, the one tamed Cheyenne?"

"I am," Emmet said.

"What are you doing here?" Moon said.

Emmet set the three wanted posters on the desk. Moon picked up the posters and carefully look at each one. "Jed, have a look," he said.

Jed came to the desk and looked at the three posters. "Any relations to the Swann family?" he said.

"He's Lettie's brother, Jake," Moon said.

"Never met him," Jed said.

"Where can I find Lettie?" Emmet said.

"It says he killed a woman," Moon said.

"That's right and I aim to bring the three of them to Stockton for trial," Emmet said.

"Lettie lives about ten miles west," Moon said. "With her husband and other brother. Jake left maybe ten years ago when this wasn't much more than some tents and a trading post. Lettie and her husband raise horses for the Army."

"I guess I better get started," Emmet said.

"Not alone you're not," Asper said.
"Jed, saddle the horses," Moon said.
"Yes, Pa," Jed said.

"Rose, my wife of three months, Isabella Campbell," Campbell said.
"You're newlyweds," Rose said. "I'm intruding."
"Nonsense," Isabella said. "Come in and get comfortable."
"I'll have your bags delivered," Campbell said.
"John, let's eat out tonight," Isabella said.
"Alright," Campbell said. "I'll be home by six."

"What they don't raise, they capture from these hills," Moon said. "The Army will go as high as three hundred for a good horse."
"When did you last see Jake?" Emmet said.
"Maybe sixty-six. Said he was going east to work on the railroad," Moon said. "Ain't been back since I know of."
"He probably skirted the town and rode directly to his sister's place," Asper said.
"Well find out soon enough," Moon said.
They rode up a hill and paused to look down at a canyon that was filled with wild horses.

"Must be a hundred of them," Asper said.

"Most of them belong to Lettie," Moon said.

On the other side of the canyon, on a flat stretch of land was a large home, barn and corral. A fire rose up from the chimney. A dozen or more horses were in the corral.

They rode to the hitching post in front of the porch and dismounted. Before they could walk up to the porch, Lettie Swan, a Greener shotgun in her hands came out.

"Sheriff Moon, what are you doing here?" Lettie said.

"Looking for your brother Jake," Moon said.

"Jake?" Lettie said. "Ain't seen him in years."

"Where's your husband and other brother?" Moon said.

"Out bringing in some horses for the Army," Lettie said.

"And Jake isn't here?" Moon said.

"I told you no," Lettie said.

"You're a liar," Emmet said.

"Mister, you better watch your . . ." Lettie said.

Emmet yanked the reins and rode Bull behind the house and in the distance, Jake Swann was riding toward the mountains.

"Let's go, Bull," Emmet said and yanked

hard on the reins.

As he followed Swann, Moon and Jasper came around the house and took off after Emmet. Swann had a five hundred feet lead on Emmet, but Bull was a massive, very powerful horse and closed the gap quickly.

As they neared the mountains, Swann's horse tired and the gap closed to three hundred feet. At the foothills, the gap narrowed to just a hundred feet.

Swann reached the mountains and started to climb, but after a hundred feet, his horse was spent and Swann jumped from the saddle and climbed on foot.

Emmet dismounted, grabbed his Henry rifle and started to climb. Swann was only a hundred feet ahead and gasping for air.

"Give it up, Swann, you'll never make it," Emmet yelled.

Swann turned, grabbed his Colt and fired a wild shot at Emmet.

Emmet cocked the lever of his rifle, aimed and shot Swann in the leg.

"Goddamn you," Swann cried as he fell and slid down the mountain about fifty feet.

"Stay right there, Swan," Emmet said. "Move and I'll blow your head off."

"I'm bleeding, you son of a bitch bushwhacker," Swan said.

Emmet reached Swann. "Get up," he said.

"You shot my leg, I can't get up," Swann said.

"Get up or I'll shoot your other leg and drag you behind my horse," Emmet said.

Swann got to his feet. Emmet shoved him and they walked down the mountain where Jasper and Moon waited below.

"It will be a pleasure to watch you hang," Emmet said.

"For what? I didn't do nothing," Swann said.

"Then why did you run?" Emmet said.

At the bottom, Emmet said, "You got a doctor in town?"

"We do," Jasper said.

"Tie his leg while I get his horse," Emmet said.

"Good surgical nurses are in short supply in the West," Campbell said. "A place like Fort Laramie Hospital can really use a nurse of your experience."

"I hope I can make a difference," Rose said. "In Washington I was one of a thousand. I won't be missed. Out here I'm needed."

Rose, Campbell and Isabella were having dinner at the Cheyenne House, the best restaurant in town.

"How do you like Cheyenne?" Isabella said.

"I must say I'm quite surprised," Rose said. "I was expecting a ten cents novel about gun fights and outlaws, but it's nothing like that at all."

"It was not so long ago," Campbell said. "But President Grant sent the best marshal he had to help establish law and order."

"He must have been some marshal," Rose said.

"He was," Campbell said. "His name was Emmet Boyd."

Rose nearly gasped at hearing the name.

"Did you know him?" Isabella said.

"I once treated a man named Emmet Boyd during the war," Rose said. "It couldn't be the same man."

"Boyd is a common name," Campbell said. "Anyway, he went to Washington to be on Grant's Secret Service two years ago."

"I'm curious. Was he tall, over six feet with sandy hair?" Rose said.

"Sounds like him," Campbell said.

"Small world," Rose said.

After a doctor removed the bullet from Swann's leg, Emmet and Jasper took the train back to Denver.

"Send for the US Marshal," Emmet said

to Jasper after they locked Swann up in Jasper's jail.

"You can't hang me, I didn't kill that woman," Swann said.

"Who did?" Emmet said.

"Suggs, that miserable bastard," Swann said. "We raped her, sure, but I didn't murder nobody. Suggs was afraid she would identify us, so he choked her to death."

"Where did Suggs and Frog go after you left them?" Emmet said.

"Why should I tell you?" Swann said.

"Because if you don't, you'll hang for murder," Emmet said. "Rape might get you ten years with parole in seven, but your neck won't be stretched. It's up to you. Sheriff, let's get some dinner."

"Hold on, just you hold on," Swann said. "I help you find Suggs and Frog and you'll make sure I don't swing?"

"I will speak up for you to the judge," Emmet said. "As it was my wife who was murdered, he'll listen to what I have to say."

"I want that in writing," Swann said. "And with you signature included."

"Sheriff, you have pen and paper?" Emmet said.

"At my desk," Jasper said.

"That was a lovely dinner, Governor. Thank

you," Rose said.

"My pleasure," Campbell said. "Get a good night's sleep. My train will be ready right after breakfast."

"I'll walk you to your room," Isabella said.

Once Rose was alone in her bedroom, she sat on the bed and cried.

Swann read Emmet's letter, then said, "I keep this?"

"I'll give it to the US Marshal, along with the warrant with your name on it to give to the judge in Stockton," Emmet said. "But only if you talk and right now."

"Suggs said he was going to see his folks in Nebraska," Swann said.

"Where in Nebraska?" Emmet said.

"He said they got a spread along the river west of Norfolk."

"And Frog?"

"Has a sister in Montana Territory," Swann said. "Place called Helena."

"Frog's real name, what is it?" Emmet said.

"Logan Lance, but nobody calls him nothing but Frog," Swann said.

"Sheriff, give this letter and the warrant to the marshal when he gets here in the morning," Emmet said.

"Where are you going?" Jasper said.

"Helena," Emmet said.

"Ellis, John, this is Ben," Beth said. "He takes care of my orange groves."

Ellis and John shook Ben's hand.

"Beth tells me you want twenty-five orange trees to start a grove," Ben said.

"We do," Ellis said.

"Ben will deliver them tomorrow and tell you how to plant and care for them," Beth said.

John took out an envelope from his pocket and handed it to Beth. "Five hundred as we agreed upon," he said.

"Thank you, John," Beth said.

"No, Beth, thank you," John said.

"I'll be over in the morning with the trees," Ben said.

"Bye, Beth and thanks again," John said.

After Ellis and John rode away, Ben said, "Those trees are worth four times that."

"I know," Beth said.

Isabella decided to ride to Fort Laramie with Rose and Campbell. The ride took about forty minutes and Rose and Isabella spent the time chatting while Campbell read some legal documents.

The fort had been around since 1849 and was a well-established frontier outpost. The new hospital was something of a crown jewel for the fort and the entire area.

Campbell introduced Rose to the fort commanding officer, Colonel Henry, his officers and two doctors that ran the hospital. The fort was home to two hundred soldiers and their primary mission was to provide safety and security for the territory, including a large supply train of freight wagons.

Rose was given a tour of the hospital, which was modern and clean and well stocked with medicine and surgical equipment.

"We not only service our soldiers and their families, but our doors are open to any civilian who needs our help," Colonel Henry said. "Doctor, would you show Rose her living quarters?"

"Certainly," a doctor said. "This way, Rose."

The closest the railroad in Denver could get Emmet to Helena was the border of Montana. He would have to ride Bull the rest of the way, a distance of about two-hundred-miles through lush, undeveloped country.

In a small town called Cody, Emmet loaded up on supplies and headed northwest toward Helena. Bull was still in his prime and could easily cover the two hundred miles in five days, but Emmet decided to make the journey in six to keep Bull's energy high.

Frog had no way of knowing he was coming, so an extra day wouldn't hurt anything. He stuck to the trails and freight roads and covered thirty miles by sundown. He didn't see another person the entire day.

At sundown, he found a comfortable spot off the road, made a fire and put on some beans and bacon and coffee and tended to Bull while the food cooked. After he ate, he brushed Bull and gave him two carrot sticks, the made his bedroll and settled in to sleep.

Emmet didn't tether or hobble Bull. Bull hated both and wouldn't wander more than twenty feet from the fire during the night.

Rose had breakfast with the doctors and other nurses in the fort's mess hall, along with the colonel and hundreds of other soldiers.

After breakfast, came her first full day of work at the hospital. The twelve rooms and twenty-four beds were full, half with soldiers, the rest with civilians. The waiting room was filled with twenty patients, half were civilians needing medical care.

Late in the afternoon, a soldier was brought in with a bullet in his chest. He was on a routine patrol when the squad was ambushed by Blackfeet Indians. He was the only soldier injured in the skirmish.

Rose assisted the surgeon in removing the bullet and stitching the soldier's wound. One soldier who was ready to return to the fort gave the new man his bed.

Rose had dinner in the mess hall with the hospital staff and then made night rounds with the other nurses.

It was a long and fulfilling day and for a little while she didn't think about Emmet.

Bull was feeling particularly frisky the second day in Montana and covered sixty miles of ground. Emmet rewarded him with a bag of grain when they camped for the night.

It was an interesting day. He met a freight wagon carrying supplies, several trappers and a saw a group of Indians on a ridge in the distance. They made no move against him and just watched as he rode by from the ridge.

After he made camp and had supper, Bull began acting fidgety and nervous.

Emmet tried brushing him to calm him down, but Bull's anxiety only grew worse.

"I get it," Emmet said. "Now don't you fret none."

Emmet built up the fire, propped up his saddle and placed his hat on top of it, then took his Henry rifle into the woods and waited.

It didn't take long. Two men armed with revolvers came from the woods and stood in front of the fire. One man aimed his revolver and fired, hitting the saddle, knocking the hat to the ground.

"I'll get his horse. You check and see he got any money," one of the men said.

Emmet stepped out from behind the fire, Henry rifle at the ready. "I wouldn't do that if I was you," he said.

Both men spun to face Emmet, guns drawn and ready to shoot. Emmet shot the one closest, cocked the lever and shot the other.

Emmet walked to the two dead men and stood over them. Then he walked to Bull and rubbed his neck. "I'll bury them in the morning," he said.

"That first year, discard any oranges," Ben said. "Too young. Next year you get about fifteen a tree of good stick. Year after that you might get a hundred and fifty per tree.

More than enough to crate and sell in town."

"Thanks, Ben, for everything," John said.

"Take care of them trees, they're a gold mine," Ben said.

After Ben left, John, Ellis and the entire family walked the small grove of twenty-five trees.

"We got room for a hundred more trees, Pa," Anna said.

"And who will take care of a hundred more trees while your brother, Lars and I are plowing the fields?" John said.

"We will," Ella said. "Me and Anna."

"And me," Bettina said.

John looked at Ellis. "They want to make us the orange king of California," he said.

Helena reminded Emmet of Cheyenne when he rode down the main thoroughfare. Muddy streets, wood shacks and buildings, dry good stores and saloon tents.

Two large, bearded men were fighting in the mud as Emmet rode by. They rolled around, cursing, biting, eye gauging each other. One managed to get up and he grabbed a barrel off a wood sidewalk and smashed the other over the head with it. "Take that ya bastard," he screamed and walked away.

Emmet dismounted in front of the large general store where a dozen men were buying equipment and supplies.

Two bearded men in filthy clothes approached Emmet. "Nice horse," one of them said.

"Nice rifle," the other man said.

He reached for Emmet's Henry rifle and Emmet drew his Colt and smacked the man across his skull and the man dropped to the mud.

Emmet looked at the other man. "Pick him up and go away," he said.

"Sure, mister," the man said.

A man from inside the general store came out and looked at Emmet. "You here to do some tin panning?" he said.

"No," Emmet said. "You got any law in this town?"

"Law?" the man said. "No man is fool enough to wear a badge in this place. You a lawman?"

"I'm just passing through," Emmet said. "I'm looking for the Lance family?"

"Them thumpers?" the man said.

"Thumpers?" Emmet said.

"Bible beaters," the man said.

"You have something against the bible?" Emmet said.

"I got something against thumpers sticking their noses in where they ain't wanted," the man said.

"Do you know where I can find them?" Emmet said.

"A day's ride due north," the man said. "You low on supplies?"

"A bit," Emmet said. "Bring me some coffee, bacon, beans, cornbread and grain for my horse."

"Got money?"

Emmet gave him twenty dollars. "That cover it?" he said.

"I'll bring them right out," the man said.

A few minutes later, Emmet headed due north out of Helena. A day's ride would get him there by noon or so tomorrow.

He made camp before dark, made a fire and cooked some supper, then put the fire out so anyone about wouldn't find him. In the morning, he made another fire, cooked some beans and bacon for breakfast, along with some bread, then continued north.

Around one in the afternoon, Emmet spotted a large cabin, corral and barn in the distance. He dismounted and used his binoculars to take a closer look.

A man was out front chopping wood. Four horses were in the corral. Beside the corral was a buggy. Smoke rose up from the chimney.

Emmet rubbed Bull's neck. "Well, let's get to it," he said.

Emmet rode directly to the house. The man chopping wood stopped and made a grab for a rifle leaning against the corral.

Emmet drew his Colt. "I wouldn't, friend," he said. "I mean you no harm."

The man looked at Emmet. "What's your business here?" he said.

"Is your name Lance?" Emmet said.

"Tis. What's that your concern?" the man said.

"Who's in the house?" Emmet said.

"Ma, my wife, my baby," the man said.

"Call them out?" Emmet said.

The man stared at Emmet.

"I mean no harm to anybody," Emmet said. "Call them out."

"Ma, Ellie, get out here," the man said.

The door opened and a woman of about sixty and a woman of about thirty stepped out.

"Are you Mrs. Lance?" Emmet said.

"Have you been saved?" the older woman said.

"What?" Emmet said.

"Have you been saved by our Lord and savior Jesus Christ?"

"I've been baptized," Emmet said.

"Have you taken Jesus Christ into your

heart?" the woman said. "That's the only true salvation."

"Mrs. Lance, I'm looking for your son Logan," Emmet said.

"Logan is a sinner," the woman said. "It's too late for him, but if you accept Jesus Christ into your heart it's not too late for you."

Emmet sighed. "Is he here?"

"He is," the woman said.

"Where?"

"What's your interest in my son?" the woman said.

"He raped and murdered my wife," Emmet said.

"So you're the one," the woman said.

"He told you?" Emmet said.

"He confessed his sins," the woman said. "Threw himself on his knees before God and asked for forgiveness for his wrong doings."

"And he told you he murdered my wife?" Emmet said.

"Confessed he consorted with evil women while working on the railroad. Stole, cheated and finally rape and murder," the woman said. "Blamed it on falling in with bad company, but it was his own weakness that drove him against God."

"Where is he now?" Emmet said.

"Resting beside my husband," the woman said.

"He's dead?" Emmet said.

The woman looked at her son near Emmet. "Show him," she said.

"This way," the man said.

Emmet dismounted and walked his horse to a gravesite near the house. Two graves were protected by a picket fence. One grave was marked **Logan Lance.**

"What happened?" Emmet said.

"Ma hung him from that big oak over there," the man said.

"Hung her own son?" Emmet said.

"He was a sinner," the man said. "Like Pa."

Every day, Anna, Emma and Bettina carried water from the creek to the wagon, then drove the wagon to the grove and watered the twenty-five orange trees.

"I was doing some figuring," Anna said. "One-hundred and fifty oranges a tree times twenty-five trees is three thousand, seven hundred and fifty oranges. Imagine if we had a hundred trees how much we could make selling them in Stockton."

"Where are we going to get another seventy-five trees," Emma said.

"From the seeds inside the oranges," Anna said.

"Girls, I think we better discuss this with the men before we get carried away," Bettina said.

"Well, let's go find the men," Anna said.

Once John, Ellis and Lars were gathered on the porch, Anna said, "Pa, we've been talking and . . ."

"Who is we?" John said.

"Us. Emma and Bettina and me."

"And what have you been talking about?" John said.

"We have the land for another seventy-five orange trees," Anna said.

"If each tree grown one hundred and fifty oranges, that's three thousand, seven hundred and fifty oranges," Emma said. "Imagine how much we can sell if we had a hundred trees."

"And where are we getting another seventy-five trees?" John said. "Beth is not . . ."

"From the seeds, Pa," Anna said.

"Grow them from scratch?" John said.

"Why not?" Emma said.

"Ellis?" John said.

"It could work, Pa," Ellis said.

"Lars?" John said.

"I've grown just about everything else,"

Lars said.

"As we don't know the first thing about growing orange trees from seeds, I suggest you four take a trip to Sacramento to the Department of Agriculture and learn all you can," John said.

"We're going to Sacramento?" Anna said.

"Well, it's not going to come to us," John said.

"We better go back," Emma said.

"And get our best dresses cleaned," Anna said.

"Wait, we're taking the train, right?" Anna said.

"Unless you'd rather a fifty-mile ride in the wagon?" John said.

Emmet returned to Helena and stopped at the general store.

"How was your trip, young fellow?" the man in the general store said. "You meet the Lance family?"

"I did," Emmet said.

"Did you get saved?"

"In a sense she saved me the trouble," Emmet said. "Let me get two weeks' worth of supplies."

"Where you headed?"

"Nebraska," Emmet said.

■ ■ ■ ■

John and Sarah drove Ellis, Bettina, Anna and Emma to the railroad depot in Stockton to catch the train to Sacramento.

On the platform, Sarah looked at her daughters. "John, they're young women. When did this happen?"

"Right under our noses," John said. "Now say goodbye or they'll miss the train. And for God's sake, don't cry."

The hourlong ride seemed to whiz by in a blink as Anna and Emma spent the entire trip looking out the window.

When they reached Sacramento and walked from the railroad depot to the city, Anna and Emma had never seen anything as pretty as the streets, trees and river.

"Ellis, it's beautiful here," Anna said.

"It's the capital of California," Ellis said.

"I know from school, but I never expected it to be so pretty," Anna said.

"Let's find the Agriculture Department and maybe we'll have time to sightsee a bit," Ellis said.

As he at lunch, Emmet studied his maps. Without the railroad, he had to ride three weeks or more to Reach Fort Laramie where he could get the railroad to Nebraska.

He could re-supply in Casper and hopefully send a telegram home. By the time they reached Casper, Bull could use a new pair of shoes.

After Bull rested for an hour, Emmet mounted the saddle. "We need thirty miles before dark," he said.

The freight roads were well marked and groomed by years of heavy freight wagon traffic and made the ride easier than unmarked terrain.

All he had to go on to find Suggs was his family lives somewhere along the river near Northfork. Unless they were well known, finding them could take weeks, maybe even months.

He was prepared to spend the rest of his life searching for Suggs. Was Suggs prepared to spend the rest of his life hiding?

Ellis, Bettina and the twins spent several hours with a specialist in the Agriculture Department at the state capital building.

He explained the proper way to pot the seeds indoors until the fully sprouted and then how to transport them into the ground.

The special care they required until they grew large enough to grow fruit and how to spot and take care of a sickly tree. Ellis made pages of notes before they left just in time for lunch.

They found a nice restaurant nearby, had lunch and then did some sightseeing before catching the six o'clock train home.

John and Sara waited on the platform for the train to arrive and Ann and Emma told Sarah all about Sacramento on the ride home.

That night, after dinner, John, Ellis and Lars sat on the porch with coffee and discussed the possible expansion of the orange grove.

"We'd have to clear out a section of the barn and pot the seeds until they sprout and are ready to grow in the ground," Ellis said. "Then we plant them five feet apart like we did the twenty-five trees."

"What do you think, Lars?" John said.

"I think we have some work to do getting that grove ready for new trees," Lars said.

Every second of her day, Rose was occupied either in surgery or with taking care of patients both Army and civilian.

In Washington, she did the same but she wasn't needed, not really. That hospital had a hundred nurses and fifty doctors and was a face in a sea of faces.

In Fort Laramie, she was needed and

made a difference and that's why she became a nurse in the first place.

It was fulfilling and satisfying work, but at night, alone in her room her thoughts turned to Emmet. At the time, there was nothing to do but let him go. She had to care for her dying husband and Emmet understood that and accepted it.

But for seven years she wondered where he went and what happened to him. That he was a US Marshal in Cheyenne and then a Secret Service Agent for Grant meant he actually accomplished something with his life.

In Washington, right under her very nose.

She didn't know if she should laugh or cry.

Emmet entered Wyoming near Fort Casper and rode southeast for a few days before stopping at a small settlement called Riverton. A trading post more than anything else, Emmet was glad to see it as this late in the year, the weather was turning cold, especially at night and he bought a warm jacket and thick blanket for Bull and extra supplies.

He decided to give Bull a two-day rest as he earned it, having ridden close to fifteen hundred miles the last two months.

Emmet got a shave and a bath and had his dirty laundry washed and even picked up a few new shirts and underwear.

For a dollar he got a tent and a cot and fifty cents paid for a corral for Bull.

Before leaving the settlement, Emmet had breakfast and studied his maps. He was only two hundred and fifty miles from Laramie and the railroad and traveling at a slower pace, would be there in a week.

John and Lars worked for two weeks building seventy-five little boxes to plant the seeds, while Ellis and the twins cleared the necessary land to plant the saplings when they grew tall enough to transfer.

After that it was just a matter of planting seventy-five seeds into the square boxes, watering them, giving them nutrients and giving them plenty of sunshine.

After the seeds were all planted, Ellis said, "In a year, we'll have trees in the ground."

Emmet rode past Fort Laramie and noted the changes since he last visited. The fort for one thing had been expanded and now had a hospital. He didn't stop and rode into the town of about a thousand people.

At the railroad depot he bought a ticket west to Stockton. Winter was no place to be tracking Suggs along the South Dakota and Nebraska border. A man could get snowed in and never been heard from again.

The train was due in two hours. Emmet took a seat on a bench, dug a book out of his saddlebags and read until the train arrived.

A few months earlier, Beth had developed a nagging cough that just wouldn't go away. She went to town to see the doctor, who examined her thoroughly.

"Beth, I can't be sure," the doctor said. "I'm sending you to San Francisco to see a specialist in such matters."

"What matters?" Beth said.

"Tuberculosis," the doctor said. "Maybe worse."

"I'm only thirty-years-old," Beth said.

"Age is not a factor I'm afraid," the doctor said. "I'll wire him today and tell him to expect you. His name is Doctor Fritz."

"Alright," Beth said.

That night, Beth told her six-year-old son Robert that she had to go to San Francisco on business and to be good for grandma and grandpa.

In the morning, she took her buggy to the train station to wait for the ten o'clock train to San Francisco.

As she sat on a bench waiting, another train arrived and she watched passengers exit the train and walk along the platform. Then, out of nowhere, Emmet appeared with his tall horse. He stopped at the bench.

"Beth?" he said.

She stood and they embraced for a moment.

"What are you doing here?" Emmet said.

"Just a short trip to San Francisco on business," Beth said. "My train is due at ten."

"Let me tether Bull and I'll wait with you," Emmet said.

Beth watched as Emmet walked to the end of the platform and tied Bull to a hitching post, then turned and walked back to her. His shoulders were broad and he carried himself as a strong, secure man, but the memories of them as children were still vivid.

They sat on the bench.

"I won't ask where you've been," Beth said.

"Traveling," Emmet said. "How's things with you?"

"Oh, you know," Beth said. "Robert is six now and all I do is run the businesses."

"I meant how are you?"

"I know what you meant," Beth said.

"And the answer is lonely. I used to believe that having money was the solution to all my problems when we were young."

"And now?" Emmet said.

"I've come to realize that all my problems were self-made," Beth said.

"Most usually are," Emmet said.

Beth sighed. "Emmet, do you ever miss home?"

"You mean the Big Woods?" Emmet said. "I think about it from time to time."

"Me too," Beth said.

"Your train is here," Emmet said.

They stood. 'I'll see you later," Beth said.

"Yeah," Emmet said.

Anna and Emma were watering the orange grove when they spotted Emmet riding Bull on the road. They dropped the buckets and ran to the house.

"Map, Pa, Emmet's home," they shouted.

John and Sarah came out to the porch. "Fetch your brother," John said.

"Wait, he found him," Sarah said.

On the road, Emmet walked Bull while Ellis walked beside them. They turned off the road and walked to the house where Anna and Emma greeted Emmet with hugs.

At the steps to the porch, Emmet looked

at Sarah, "Hi, Ma. We have a lot to talk about."

"After a shave and a bath," Sarah said. "Girls, put on some hot water."

After Beth dressed, she met Doctor Fritz in his office.

"Beth, you're a very sick woman," Fritz said.

"How sick?" Beth said.

"This part of my job never gets any easier," Fritz said. "You have a cancer in your lungs. Advanced."

"Is there anything you can do?" Beth said.

"I'd have to cut you open like a fish," Fritz said. "I'm sorry, but medicine just isn't advanced enough to deal with this type of cancer. Maybe someday but not now.

"How long do I have?" Beth said.

"Four months. Six," Fritz said. "That pain you feel in your chest will get worse. You'll have to be medicated just to get through the day. Then you won't want to."

Beth stared at the doctor.

"I'm sorry for my bluntness, but it's best you know what you're in for."

"What . . . what will I be able to do?" Beth said.

"For the next month, anything you want," Fritz said. "Less after that. Then you won't want to do anything."

"Thank you for your honesty," Beth said.

"I'll give you some laudanum," Fritz said. "Take it when you need it and have the doctor in Stockton bring you what you need. I'll write him a note."

They put two tables together and Bettina, Ellis and their two children had dinner with John, Sarah and the twins.

"So what happened on your trip, Emmet?" John said.

"It's not meal time talk, Pa," Emmet said. "Especially in front of the twins."

"Emmet, in a few months we're seventeen," Anna said.

"When did that happen?" Emmet said.

"Girls, put on a pot of coffee," Sarah said.

After dinner, while the twins did the dirty dishes, everybody else took coffee on the porch.

"What happened to the one called Swann?" Emmet said.

"They had a trial at the courthouse," John said. "The judge gave him ten years of hard labor in a federal prison. It would have been worse but your letter of consideration helped reduce the sentencing."

"And the others?" John said.

"The one called Lance, I tracked him to

Montana, but I was too late," Emmet said. "His mother and brother hung him for being a sinner."

"My God," John said.

"And the third?" Sarah said.

"Suggs is hiding somewhere along the river in north Nebraska, possibly South Dakota," Emmet said. "He's just going to have to wait until spring because there's no way to navigate that area come snowfall."

"You'll stay here?" John said.

"I could use a little hard work," Emmet said.

"It's dark now, but in the morning I'll show you the oranges," John said.

"Oranges?" Emmet said.

"The doctor must be wrong,' Beth's father said.

"He's not wrong," Beth said. "I can feel the cancer eating away at me."

"Oh my God," Beth's mother said and burst into tears.

"Now listen you two," Beth said. "I don't have a lot of time. Four to six months at best, so I have many things to put in order. My son will need you to raise him and I will need you to care for my businesses."

Beth's father poured a tall drink of whiskey and slumped into a chair.

■ ■ ■ ■

Sarah was on the porch when Beth arrived in her buggy.

"Beth, what are you doing here?" she said.

"I've come to see Emmet," Beth said.

"He's with Ellis in the fields," Sarah said.

"I'll find him," Beth said. She rode her buggy to the field where Emmet and Ellis were plowing behind a team on mules.

"Emmet, can I see you for a few minutes," Beth said.

Emmet tossed the reins to Ellis and went to the buggy. "What are you doing here?" he said.

"We need to talk," Beth said.

Emmet walked to the buggy and climbed aboard.

"Emmet, I'm dying," Beth said.

"What?"

"I have a cancer. In my lungs. The doctors can't do anything," Beth said.

Emmet stared at her. He wanted to speak but there were no words.

"It's okay," Beth said. "I've come to ask a favor. More than one favor, actually."

"Anything," Emmet said.

"I've given this a lot of thought," Beth said. "My parents will care for little Rip, but they are in their sixties now. If something happens to them, I would like your family to raise him as their own. He will be very wealthy but not until he is twenty-one. I've had my lawyers taken care of that."

Emmet nodded. "You know we will," he said.

"I know," Beth said. "And now for the other favor I have to ask of you. My family still owns the farm in The Big Woods. I would like you to take me there and bury me under that giant oak tree beside the house. Remember?"

"You had a swing on it," Emmet said.

"That's the one," Beth said. "Promise?"

"I promise," Emmet said.

Beth reached out and kissed Emmet on the lips. "Go back to work, I have things to do," she said.

Chapter Fourteen: 1873

In April, Beth's father rode to the Boyd farm to fetch Emmet. It was a fine day and he was clearing a field with Ellis while the twins watered the orange grove.

"It's her time, Emmet," Beth's father said. "She asked for you."

"I'll take my horse," Emmet said. "It's faster."

For the past five months, Emmet had visited Beth a great deal. For a month, except for the laudanum, she seemed like Beth. Then the cancer started eating her away and she grew frail and weaker and this last month, she barely could sit up in bed.

Sometimes he wasn't sure if she was awake or not but he would sit beside the bed and read to her for hours.

When he was sure she was asleep, he would stop reading and with her eyes closed, Beth would whisper for him to continue.

Emmet reached Beth's house an hour before her father and found her in her room with her mother and the doctor.

He pulled up a chair and took her hand. "Beth, it's Emmet," he said.

She opened her eyes, smiled at him and then was gone.

Beth's death shocked Stockton. It's not every day a city loses it wealthiest woman citizen.

The church service was maximum capacity.

The next day, her coffin was loaded onto the train, Bull was loaded into the box car and Emmet said goodbye to the family.

"I'll be back when the job is done," he said.

The ride to Wisconsin took three days.

He passed the time reading several new books. At stopovers he would visit Bull in the box car and brush him.

The closest to The Big Woods the railroad could get him was Milwaukee.

Milwaukee was a major city now of seventy-five-thousand people and a port city of some importance.

Emmet had Beth's coffin stored overnight at the city's morgue, then rented a wagon and team of horses. After that he boarded

Bull at a large stables.

"I would like him walked every day and groomed," Emmet told the stables manager. "I'll be back in two weeks." He gave the manager one hundred dollars and told him if there was anything extra he would pay it on his return.

Emmet spent the night at a small hotel near the stables and got an early start in the morning after buying enough supplies to last the trip.

The first day, Emmet covered thirty miles on a freight road west. He camped off the road and made a fire and put on some supper and tended to the horses while supper cooked.

After supper he took out a book he never finished reading to Beth. Around the World in Eighty Days, a novel by Jules Vern.

He picked up from the last page he read to Beth and read out loud to her until he grew sleepy and went to sleep.

Much had changed in The Big Woods. The small settlement center was now a town of three hundred people. There was a large church and school. He barely recognized the place and no one recognized him.

Before reaching Beth's property, he passed his old house and stopped for a few moments. The house was larger and there was a picket fence with flowers growing. A man was working the fields and he nodded to Emmet as he rode by.

Then he reached the Olson house. It was in a sorry state of repair. Weeds dominated the front yard. He rose around to the side where the big oak stood and parked the wagon.

"Well, Beth, you're home," Emmet said as he stepped down from the wagon.

He removed the pickax and shovel from the wagon and got to work. The grass was thick and the ground was hard and full of roots. By dark, the grave was half dug. He made a fire and cooked supper and tended the horses.

After eating, he took out the book and read to Beth by the light of the fire.

In the morning, after breakfast, Emmet finished digging the grave and then dragged Beth's coffin to her final resting place. The afternoon passed covering up the coffin and by nightfall, the headstone was in place. It read **Elizabeth Olson-Taylor 1842–1873.**

The next day, Emmet headed back to Milwaukee.

Ellis had the ground ready for planting the young orange trees, which were barely a foot high. He and John carefully removed each sapling from its box and placed them in the ground and covered them up.

Anna and Emma carried out new trees and the process went on for two days until all seventy-five were in the ground.

Once all the trees were in the ground and watered, the entire family looked at the new grove.

"Well, how do you like Beth's grove?" John said.

"That's it, Pa," Anna said. "We'll call it Beth's Grove."

"By God, she'd like that," John said.

Emmet stayed overnight in Milwaukee at the same small hotel. After a bath and a shave, he had his clothes laundered and broke out his lone suit and had that cleaned as well.

In the morning, he caught the ten o'clock train to Washington. There was one long stop and he went to the box car to brush Bull and feed him a few carrots.

He arrived in Washington after midnight and was able to find a decent hotel and livery not far from The White House.

After breakfast, he shaved and dressed in his suite and walked to The White House and requested to see President Grant.

Grant was in a meeting until noon but left word for Emmet to join him for lunch in the Oval Office.

Emmet waited outside until a page called him and he was escorted to the Ovel Office where Grant waited for him.

"Emmet, how are you?" Grant said.

"Fine, sir and you?" Emmet said.

"Feeling my age and ever growing weight," Grant said. "Lunch is on the table, you can tell me what you've been doing the past year."

As they ate a lunch of baked chicken, Emmet told Grant about the three men who murdered Eva and how he tracked two of them.

"Messy business, Emmet," Grant said. "But I have the feeling you came to see me with a purpose in mind."

"I would like to be temporarily reinstated at a US Marshal so that pursuing Suggs is totally legal," Emmet said.

"Temporarily?" Grant said.

"I know I'm asking to skirt things a bit, but . . ." Emmet said.

"Emmet, the west needs capable Marshals like yourself," Grant said. "I reinstate you but I want at least five years commitment from you and you pick the territory."

"Five years?"

"Minimum," Grant said.

"California, sir," Emmet said,

"I know you're not a drinking man, but . . ." Grant said.

Grant filled two small glasses with bourbon and handed one to Emmet. "A man shares a drink is the same as giving his word," Grant said.

"Yes sir," Emmet said.

"Do you still have your badge from Cheyenne?" Grant said.

"I do."

"Polish it up and go to work," Grant said.

"Yes sir."

"And by the way, I never did accept your resignation," Grant said.

Emmet spent the next twenty-four hours on the train to Omaha. He spent most of the time in his sleeper car. Reading and dozing when not having dinner and breakfast in the dining car.

Omaha was a sprawling town of fifteen-thousand people on the Missouri River. Emmet wasted no time sightseeing. He retrieved Bull from the box car, found a general store and purchased two weeks' worth of supplies and then sent a telegram home. Then he headed northwest to the Elkhorn River about ninety miles away.

Without taxing Bull too much, he could make the river in two and a half days. He rode until dark and made camp in the woods. Bull was restless, having built up an excess of energy over the past few weeks, but Emmet didn't want to travel after dark.

They got an early start and Emmet let Bull go as far as he wanted to, stopping for lunch and a rest around one in the afternoon.

Shortly after lunch, as Emmet rode Bull through a thicket of trees, a rock struck Emmet on the back of his head and he fell from the saddle. As he was trained to do, Bull stood watch over Emmet.

Emmet was bleeding but wasn't seriously hurt. When he heard the rustling of leaves, he silently drew his Colt, cocked it and held it by his side.

"Ya got him you rock throwing sum bitch," a man said.

"Let's see what he got," another man said.

"I think he's still breathing," the first man said.

"So cut his throat and grab his shit," the second man said.

"Okay," the first man said.

As soon as the man touched Emmet's shoulder, Emmet spun and shot him in the face, cocked the Colt and aimed it at the second man.

"No, wait," the second man said just as Emmet shot him in the gut.

Emmet stood up as the second man fell to the ground.

"I'm shot," the second man said.

"Yes you are," Emmet said.

"You shot me," the second man said.

"You were going to cut my throat," Emmet said.

"I'm kilt for sure," the second man said.

"About sixty miles that way is Omaha and a doctor," Emmet said as he mounted the saddle. "If you save your breath, you might make it."

"I'll find you. I'll kill you," the second man said.

"Sure you will," Emmet said and rode off.

Ellis, Bettina and the twins rode to town for supplies. At the general store, Anna and Emma decided to look around town while Ellis and Bettina did the shopping.

"Look for what?" Ellis said.

"Ellis, let them go," Bettina said.

"What are they looking for?" Ellis said.

"Boys," Bettina said.

"Oh."

"Well, get started while I get the mail," Ellis said.

Ellis walked to the post office where a telegram from Emmett waited.

Emmet reached the banks of the Elkhorn River. It was a tributary of the Platte River, but still was close to three hundred miles long.

He found a place to camp for the night, filled the gallon canteen with water from the river and put supper on and tended to Bull while it cooked.

In the morning, Emmet began the hunt.

He rode twenty miles before he came across a small settlement by the river. A trading post and general store for farmers. About thirty people were buying or trading goods, including some Plains Indians, who were trading furs for blankets.

Emmet sought out the owner of the trading post.

"Name is Clyde. What can I do for you, Marshal?" he said.

"I'm tracking an outlaw named Suggs," Emmet said. "Ever hear the name?"

"Can't say as I have and I know every name for fifty square miles," Clyde said.

Emmet showed Clyde the wanted poster.

"Sorry, Marshal."

"What about them?" Emmet said and nodded to the Plains Indians.

"Ask them. They speak English," Clyde said.

Emmet walked to the dozen Plains Indians at the table full of blankets. "I'm United States Marshal Emmet Boyd," he said. "Who speaks for you?"

"I do," a handsome brave said.

"I'm looking for an outlaw named Suggs," Emmet said. "Have you ever heard the name?"

The brave shook his head.

"Take a look," Emmet said and showed the brave the wanted poster.

"No," he said.

"Thanks for your time," Emmet said.

Emmet bought some extra supplies and said, "Where is the next trading post?"

"Fifty miles west," Clyde said.

Sarah read Emmet's telegram to the family on the porch before dinner.

"He's been reinstated as a US Marshal by Grant," Sarah said. "So he can officially arrest this Suggs outlaw. After that he'll be coming home."

"To the farm?" Anna said.

"Not quite," Sarah said. "As a US Marshal for California."

"Well, at least he'll be near," John said.

"Where does a US Marshal work, Pa?"

Emma said.

"Generally, wherever he wants to," John said.

In twenty-five miles, Emmet encountered a dozen homesteaders farming wheat and corn and none could lay claim to knowing the Suggs family.

He camped beside the river and in the morning, got a fresh start and covered another thirty miles.

The second settlement and outpost was much the same as the first one Emmet encountered. A general store and people stocking up on supplies.

Emmet dismounted and asked for the owner.

"That be me. Name is Cray. What can I do for you, Marshal?"

"I'm looking for the Suggs family. Do you know them?" Emmet said.

"Everybody within fifty square miles knows the Suggs family," Cray said.

"How many are there?" Emmet said.

"Ma Suggs and her three sons," Cray said. "One worse than the other."

Emmet took out the wanted poster. "Which one is this?"

Cray looked at the poster. "That's Billy," he said. "He's the worst of the bunch. Was wanted for murder back in sixty-six and ran off somewhere to hide. His brothers Gayland and Frank are just as bad."

"When did you last see them?" Emmet said.

"They don't come this way more than one or twice a year," Cray said. "I ain't seen them since before the winter."

"Where can I find their place?" Emmet said.

"Twenty miles west along the river, then turn south for another ten," Cray said. "They got a homestead place."

"Thanks. I need some beans, bacon, coffee, biscuits, a few cans of milk and some sugar," Emmet said.

"I get them for you right away," Cray said.

Emmet left the settlement and rode along the river until dark and made camp. The Suggs homestead was another ten miles to the south, but he would never find it in the dark.

After tending to Bull, Emmet ate and then went right to sleep. He was exhausted and not just physically. He wasn't yet thirty-one but felt twice that. Since the war, the railroad, being a Marshal and Secret Service Agent, his life was one situation after another without a real home to call his own.

Eva was a good woman. She deserved a

home and family, not what she got.

Suggs would pay.

After that, he didn't know. He gave his word to Grant and he would keep it.

Emmet fell asleep thinking about his future and Rose. He wondered where she was, what she was doing and hoped she was happy.

From a few hundred yards away, Emmet watched the Suggs house through his binoculars. The house was a typical homestead farmhouse, with small barn and corral, water pump and outhouse.

The corral was empty. Some chickens roamed about. The only sign of life was an old woman sitting in a rocking chair on the porch.

Emmet removed his badge and placed it into his shirt pocket. Then he rode Bull at a moderate pace to the Suggs homestead.

When he was in range, the woman on the porch sipped coffee and watched him with mild curiosity.

"Good morning, ma'am," Emmet said. "Are you Mrs. Suggs?"

"I be Mrs. Suggs," she said.

"I'm looking for your son Billy," Emmet said.

"Why?"

"We worked on the railroad together," Emmet said. "He said I should look him up if I was ever this way."

"You're too late," Mrs. Suggs said. "My boys left at snow melt."

"Where did they go?" Emmet said.

"Crossed the river to seek their fortune in gold," Mrs. Suggs said.

"Where?" Emmet said.

"Black Hills. You're the law, aren't you?"

"The Black Hills of South Dakota?" Emmet said.

"Is there another? I heard talk they found gold in French Creek. If they went anywhere, they went there."

"Obliged, ma'am," Emmet said.

"You watch yourself," Mrs. Suggs said. "I got no illusions about my boys. They get the chance, they'll kill you."

"I'll be careful," Emmet said.

"Mind me asking what Billy done?" Mrs. Suggs said. "A mother has a right to know."

"Rape and murder," Emmet said.

"They'll hang him," Mrs. Suggs said. "If you get the chance to kill him, spare him the noose. That's an ugly way to die even for the likes of Billy."

Emmet nodded. "Good day, ma'am," he said.

■ ■ ■ ■

Emmet needed a place to cross the Elkhorn River rather than go around it. The river went on for another two hundred miles and he couldn't afford the wasted time it would take so he would look for a crossing.

Ten miles west of the Suggs homestead, Emmet found a river crossing station. There was a cabin, a corral with six horses in it and a raft large enough to carry a dozen men and horses across the river. Two men sat on the porch of the cabin, drinking coffee and smoking pipes.

"Morning," Emmet said when he stopped at the porch. "I'd like to cross the river."

"Wait inside with the others," one man said. "Coffee's fresh."

"Wait for what?" Emmet said.

"We don't cross until we have ten to fill the raft," the man said. "You makes seven. Be about an hour."

"I'm a US Marshal on official business. I need to cross," Emmet said.

"We don't cross until we're full," the man said.

"How much to cross?" Emmet said.

"A dollar a man, a dollar a house," the man said.

"Take us seven and I'll pay the fare for a full house," Emmet said.

"You'll pay eight dollars?" the man said.

"Yes, if we can leave now," Emmet said.

"Load them up," the man said.

Once Emmet and the others were on the raft, the two men pulled the ropes that were connected to anchors on the other side of the river and they slowly crossed. It took about ten minutes to pull the heavy raft to the other side where everybody got off.

"Much obliged," the man said to Emmet.

Emmet headed northwest the rest of the day. When he made camp after dark, he studied his maps by the firelight. He had about seven hundred miles to go to reach the Black Hills, and another river to cross.

On a bright, sunny afternoon, while Anna and Emma watered the grove, Ellis toiled in the field and John worked on repairing some equipment in the barn.

Sarah and Bettina and her two children were in Sarah's house preparing lunch.

Lars walked into the grove and said, "Hello, girls."

"Hi Lars," Anna said.

"Can I help?" Lars said.

"Sure. Grab a bucket," Emma said.

Lars walked to the wagon where a dozen

buckets of water were loaded into the back. He stopped suddenly, grabbed his left arm, turned to Anna and Emma and said, "Girls," then fell to the ground.

They ran to Lars. "Ellis, Pa, come quick. It's Lars," Anna shouted.

Emmet rode a hundred miles northwest without seeing another town, settlement or person. He crossed several small streams and creeks and finally reached a settlement of a hundred people called Broken Bow.

It was much like other settlements, tents, a few wood structures, a place for farmers to come together and buy what they needed.

Plains Indians were trading for blankets and food with the general store.

Emmet stocked up on supplies and was on his way. He still had about two hundred miles before he would reach South Dakota Territory.

He prayed Mrs. Suggs was correct in that it was the destination of her three sons.

"It was his heart," the doctor from town said. "Lars was sixty-six and it must have been bothering him for quite some time. He never said anything?"

"Not a word," John said.

"He might have lived a bit longer if he had."

They held services on the grounds and Lars was buried next to Eva in what would become the family resting place.

After the service, Beth's parents took John and Sarah aside.

"John, I'm a year older than my brother Lars," Beth's father said. "I can look after Beth's business interests, but we're just not fit to raise young Robert. I'm afraid we'll leave him alone or fail him in some way. Beth wanted you and Sarah to raise him in case we weren't capable and to be honest, we're not."

"Ellis," Sarah said and he came across the living room.

"Yes, Ma?" Ellis said.

"How would you feel about having a younger brother?" Sarah said.

"What?"

Emmet crossed into South Dakota near the Badlands. He was maybe a day's ride from French Creek, a tributary of the Cheyenne River.

The badlands were strange mountains and hills formed thousands of years ago. It was a harsh environment to live in, but damn pretty to look at.

After dark, he made camp, built a fire and tended to Bull while beans and bacon cooked. He had some fresh cornbread and ate some of it with supper.

Bull, sensing coyotes in the area was nervous, so Emmet hobbled him and built up the fire before going to sleep.

The he rested against the saddle near the fire and watched the moon rise over the Badlands.

It was quite a beautiful sight.

"I don't understand why I'm here," Robert said. "Have I done something wrong?"

"Oh no, Robert," Sarah said.

"My mother called me Rip," Robert said.

"Alright, Rip," Sarah said.

"If I didn't do anything wrong, why did Grandpa and Grandpa send me away?" Robert said.

"They didn't send you away," Sarah said. "We're part of your family as well. You see, they're getting on in years and after your uncle died they worried that if something happened to them you wouldn't be raised right. Understand?"

"I guess so," Robert said.

"There are things you learn in school and things you learn by doing," Sarah said. "When you become a man, you'll be in charge of your mother's businesses. It helps to know a great many things."

"Things like what?" Robert said.

"Well for instance, do you see your Uncle John and Ellis working in the field over there?" Sarah said.

"I see them."

"And Anna and Emma tending to the orange trees?"

"I see them too."

"Well, your mother has left you just about the biggest orange grove in the county," Sarah said. "How will you know how to take care of them without learning by doing?"

"Like learning how to dress yourself?" Robert said.

"Exactly like that," Sarah said. "And do you know what else a man needs to learn how to do?"

"What?"

"Cook."

"Cook? Men don't cook," Robert said.

"Sure they do," Sarah said. "In all the best restaurants and fancy hotels, the cooks are always men. They call them chefs."

"Can Ellis and Uncle John cook?" Robert said.

"As well as me," Sarah said. "Tell you what. Let's go inside and start lunch for everybody and I'll show you some things about cooking."

The French Creek ran for about sixty miles and wound through the Badlands into The Black Hills.

There was no easy way to smoke Suggs out from wherever he was holed up, if he was holed up, so he would have to check every camp and prospector along the river. With sixty miles to cover, that could take months.

The first night along the river, he was alone with just Bull and the stars for company.

The second night, before dark, Emmet came across a group of prospectors camped along the river. They had their claim stakes out and were friendly enough when he stopped by their camp.

"A US Marshal," one of them said. "None of us has done anything again the law."

"I know," Emmet said. "I'm just passing through."

"Be dark in a few minutes, stay the night," the man said.

Emmet stayed, shared their fire and food and they told him they had panned about fifteen-hundred-dollars in gold so far.

In the morning, after breakfast, Emmet continued along the river.

He stopped by three more camps, but Suggs wasn't visible at any of them. The men in these camps were friendly enough, offering him food and coffee, but there must be a hundred or more claims along the river alone.

If Suggs and his brothers were in the Black Hills, he might never find them.

The Chief Surgeon at Fort Laramie Hospital was Doctor Stephen Porter and he was around fifty and one of the kindest men Rose had ever met.

Rose had assisted him dozens of times during the past seven months, so it was no surprise to her when he sought her out to accompany him to Cheyenne.

Governor Campbell sent his private train for them and they used the local doctor's office to perform the surgery.

A prominent local rancher had been held up on his way to town and took a bullet in his back that lodged in his spine. The General Practitioner in Cheyenne knew it required a specialist to remove the bullet and asked Governor Campbell to send for Porter.

The surgery took two plus hours, but once it was over, Porter was optimistic about a full recovery.

Afterward, Campbell invited Porter and Rose to dinner at his home.

"Nice to see you again, Rose," Campbell said. "Doctor Porter, how is the patient?"

"A great deal better without that bullet in his back," Porter said. "I expect him to make a full recovery, although a slow one."

"Good," Campbell said.

Isabella, Campbell's wife, presided over dinner. After dessert and coffee, Rose asked to speak to Campbell privately.

They went to his study.

"Is something wrong?" Campbell said.

"No, Governor," Rose said. "Forgive me for sounding like a schoolgirl, but I was wondering what happened to Marshal Boyd. You see, if it's the same man as I'm thinking, we were sweethearts a long time ago."

"I see," Campbell said. "Well, he left to work for President Grant on his Secret Service department. He was married."

"I didn't know," Rose said.

"Unfortunately, while Marshal Boyd was on an assignment down south, his wife went to stay with his family in California where she was murdered," Campbell said.

"Oh no," Rose said.

"That's all I know, I'm afraid," Campbell said.

"Thank you, Governor," Rose said.

"I wish I knew more," Campbell said.

Emmet turned north and headed toward South Dakota Territory. His quest to find Suggs so far had been a failure. He had spoken to hundreds of prospectors and stopped at a dozen settlements and outposts and turned up nothing,

They either rode directly into the Badlands, or didn't go at all.

An hour or so before dark, Emmet came to a small settlement of tents and a few wood structures, one of which was a trading post.

He dismounted at the trading post where dozens of people were shopping.

"What can I do for you, Marshal?" the owner of the trading post said.

"How far to South Dakota?" Emmet said.

"A day's ride north. I'm guessing you're not out here in the middle of nowhere for the sights," the owner of the trading post said.

"I'm after three wanted men," Emmet said. "I believe they came this way on their way to the Badlands."

Emmet showed him the poster of Suggs.

"I can't swear to it, but he looks like a fellow came through here maybe six, seven weeks ago," the owner of the trading post said.

"Was he alone?"

"Two other men as I recall."

"Thanks. What do you have in the way of supplies?" Emmet said.

"What do you need?"

"Supplies, a hot bath, a shave and a good meal," Emmet said. "And a good night's sleep."

"Go tie your horse."

On the return trip to Fort Laramie Hospital, Rose looked out the window beside her seat and thought about Emmet.

She wondered what kind of woman he married, how she was murdered and where he was now. She knew his family was from Wisconsin, so they obviously relocated to California.

Was he there now? Farming?

The Emmet Boyd she knew and fell in love with was the bravest man she had ever met. He was not the type to do nothing after his wife was murdered.

Her guess was that he was out hunting whoever was responsible.

Robert was too small to carry a bucket of water from the wagon to the orange trees, but while Ellis and the twins did that, he worked the ladle.

Each small sapling got one full ladle of water. Each larger tree got three. Watering all one hundred took hours, but he didn't mind and felt good when the job was done.

On days when it rained and the trees didn't need watering, Robert helped John and Ellis in the barn with chores and sometimes helped Sarah and Bettina in the kitchen.

His grandparents visited often and sometimes had long talks with John about his future. About money, his education and the businesses, mostly things he didn't understand too much about.

When school started up again, John or Ellis and sometimes Sarah and Bettina would ride him to town and drop him off and then pick him up at three o'clock.

He missed his mother something awful but he always felt like she was with him and that feeling gave him comfort.

Uncle John and Aunt Sarah loved him and treated him like he was their own and that also gave him comfort.

South Dakota was some rough territory, but also beautiful as well. As he rode to the Black Hills, Emmet decided that the Suggs brothers weren't the type to break their backs mining for gold.

Word of gold in the hills made the newspapers about a year ago and attracted people from everywhere all looking to get rich overnight. Panning was hard work. Backbreaking sunup to sundown, hard work. Mining with a pickax was even harder.

Suggs had his share of hard work laying iron rails for the railroad. He wasn't about to resort to breaking his back again.

If he's in the Black Hills with his brothers, they'll target a rich claim and rob it. Find someone who struck a vein who was robbed afterward and that's how you find the Suggs.

After several days, Emmet was deep in the Black Hills. The Hills belonged to the Lakota people after the treaty of Fort Laramie in 1868. To the Lakota, the land was sacred.

Early one morning, Emmet awoke when Bull nervously snorted. He sat up and saw why. A dozen Lakota warriors were mounted on Indian ponies, watching him from a distance of twenty feet.

"Good morning," Emmet said. "Speak English?"

"Yes," one warrior said.

"Mind if I make a fire and put on some

coffee?" Emmet said.

"Go," the warrior said.

Emmet stood and grabbed some wood from the pile he gathered the previous night and struck a match. "You're welcome to join me," he said.

The warrior spoke to the eleven others and they rode away as he dismounted and walked to Emmet.

"You wear a badge," the warrior said. "You are a lawman."

"I am a United States Marshal," Emmet said. "My name is Emmet Boyd."

"I am called Takes His Horse."

Emmet put on coffee and a pan of bacon. "Nice to meet you, Takes His Horse," he said.

"You must be after someone to be out here alone," Takes His Horse said.

"I'm after a murderer," Emmet said. "Do you know this word?"

"Someone who kills."

"That's right."

Emmet put bacon in a pan to cook and removed several biscuits from a pouch and placed them in a pan over the fire to warm them.

"When you find him, what do you do?" Takes His Horse said.

"Arrest him. Bring him back for trial."

"Will he be put to death?"

"Most likely."

The coffee was ready and Emmet filled two cups. "Sugar?" he said.

Takes His Horse nodded and Emmet added a spoonful from the sugar bag. He stirred the bacon as they sipped coffee.

"Where are the white men panning for gold?" Emmet said.

"In the gulch with the dead trees," Takes His Horse said. "A day's ride to the northwest."

"You've seen them?"

"Everybody has seen them," Takes His Horse said. "They are on our land."

"Why don't you get the government to get them off?" Emmet said.

"The government man from the reservation has gone to Washington to speak with the chiefs," Takes His Horse said. "We will give them time, but if they do nothing, we will take matters into our own hands."

"That would be a mistake," Emmet said. "The white man's Army is large and powerful. Many of your people will die."

"You are a lawman. You know there are things worse than death," Takes His Horse said.

"I do know that," Emmet said. "I also know there is no future in dying."

The bacon was done and Emmet filled two plates and added biscuits.

"Where did you learn English?" Emmet said.

"The missionaries on the reservation," Takes His Horse said.

"A day's ride to the northwest you said?" Emmet said.

"I'll ride with you," Takes His Horse said. "A man can get twisted around in these mountains."

"What about your hunting party?"

"They will return to the reservation."

"Well, let's finish up and get moving," Emmet said.

An hour before nightfall, Emmet and Takes His Horse stood on a cliff and looked down upon a makeshift settlement in the gulch below.

Maybe thirty large tents, some with wood frames and several hundred prospectors.

"The white man's desire for gold is great," Takes His Horse said.

"It is," Emmet said.

"My people don't understand that," Takes His Horse said. "Gold is too soft to make weapons or tools with. Our women don't even want it for decoration. What does the white man do with it?"

"Most of it is put into a bank," Emmet said. "The rest is used to make money and jewelry for women."

"You put gold into a bank?" Takes His Horse said.

"Most of it," Emmet said. "A special bank called a reserve. Doesn't make much sense, does it?"

"No."

"Well, let's get a fire going and make some supper," Emmet said.

Emmet had some fresh beef and put it and beans into a pan with some water and put on a pot of coffee. While supper cooked, Emmet and Takes His Horse tended to their horses.

After dark, they watched a hundred torches and lanterns dot the landscape below in the gulch. Noise from the camp filtered up to the cliffs. Banjo music, women laughing, men talking, it carried on the wind.

"Why do white people always make so much noise?" Takes His Horse said.

"That is another thing I have never been able to figure out," Emmet said.

In the morning, after breakfast, Emmet and Takes His Horse parted ways.

"I have enjoyed your company," Emmet said.

"If you ever get back this way, you are welcome on our land," Takes His Horse said.

After Takes His Horse left, Emmet followed a trail down to the settlement in the gulch. The sun was up just an hour and already men were drunk in the muddy streets between the tents.

One large tent had a wood sign on it that read **Saloon.** Another read **Hardware.** Two men were fighting in the mud, another group of men were arguing outside the hardware tent over pickaxes and shovels.

Emmet dismounted at the hardware tent. "Who is in charge here?" he said to a thin, balding man standing in front of the tent.

"Who wants to know?" the man said.

"I do," Emmet said. "US Marshal Emmet Boyd."

"Him," the man said and nodded to a short, stout man wearing a six-gun on his right hip. "Name is Trent."

Emmet walked to Trent. "Mr. Trent?"

"Wait your turn, boy," Trent said.

"It's US Marshal and I'm not here to buy a shovel," Emmet said.

Trent looked up at Emmet.

"Them damn Indians complaining again?"

Trent said.

"I suppose there's no law around here," Emmet said.

"We keep our own law," Trent said. "Somebody gets out of line and we string him up."

"Is there a place we can talk privately?" Emmet said.

"Pete, take over," Trent said.

The balding man took Trent's place as Trent led Emmet to his tent in the rear. "Tie your horse there," Trent said.

Emmet tied Bull to a hitching post, then they entered the tent.

The tent had a wood cot, a dresser and a footlocker. Trent opened the footlocker and took out a bottle of whiskey. "Care for a snort?" he said.

"It's nine in the morning," Emmet said.

"Well, it's dark somewhere," Trent said and took a swallow.

"I'm after three men," Emmet said. "One of them looks like this."

Emmet showed the wanted poster of Billy Suggs to Trent. "Maybe. I don't know," Trent said. "The ones you should ask is the whores."

"Where are they?" Emmet said.

Trent took another swig of whiskey. "Follow me," he said.

Trent led Emmet to six tents strung together behind his tent. "The ladies," Trent said.

"Still asleep?" Emmet said.

"They work nights you know."

"Get them up," Emmet said.

Trent stuck his head into each tent. "Rise and shine, ladies, the law wants a word with you," he said.

One at a time, robes over sheer nightgowns, six women exited the tents.

"We ain't broke no law, what you want with us" one of them said.

"I'm not here for any of you," Emmet said. "I need your help."

"Least get us some damn coffee," another of the women said.

"We can go over to the mess tent," Trent said. "Follow me ladies."

Trent led them to the mess tent, a tent with wood construction and tables and chairs. "Hey, Jed, bring us a large pot of coffee and eight cups," Trent said.

After the six women were seated at a table and had cups of coffee, Emmet said, "I need your help with an . . ."

"We get paid five dollars for a straight roll, seven for extra," one the women said as she lit a cigar. "Who's paying us?"

"I'll pay each of you ten dollars for your

time," Emmet said.

"You heard him, Trent. Ten dollars," the cigar smoking woman said.

Emmet took out the wanted poster and gave it to the cigar smoker. "This man, have any of you seen him?" he said.

Each girl looked at the poster.

"Me," the fifth girl said. "I had him."

"Are you sure?" Emmet said.

"I'm sure."

"Did he tell you his name?"

"No, but he with two other men and one of them called him Billy," the girl said.

"How long ago?" Emmet said.

"No more than three weeks," the girl said.

"How come you remember him three weeks later?" Emmet said.

"I always remember the men who pay for extra," the girl said.

"Extra?" Emmet said.

"He likes to spank girls," the girl said. "He paid an extra three dollars to put me over his knee and paddle me with a hair brush."

The other girls giggled.

"I had one cowboy always wanted me to . . ." one of the girls said.

"That will do, Cora," Trent said.

"Anybody see which way they went when they rode out?" Emmet said.

"Up towards the hills where the gold is,"

Cora said. "I know cause I seen them."

Emmet put sixty dollars on the table. "Thank you, ladies," he said.

"Hey Jed, as long as we're up, how about breakfast?" Cora said.

Emmet retrieved Bull and went to Trent's supply tent. "What do you have for supplies?" Emmet said.

"What do you want?" Trent said.

"Beans, bacon biscuits, coffee, sugar, canned milk, any fresh meat and grain for my horse," Emmet said.

"Cost you twenty dollars," Trent said.

After the supplies were loaded, Emmet said, "Where would you go for gold?"

Trent pointed to the north slope of the Black Hills.

"Obliged," Emmet said.

Gold fever was everywhere. Men panned in streams and creeks, others worked cliffs and caves with pickaxes and shovels, some did both.

After two days and nights, Emmet had to admit that he had no idea where Suggs and his brothers went.

It would take a stroke of luck, an accident or an act of God to find Suggs.

On the third day in the Black Hills, an accident led to a stroke of luck. Emmet took a turn into a gully when he was looking for a pass.

Buzzards were flying overhead in the gully. "Let's go take a look, boy," Emmet said and rode Bull further into the gully.

He stopped and dismounted twenty feet from a pack of buzzards that were picking at a dead man and his dead mule.

Emmet withdrew his Henry rifle and shot three buzzards and the rest flew away. The man was a prospector. He had been shot several times. The mule was shot once in the head.

There were three sets of tracks leading west away from the body. He inspected the tracks carefully. They were a week old, no more than that.

The mule had a shovel in its pack and Emmet covered the prospector and mule with dirt. When he left the buzzards returned to feast on the three buzzards Emmet had shot. He followed the tracks until dark.

After eating supper, Emmet sat in front of the fire with a cup of coffee and thought about the prospector. He must have been carrying a load of gold and was an easy target for the Suggs brothers.

He had the feeling that prospector was not the only one they would kill.

■ ■ ■ ■

A few days later, while on a ridge, Emmet spotted an Army patrol below near French Creek. Emmet used his binoculars and recognized the man leading the patrol, General George Armstrong Custer.

They were miles away and Emmet didn't have time to waste, so he moved on and continued tracking Suggs.

A few days later, he came across two more dead men and their dead mules. Prospectors. Robbed and murdered for their gold.

They had been dead a week and there wasn't much left of them or their mules after the buzzards got through with them.

Suggs and his brothers were as bad a bunch as Emmet could remember. Their own mother so much as told him they needed killing.

The Black Hills extended into central Wyoming and Emmet was sure, after studying his maps that he had crossed over.

They had gold and they had time. They needed a place to spend it.

They would head to Cheyenne.

They were taking it easy, feeling safe in the knowledge no one knew of their crimes.

That gave Emmet an advantage, the advantage of surprise.

As he rode through a clearing, Emmet spotted buzzards circling overhead. "Let's go see," he said and rode Bull hard and reached a man who was on his back, but still alive.

Emmet brought the man water and dabbed some on the man's lips. He opened his eyes, looked at Emmet and whispered, "Nice to meet you."

Around a campfire, the man ate two plates of beans and bacon and told Emmet what happened. "Two days ago, me and my partner were headed south to Cheyenne with our strike to cash it in," he said. "I set out to find a stream to fill our canteens. I heard shooting. When I got back, I hid in some rocks. Three men had shot my partner and our mules. I stayed hid until they left and set out on foot. I must have got turned around and lost I suppose."

"Did one of the men look like this?" Emmet said and showed the man the poster of Billy Suggs.

"That's him. I'll never forget that face," the man said. "The murderous bastard."

"How much gold did you have?" Emmet said.

"Tween us, maybe fifteen thousand."

Two days. Suggs was close. "Mister, I'm going to leave you food and my extra canteen," Emmet said. "Walk west until you reach a town."

"You catch them, Marshal," the man said. "And you hang them for what they did to my partner."

Emmet rode off and didn't stop until dark and then made camp.

He watched the stars after eating and thought of the nights in The Big Woods when he and Ellis would sit on the porch and try to count them.

Ellis hated the farm and wanted to get away and Emmet always thought the farm would be all he ever knew.

How different everything turned out.

Beth and Eva were gone too soon.

Rose, how he loved Rose. When she told him her husband wasn't dead, a little piece of Emmet died at the news.

He grew to love Eva, but not the way he loved Rose. He was thirty-one now and doubted he would ever marry again because he doubted he would ever love another woman the way he loved Rose.

They were coming out of the hills now on the Cheyenne side. Mountains loomed in the background and most of the hills didn't reach a thousand feet.

Suggs and his brothers were close, no more than a day in front.

He stepped up the pace, pushing Bull to give more and the massive horse responded, giving him more.

He camped on the side of a hill, made supper and watched the stars. It was a warm night and after eating, he put the fire out and settled in to sleep.

About to drift off, Emmet's eyes bolted open when he caught the scent of another fire. He stood up and searched the dark, but he couldn't see a fire anywhere. The scent came from the west. They were close enough for their smoke to reach him, but too far away to see flame.

Twelve hours. They were twelve hours in front of him.

In the afternoon, Emmet found where they camped the night before. They were traveling slow, their horses weighted down with sacks of gold.

By nightfall, Emmet was close enough to see their fire.

He ate a cold supper of biscuits, a can of peaches and water. Then, after midnight, he walked Bull to their campfire.

Emmet took the Henry rifle with him as

he walked into their camp.

In the light of the fire he could see Billy Suggs asleep in his bedroom between his two brothers.

Emmet cocked the lever of the Henry rifle and fired a shot into the dirt.

Billy, Gayland and Frank jumped up with their revolvers in hand. Emmet shot Gayland in the chest and Frank in the face, but not before Billy put a bullet in Emmet's lower, left abdomen.

Emmet returned fire and shot Billy in the stomach. He slumped to his knees and dropped his gun. "You gut shot me, you murdering ambusher," Suggs said.

"You're under arrest for murder," Emmet said.

"You kilt my brothers," Suggs said. "We never hurt nobody."

"I'm more convinced by the woman you raped and strangled in California and the trail of dead men you left behind clear across the Black Hills," Emmet said. "Get on your feet."

"I'm bleeding," Suggs said.

"Me too," Emmet said. "Get on your feet."

"I can't. I'm gut shot," Suggs said.

Emmet grabbed Suggs by the shirt and yanked him to his feet.

"Goddamn you," Suggs yelled. "My insides are on fire."

Emmet grabbed a rope from Bull and tied Suggs by the wrists and ankles, then shoved him to the ground.

"Is that coffee hot?" Emmet said.

"You gut shot me you asking about coffee?" Suggs said.

Emmet picked up the coffee pot from the fire and filled a cup. It was still hot and he took a sip. "When the sun comes up, we're riding to Fort Laramie."

"That's forty mile from here," Suggs said. "I'll die before we get there."

"That's up to you, but that's where I'm taking you," Emmet said.

"What I do, you gut shot me and kilt my brothers?" Suggs said.

Emmet took a sip of coffee. "For starters, you raped and killed my wife," he said.

"You lie," Suggs said. "Me and my brothers are prospectors. We never harm nobody."

"All that gold you got there in those sacks, you killed a half dozen people to get it," Emmet said. "I buried the bodies the buzzards didn't eat. I found the partner of the last man you killed and he got a good look at you."

"You lie," Suggs said.

"Want to open the gold sacks and see

whose names are written on the inside?" Emmet said. Emmet dumped the coffee. "And you make terrible coffee."

Emmet put on a fresh pot of coffee and then found a bottle of whiskey in Suggs' saddlebags and poured some on a neckerchief and plugged the hole in his left side with it.

"What about me?" Suggs said.

Emmet walked to Suggs and poured whiskey onto his open wound and Suggs screamed. "There, all better now," Emmet said.

At sunup, Emmet saddled a horse for Suggs and helped him into the saddle and tied his hands to the saddle horn. Then he loaded the sacks of gold onto a second horse, took all the canteens and looped the horses with a rope.

"Let's go, Bull," Emmet said.

By noon, they had covered twenty miles. The sun was high and hot and Emmet dismounted to give the horses water and a one hour rest. Suggs had passed out in the saddle, but was still alive.

He sat against a tree and closed his eyes.

Ellis returned to fishing while Emmet and Beth took a walk along the creek. After about a quarter mile, Beth stopped under tall tree.

"Why did you stop?" Emmet said.

"Don't you know anything, Emmet Boyd?" Beth said.

"I don't know what you're talking about," Emmet said.

"You're supposed to kiss me, stupid," Beth said.

"Well, how am I supposed to know?" Emmet said.

"You're a boy, you're supposed to know."

"Well I don't."

"Oh, never mind," Beth said. "Let's go back."

"Wait, tell me what to do," Emmet said.

"You kiss me."

"Where?"

"On the lips."

"Well who starts?"

"The boy always starts."

"Okay."

Beth looked at Emmet. "Well, go ahead."

Emmet leaned forward and pecked Beth on the lips.

"Well that wasn't very much," Beth said.

Emmet looked at Beth and then grabbed her and kissed her full on the lips for twenty seconds. When they came apart, Beth was flushed and out of breath.

"Emmet," she said.

"I know," Emmet said.

"We better get back," Beth said. "Hold my hand."

Emmet took Beth's hand and they walked back to Ellis.

Emmet opened his eyes. He was drifting and stood up and took some water. He checked on Suggs. Somehow he was still breathing.

Emmet mounted the saddle and said, "Let's go, Bull.".

Emmet left Grant and walked to his private car. The camp was alive with men singing in the saloon and others sitting in front of campfires.

Men nodded to Emmet as he walked past them until he reached the private car that was somewhat secluded.

As he took the first step, Eva came out of the shadows on the platform. "I've been waiting for you," she said.

"Why?" Emmet said.

"Let's go inside and I'll show you."

"Not a good idea," Emmet said.

"Relax, Captain," Eva said. "I'm the madam, not a whore. I choose who shares my bed, not who pays for it."

Eva opened the door. "You first," she said.

He was drifting again. He looked at his pocket watch. They had traveled another five miles. Just five more miles to Fort Laramie.

"Come on, Bull, take us there," Emmet said.

Emmet arrived in Washington in early June and raced to the hospital with his heart pounding at the thought of seeing Rose again.

Since the day she gave him the Saint Christopher medal, he had never taken it off.

He burst through the front door of the hospital and walked from ward to ward, looking for her until he spotted her in a room full of wounded men.

He opened the door and walked in and she saw him and her eyes went wide and she walked quickly to him and ushered him outside.

Emmet tried to kiss her but she pushed him away.

"What's wrong?" Emmet said.

Rose pointed to a sick soldier in a bed. "Do you see that man? He's been in a Confederate prison camp for four years," she said.

"I see him."

"He's my husband," Rose said.

"What?" Emmet said.

"My husband," Rose said. "He's been in a prisoner of war camp all this time. I'm still a married woman, Emmet."

Emmet stared at her. He was completely numb at the news.

"I don't know what to say," Rose said.

Emmet backed away. He removed the Saint Christopher medal from around his neck and placed it into her hands.

Rose closed her fist around the medal and cried as Emmet walked out of her life.

Emmet woke up when he fell out of the saddle. He held onto the reins and forced himself to stand up. The sun was in his eyes and he could see Fort Laramie directly ahead, but he wasn't sure if it was really there or if he was drifting again.

Then he saw a group of soldiers running towards him.

"US . . . Marshal . . . Emmet Boyd," Emmet managed to say before he passed out.

"Rose, scrub up, we have an emergency," Doctor Porter said as he entered the mess hall.

"Who?" Rose said as she stood up from the table.

"A US Marshal with a bullet in him," Porter said.

Rose followed Porter into the hospital where she put on her gown and scrubbed up. Then she entered the operating room and looked at the man on the operating table.

"My God," she said.

■ ■ ■ ■

Emmet drifted in and out of consciousness for several days. Sometimes he heard voices. Muffled and soft. A man saying, "How is he?" A woman saying, "Weak but getting stronger." Another man's voice that sounded like Governor Campbell saying, "By God it is him."

"What's that big star overhead, Emmet?" Ellis said.

"Pa says that's the North Star," Emmet said. "Pa says as long as you follow that star you'll never get lost."

They were in a field of tall grass behind the house in The Big Woods.

"Let's go fishing tomorrow," Ellis said. "Ma would love it if we caught a mess of fish for her to fry up."

"We'll go early and dig for bait," Emmet said.

"Boys, time to come in," Ma called from the porch.

"Be right there, Ma," Emmet said.

Emmet opened his eyes and the light stung and he shielded his face with his hand. He looked to his left and Rose was beside the bed, asleep in a chair.

Was he drifting again or was she really there? "Rose?" he said.

Rose opened her eyes, smiled, took his hand and started to cry.

"Am I dreaming?" Emmet said.

"No," Rose said. "You're not dreaming, Emmet."

"My prisoner?"

"He didn't make it."

"I have so much to tell you," Emmet said.

"Later," Rose said. "Right now I have to get the doctor."

Rose left the room and returned with Doctor Porter and Governor Campbell. Porter checked Emmet's pulse and listened to his heart and then said, "Rose, I'm leaving him to you."

"Marshal, maybe you could tell me what this is all about?" Campbell said.

"Any chance I can get something to eat first?" Emmet said.

"I'll tell the mess sergeant to bring you a steak and eggs," Campbell said.

After Porter and Campbell left the room, Rose took Emmet's hand. "I thought I would never see you again," she said.

Anna and Emma waited on the porch with Robert. It was Sunday and as soon as Pa brought the wagon around, they would all ride to church.

"Can I go fishing after church?" Robert said.

"Ask Ellis," Anna said. "We're young ladies now, Robert. You can't expect us to smell like fish all the time."

"Hey, somebody's coming," Robert said.

Anna and Emma looked down the road. A man was on horseback, a woman on horseback rode beside him.

"Is that . . . ?" Emma said.

"Robert, go get Ma," Anna said. "Hurry."

As Robert went inside, Anna and Emma jumped off the porch and ran down the road to meet Emmet and Rose.

ABOUT THE AUTHOR

Al Lamanda was born in The Bronx, New York and lived most of his life in Manhattan. His debut novel *Dunston Falls* received high praise from *Kirkus* and *Publisher's Weekly* and from there he was hooked, writing more than twenty novels and several screenplays.

The employees of Thorndike Press hope you have enjoyed this Large Print book. All our Thorndike Large Print titles are designed for easy reading, and all our books are made to last. Other Thorndike Press Large Print books are available at your library, through selected bookstores, or directly from us.

For information about titles, please call:
(800) 223-1244

or visit our website at:
gale.com/thorndike

Printed in the USA
CPSIA information can be obtained
at www.ICGtesting.com
JSHW080148040424
60478JS00004B/4

9 798885 798914